Conham reached out and briefly squeezed one of her hands.

Rosina froze, her heart thudding so hard again that it was suddenly difficult to breathe. She kept her eyes on the road, fighting for calm. What she was feeling now was nothing like her revulsion at the thought of her brother. This was entirely different. Her whole body felt alive with a sudden, blinding awareness of the man sitting beside her.

They had been driving together all day, chatting companionably, his shoulder sometimes rubbing against hers when the gig bumped over the uneven roads. It had been relaxed, enjoyable, but now she was almost overcome by unexpected sensations. A sudden tension inside her, a powerful yearning for him to pull her into his arms and kiss her, as he had done on their very first meeting. She had never felt such strong, primal feelings before, and they frightened her.

"Are you ill, Rosina? Would you like me to drive?"

"No. Thank you. I can manage now."

It took a supreme effort to drag her thoughts away from the desire pooling inside her, but somehow, she succeeded. The earl had employed her as his land steward, a role normally performed by a man. To betray weakness, instability, would be disastrous. She could not afford to lose this position now. From somewhere deep inside, she hauled up a smile.

Author Note

This book started life with a trip to my home city, Bristol. I wanted to walk around the city dockland. In 1816, when my story starts, Bristol was a bustling port with ships sailing off from there to around the world—and that was what I needed for the start of my story.

In the heart of the harborside is Queen Square, its Georgian houses surrounded on three sides by the River Avon, and I decided it was the perfect place for Conham, the Earl of Dallamire, to meet Rosina, who is fleeing for her life.

Conham has inherited a mountain of debt from his father, and it is his job, his duty, to put it right, so he must marry a fortune. Rosina spent years helping her father run the family estate and knows only too well what is required of a responsible landowner.

A friendship develops between Rosina and Conham, but even when it threatens to turn into something stronger, she knows nothing can come of it. She must fend for herself and maintain her independence. Unless, of course, she and Conham can find a way out of their dilemma...

Writing Conham and Rosina's story has been a complete joy, and I do hope you enjoy reading it as much as I enjoyed creating it!

THE EARL'S
MARRIAGE DILEMMA

SARAH MALLORY

HISTORICAL

Harlequin®
HISTORICAL

ISBN-13: 978-1-335-53989-2

The Earl's Marriage Dilemma

Copyright © 2024 by Sarah Mallory

Recycling programs for this product may not exist in your area.

For questions and comments about the quality of this book, please contact us at CustomerService@Harlequin.com.

TM and ® are trademarks of Harlequin Enterprises ULC.

Harlequin Enterprises ULC
22 Adelaide St. West, 41st Floor
Toronto, Ontario M5H 4E3, Canada
www.Harlequin.com

Printed in U.S.A.

Sarah Mallory grew up in the West Country, England, telling stories. She moved to Yorkshire with her young family, but after nearly thirty years living in a farmhouse on the Pennines, she has now moved to live by the sea in Scotland. Sarah is an award-winning novelist with more than twenty books published by Harlequin Historical. She loves to hear from readers; you can reach her via her website at sarahmallory.com.

Books by Sarah Mallory

Harlequin Historical

His Countess for a Week
The Mysterious Miss Fairchild
Cinderella and the Scarred Viscount
The Duke's Family for Christmas
The Night She Met the Duke
The Major and the Scandalous Widow
Snowbound with the Brooding Lord
Wed in Haste to the Duke

Lairds of Ardvarrick

Forbidden to the Highland Laird
Rescued by Her Highland Soldier
The Laird's Runaway Wife

Saved from Disgrace

The Ton's Most Notorious Rake
Beauty and the Brooding Lord
The Highborn Housekeeper

Visit the Author Profile page
at Harlequin.com for more titles.

To Sue, who is not only an excellent host
but a great tour guide, too!

Chapter One

She refused. She refused me!

The words pounded through Conham's head as he strode out of the house. He had come to Bristol solely with the intention of proposing to Alicia Faulds, and she had turned him down.

She had been his mistress for six months and he had thought they were ideally suited. She was a widow, experienced, entertaining and witty. She was also very wealthy. As the Eleventh Earl of Dallamire, he had an impressive lineage and a large house in Berkshire, together with extensive estates around the country. True, he was sadly short of funds, but he had never made any attempt to hide the fact from her.

He had barely stepped out of the house when the door closed behind him with a thud. That was it. He was done with the rich Mrs Faulds. He almost winced as he recalled how she had laughed at him when he had admitted that his fortune was somewhat depleted.

Depleted? My dear Conham, it is nonexistent! The Dallamire estates—those that are not entailed—are riddled with debts. And you greatly misled me with talk of your latest inheritance, I have seen it. An insignificant property in the wilds of Gloucestershire and a ramshackle collection

*of run-down buildings on a few acres of land to the north
of Bristol. Ha! There is nothing there to tempt me.*

Suddenly, the lady he had thought might make him a
good wife had been more like a stranger. She had travelled
ahead of him to Bristol in order to assess the properties his
godfather had left him. Confound it, he had not even seen
them for himself yet!

A chill breeze sprang up, rousing Conham from the useless reflections. He looked about him. He had planned to
escort Alicia to a masquerade tonight, but that was clearly
out of the question now. He would not go alone, but neither did he want to go back to his rooms at the Full Moon
just yet. He felt too tense, too restless, and it was more than
likely Matt would still be awake. He would want to know
why Conham was back before daybreak and what had put
him in such a foul mood.

*That's what comes of bringing Matt Talacre with me
on this journey,* Conham thought irritably. It was impossible to snub a man who had fought beside you at Waterloo.

Across the street, Queen Square silent in the moonlight,
and the walks dissecting the lawns were deserted. It was
an ideal place to collect his thoughts and cool his temper.
Conham threw the domino around his shoulders to keep
out the chill of the November night and crossed the road.
After jumping over the low wooden rail and onto the grass,
a few steps took him to the gravel path that ran around the
square beneath the trees.

It was very quiet, although he could hear faint noises
from the floating harbour that surrounded Queen Square
on three sides. Shouts and thuds drifted over the terraced
houses that separated the elegant square from the docks,
and he guessed a ship was getting ready to depart and
catch the tide. From the clear sky, a full moon shone down

through the bare branches of the trees, casting dappled shadows on the path. By the time Conham began a second circuit of the square he could feel his mind settling.

He could not deny that Alicia's rejection was a disappointment. She was a luscious brunette and knew how to drive a man wild with desire. She also possessed a considerable fortune, but he had genuinely thought marriage would suit them both. It would not be a love match, but they liked one another well enough, which was as much as Conham expected from a wife. As an earl, marriage was a duty and, in his case, a rich bride was a necessity. However, it appeared the wealthy widow valued her independence above a title.

Conham could not blame her. He *was* impoverished, and a fool not to have done something about it. He had received the news of his father's death shortly after Waterloo, but had gone on to Paris with the Army of Occupation, believing there was no immediate need for him to rush home. However, when he had returned to England some six months ago, he discovered that the old earl, an inveterate gambler, had left him neglected estates and a mountain of crippling debt.

True, the Berkshire property was extensive, but years of bad management had left Dallamire Hall in a poor condition, and the combined income from all his lands was barely enough to provide for his stepmother and his two half-sisters, who were still in the schoolroom.

'Damme,' he muttered. 'I should have quit the army and come back earlier. I always knew Father was a gambler. I should have made more effort to keep an eye on him before he gambled away almost everything!'

The pill had been somewhat sweetened by the acquisition of his godfather's properties, which had been held in trust for him until his twenty-eighth birthday. That event had occurred in August, and was the reason Conham had come to the West Country, to inspect his inheritance.

The news that Alicia had gone ahead and rented a house for herself in Bristol he had taken as a good sign, until she had dashed all his hopes tonight. He flicked his cane at an errant weed in the grass. What was it she had called it? *Another ramshackle property.* From his lawyers' cautiously worded report, he suspected Alicia's description would prove to be correct.

He sighed and stared up at the moon. Well, what was done was done. His years in the army had shown him that a fellow must be philosophical about these things. There were any number of people who depended upon the Earl of Dallamire for their livelihood and he could not let them down. He must now look elsewhere for a rich bride. It shouldn't be too difficult. There were numerous tales of rich men willing to settle a fortune on their daughter in return for a title.

'*Oof!*'

His meanderings were cut short as a body cannoned into him, knocking his ebony cane from his hand. Instinctively, he grabbed the culprit.

'Oh, no, you don't!'

He expected oaths and curses from his struggling attacker. Instead, a soft female voice begged him to let her go.

'What the devil!'

Conham swung his captive into the moonlight and found himself looking at a pale, heart-shaped face set about with an untidy mass of fair curling hair. She wore no coat, but the sleeves beneath his hands felt very much like silk. At that moment he heard shouts coming from the Grove.

'Please, sir. They must not see me!'

A pair of wide eyes gazed anxiously up at him and he

pulled the girl back into the shadows just as four men came running into the square.

'Too late for that,' he muttered, shrugging off his domino. 'Here, put this around you.' He threw the cloak around her shoulders and lifted the hood over her fair hair. 'Now, put your arms around my neck.'

And with that he bent his head and kissed her. She froze, but did not push him away. Instead, she clung tighter at the sound of boots pounding along the path. Someone was approaching at a run. Conham raised his head.

'Stay close to me,' he whispered.

He turned, keeping the woman behind him, in his shadow. The men had split up and only two were coming towards him. He moved forward, one hand pretending to straighten the fall flap of his breeches as he hailed them cheerfully.

'You are in the devil of a hurry, sirs. Are the pressmen abroad?'

The men stopped.

'And who might you be?' demanded one.

'I am Dallamire,' he said, with a touch of hauteur. 'The Earl of Dallamire.'

He saw them eyeing him, taking in the black woollen evening coat with its gilt buttons embossed with a coat of arms, the tight-fitting black trousers and dancing shoes. The second man touched his forelock, clearly impressed.

'No, my lord, not the press gang. We're after an escaped prisoner. But 'tis only a whore who slipped off the ship,' he added when Conham feigned alarm. 'Have you seen or heard anyone go past you?'

'Well, no.' Conham pulled his cloaked companion into his side. 'But as you can see, I have been rather…occupied.'

The man laughed coarsely. 'Aye, well, we'll not keep you from your pleasures, my lord. Come on, Joe!'

Conham watched the sailors until they were out of sight and he and the woman were alone again in the square.

'Well, now,' he said, 'I think you had best tell me what this is all about.'

'And I think you should let me go,' she retorted, struggling against his hold.

He tightened his grip. 'But I have yet to be convinced that you are innocent.'

'How dare you!'

'And besides that,' he said as she continued to fight him, 'it is not safe for a young woman to be wandering around unattended. We are in the docklands, there are some very rough characters abroad.'

'I am well aware of that!'

'Not me, you wildcat,' he exclaimed, catching her free wrist before she could claw at his eyes. 'There are those in the alleys around here who would kill you for the clothes on your back. And then there are your pursuers.'

She stopped struggling and eyed him resentfully. He went on.

'That's better. Let's go to an inn and you can tell me your story. Who knows? I may even be able to help you.'

For a moment she was silent. Then, 'Very well, I will come with you.'

'Good.' He retrieved his cane, saying, 'You had best keep my domino about you, too.'

'But it is far too long,' she objected. 'It will drag in all the dirt.'

Her concern for his property surprised him but he merely shrugged. 'Better that than you freeze to death.'

He heard a faint chuckle. 'Very true.'

'Come along, then.'

Conham pulled her hand onto his sleeve and set off, very much aware that she was not putting any weight on him at all. They had not gone far before she stumbled and he quickly put his arm around her.

'I beg your pardon,' she muttered. 'I feel a little dizzy.'

'It's not far to King Street. You will feel better once you are sitting down. And then you can tell me what all this is about.'

They had reached the edge of the Square when he saw the sailors coming back. He glanced down at his companion, to assure himself that the voluminous hood of the domino concealed her face. She had hesitated at the sight of them, but Conham put his hand on her arm, where it rested on his sleeve, and kept her moving, He addressed the men as they drew nearer.

'No luck finding your quarry?'

'There's no sign of the wench.' A rough curse followed the words. 'And we dare not wait any longer to cast off or the lock gates will be closed against us.' He spat into the gutter. 'She's disappeared into the stews. She'll not last long there.'

'No. Good night to you, then.' Conham touched his hat and strolled on, whistling nonchalantly and resisting the urge to look back until they had reached the corner of King Street.

'Have they gone?' came a whisper from beside him.

'Yes. They are scurrying back to their ship. You are safe from them now.'

'Thank goodness,' she said, and with that she crumpled against him.

As Conham swept her up into his arms, the hood slipped

back and her fair hair cascaded over his sleeve like silk. Her eyes were closed and he gazed down at her, taking in the straight little nose and a mouth that he had already discovered was eminently kissable. Under the flare of the street lamp she looked older than he had first thought, but still defenceless. And far too young to be abroad unprotected.

'Oh, Lord,' he muttered. 'What the devil am I going to do with you?'

Chapter Two

Rosina stirred. Her head ached prodigiously and her mouth felt very dry. She was in bed, the covers pulled up snugly around her shoulders. She opened her eyes, wincing at the light from the unshuttered window. This was not her bedchamber. A chill ran through her as she began to remember parts of her ordeal.

She looked up at the plain wooden canopy above her head, then at the furniture around the room. Finally, her eyes came to rest upon the man standing by the hearth, looking down at the fire. He was tall, with broad shoulders and chest that tapered down to the flat plane of his stomach. A sportsman, perhaps, his glossy red-brown hair curling down to his collar like the drawings she had seen of fashionable Corinthians. He was not wearing a coat, and snowy white shirtsleeves billowed out from a fine silk waistcoat. That and his black trousers suggested evening dress, even though it was now full daylight.

As if aware of her gaze he turned to look at her and she noted a strong face with an angular jaw and piercing, grey-green eyes. She did not recognise him as her rescuer, but then the night had been fearsome, all blue-grey moonlight and dark shadows. However, when he spoke, his smooth, deep voice was familiar.

'So, you are awake at last.'

'How long have I been here?'

'Since midnight.'

'Midnight.' She frowned, struggling to remember. 'You are an earl...'

'Conham Mortlake, Earl of Dallamire, yes.'

He rose and came across to her, picking up a glass from the table beside the bed, but as he came closer she shrank away.

'Don't be afraid. It is only water.'

'Of course, but I can hold it for myself,' said Rosina, fighting down her momentary panic.

She reminded herself that this man had helped her, but even so, her hand was shaking when she reached out for the glass.

The earl laughed, but not unkindly. 'I think you should let me help you.'

He sat on the edge of the bed and slipped one hand behind her shoulders, the other holding the glass as she took a few sips.

It *was* water. No unpleasant taste or pungent smell; no one was trying to drug her now.

'Thank you,' she said. 'Where am I?'

'In my rooms at the Full Moon.' He arranged the pillows behind her so she could sit up more comfortably. 'You collapsed as we were leaving Queen Square and I thought it best to bring you here. You have slept the morning away. That was probably the result of all the laudanum you had taken. I could smell that, or something like it, on your breath.' He straightened. 'There, is that better?'

'Yes. Thank you.' Rosina realised she was only wearing her shift and she pulled the sheet up to her chin.

'The chambermaids undressed you, not I,' he told her.

'Unfortunately, the inn is full and they had no choice but to put you in my bed. No need to look so startled. I had another bed made up in my companion's bedroom. I came in here only to build up the fire. I am sorry if I woke you.'

He paused, but she was still too dazed to make a sensible reply, and after a moment he continued.

'I have to go out. I will send up a maid with some tea and bread and butter. Anything else you need, just ask her. This room and the adjoining parlour are at your disposal for as long as you need it. No one will disturb you, unless you ring for a servant.'

'Thank you.' She looked up at him, then said in a rush, 'You will come back?'

'Of course.' His crooked smile was kind, reassuring. 'I shall be gone for a few hours but I will look in on you when I return. Oh, and I have told everyone here you are a cousin of mine. A Mrs Alness. I said that your carriage overturned and all the trunks fell into the river, which accounts for your dishevelled state and lack of baggage. They may not believe that, but they will accept it, trust me.'

'Because you are an earl?'

'Because I am an earl.' He was still smiling, but she thought there was a hint of derision in it now. 'May I know your name?'

'Rosina.'

He waited, but she closed her lips, unwilling to give him any more information, and at length he nodded.

'Very well, Rosina. I will bid you *au revoir.*'

When Lord Dallamire had gone, Rosina lay back against the pillows, trying to put her thoughts into some order. When she had collided with him last night, she had been flying for her life. He had saved her; there was no doubt of that. And strangely, she had not been frightened when he kissed her. It had been shocking, very much as she imagined it would feel to be struck by lightning. But it had been energising and exciting, too. No one had ever kissed her like that before, so she had no idea if it was always that way.

Last night she had been wary of the earl, afraid he might be helping her for his own ends, but it seemed he had taken care of her. She closed her eyes. She had no idea what she was going to do, but for the moment she felt safe. Her arms were bruised, but that was the rough treatment of the sailors and from... Rosina shuddered. She did not want to think of how she had come to be on the ship. Not yet.

She threw back the covers and swung her legs to the floor, standing up cautiously. She felt a little dizzy, but her legs supported her. She did not want to lie in bed any longer. Carefully, she walked over to the bell-pull and tugged at it.

It was late afternoon and growing dark when Conham returned to the Full Moon and the landlady told him his cousin was waiting for him in the private parlour. He went upstairs to find the room glowing with candlelight and Rosina standing before the fire, warming her hands. For a moment he had a clear view of her profile, that glorious hair piled up loosely, one or two golden tendrils hanging down around her face, the dainty nose and chin and sculpted lips that looked made for laughter but were now drooping slightly.

Then she turned to look at him, and Conham's breath caught in his throat.

'You are dressed.' He said the first thing that came into his mind.

'Yes.' She glanced down at her skirts. 'The maid cleaned

my gown as best she could and found me a brush and pins, so I could tidy my hair.'

Despite her shy smile, she still looked pale and drawn.

'Are you feeling better?'

'Very much so, my lord, thank you.'

'And have you eaten?'

'Yes, thank you.'

'How much?' he asked, giving her a searching look.

'A piece of bread and butter.'

'That is hardly enough to sustain you.'

An uneasy silence fell and his glance went to the small purse on the table. He had left it there deliberately, half expecting her to take the money and leave.

'I thought you might have gone by now.'

'You wanted an explanation.' Her shoulders lifted slightly. 'I owe you that much.'

He nodded. 'I will ring for refreshments.'

A servant entered and Rosina studied the earl as he gave his orders. He was no longer wearing his evening clothes but was dressed in pantaloons and Hessians, with a blue coat over his dove-grey waistcoat and snow-white linen. She had rarely seen such well-fitting clothes outside the pages of a fashion journal. Her brother Edgar's finery, the nipped-in waist of his coats, the high shirt points and pomaded hair, had always struck her as rather flamboyant. Edgar assured her it was the height of fashion but she had always thought he looked a trifle ridiculous.

There was nothing ridiculous about Lord Dallamire. The shoulders of his coat required no additional padding, while the flat plane of his stomach and muscular thighs hinted at a body honed by exercise. Not at all like Edgar or the friends he occasionally brought to the house. They were without exception overfed and overdressed, their faces already showing signs of dissipation. Just the thought of them made her shudder.

'Well, madam, is my presence here so offensive to you?'

The servant having withdrawn, the earl had turned back towards her and was regarding her coldly, his brows raised. He must have seen her look of revulsion and thought it was directed at him! Rosina felt the heat of a blush burning her cheeks.

'No, no, I was just…' She stopped and tried again. 'Your clothes. That is not what you were wearing when I saw you this morning. I did not expect…'

'I slept in my evening dress.' The icy look had gone and his lips twitched. There was even a gleam of amusement in his eyes as he explained. 'I knew I would be looking in on you several times in the night, and thought you might be alarmed if you woke and saw me dressed in a nightgown.'

As he pulled out a chair for her at the table, she suddenly remembered the domino he had wrapped around her.

'Oh, you were on your way to a ball last night! I beg your pardon, I am very sorry if I ruined your evening.'

He sat down opposite her, waving aside the apology. 'It is not important, I had already decided not to go. But let us return to the matter in hand. Why were those men chasing you? And no lies now!'

Rosina bridled a little at his tone, but decided it was a perfectly reasonable question. When she thought of how she must have looked, with her dusty gown and untidy hair, it was quite understandable that he should be cautious. But she needed to be wary, too.

'Forgive me, sir, but how do I know you are who you say?'

He took out a silver case and extracted a card for her.

'That will have to suffice for now,' he said. 'Until six months ago I was with the army in France.'

The entry of a servant with a tray caused a diversion. Rosina read the card and set it down while Lord Dallamire was pouring wine for them both. When the servant had retired again, she accepted a glass from the earl, but refused the sweet biscuits.

'Were you at Waterloo, my lord?'

'I was.' A shadow crossed his face, as if he found the memories disturbing. 'It was hailed as a glorious victory, but it was the end of so many good lives.'

'I am very sorry.'

He acknowledged her words with a nod, but said briskly, 'Now, are you going to tell me your story?'

Rosina sipped at her wine, trying to decide what to do. She was in a fix, and instinct told her she could trust this man.

'My name is Rosina Brackwood,' she said at last. 'My father was Sir Thomas Brackwood, of Brackwood Court in Somerset. It is some miles south of Bristol.'

'I do not think... Wait, I heard the name Brackwood recently in town.' He frowned. 'But that was a young man.'

'My brother Edgar.'

'Ah, yes, that would be it. I came across him once or twice, at the gaming tables.'

Her lip curled. 'That does not surprise me. He lives only for pleasure. While Papa was alive Edgar rarely visited Brackwood, except when he had outrun his allowance. He was at home when Papa died in April and when he stayed on, I thought it was to take up his responsibilities at last, but he was only interested in releasing funds from the estate to pay his debts. He has no interest in the people or the land, but my father did! Papa cared passionately. As do I, having lived at Brackwood all my life.' Her little spurt of defiance faded and she sighed. 'I had grown accustomed to running Brackwood as if it was my own. I suppose it was inevitable that Edgar and I would quarrel when he came home.'

She took another sip then put the glass down. She felt a little light-headed, and she needed to keep her wits about her if she was to explain everything.

'My father was concerned about what would happen to Brackwood when he died, so he drew up new agreements with some of the villagers and tenant farmers, giving them more security. When Edgar tried to force them to leave, I made sure they knew he could not do so without due compensation. He has also tried to borrow money from Papa's friends, which I knew, as well as Edgar, that he would not be able to repay for years. If ever.' She glanced across at the earl and noted the slight frown on his brow. 'I did nothing illegal, merely told our friends the truth. Papa would have wanted them to know the risks. Edgar did not like that. He said I was interfering.'

'I can imagine.'

Conham remembered his own homecoming earlier in the year. Having been assured by his stepmother that they were managing very well at Dallamire, he returned to find that was very far from the truth.

'Do you think I was wrong?' she asked him. 'My father was an honest man, he would be ashamed of Edgar's duplicity towards our friends. As for the villagers, they are mostly poor people and ill-educated. What will become of them if they are turned out of their houses? Where could they go? My brother's actions would have ruined their lives, and all for a short-term gain because he wants to sell the houses and the unentailed land.'

'It is understandable that your brother will have his own

ideas about his inheritance,' he replied, thinking of his own predicament.

'But he should be *protecting* it! Papa bought the extra land to help ensure Brackwood can survive and profit. If Edgar would only implement Papa's plans, then, in time, everyone would benefit. The farms would be improved, yields increased.' She went on, warming to her theme, 'I used to help my father with the estate business and before he died, he shared many of his ideas with me. He knew they would take time, of course but—' She stopped. 'You look sceptical. Do you not believe me?'

He said, gently, 'I believe you mean well, Miss Brackwood, but perhaps you do not understand the situation.'

The wine appeared to have put some heart into his companion.

'Lord Dallamire, I am five-and-twenty, four years older than my brother, and I understand the situation very well,' she said, sitting up very straight. 'I began helping my father before I left the schoolroom and when he discovered I had an aptitude for figures and for dealing with legal matters, too, he passed even more of the work over to me.'

'Did you not have a season in London?'

'I never wanted one. I was quite content looking after Brackwood.'

'But if you had married, you would have an establishment of your own.'

'That would be my husband's property, never mine.'

'Ah. Very true.'

He smiled and saw a shy twinkle appear briefly in those blue eyes, then she grew serious again.

'I *would* have stepped back and let Edgar take control of the estate, my lord. If only he had shown the slightest interest. Papa was deeply disappointed when my brother said he wanted to see more of life before settling down. He went off to town again and we rarely saw him after that.'

'You can hardly expect me to condemn him, Miss Brackwood. My own father died more than twelve months ago, and I have only just taken up my inheritance.'

'But you were in the army, my lord. You had responsibilities. My brother had no such claims upon his time. He only ever came home when he was obliged to do so, to escape his creditors. While Edgar was in London, squandering his allowance, I was working with Papa, discussing the improvements he wanted to make, drawing up plans and working out the costings. In fact, for the last year of my father's life, when his health was failing, I looked after everything for him.'

'Very commendable.'

She went on eagerly. 'Some of Papa's improvements have already been implemented and are bearing fruit, like the drainage of the long meadow and encouraging the farmers to use the Scotch plough on the heavy soils. Then there is the crop rotation—'

Conham threw up his hands. 'Enough! There is no need to go on. I stand corrected, you understand these things far more than I!'

Rosina saw the amusement in his face and sat back, chuckling. 'I beg your pardon. I do tend to get carried away once I begin talking of these things!'

'But your brother wants none of it.'

Rosina shook her head, all desire to smile gone.

'That is very sad, ma'am, but if he is master now, it is surely his choice what is done.'

'I know that, I had accepted it. I did not argue when he sold off the fields to the north of the village, nor the three houses in Wood Lane.' She drew a breath. 'But when it comes to our friends, I could not let Edgar dupe them into lending him money. He told them it was for improvements to Brackwood, but that was a lie. He needed it to settle the most pressing of his gambling debts!'

'And he was angry because you intervened.'

'More than angry.'

Rosina clasped her hands tightly in her lap. Lord Dallamire wanted the truth and she owed Edgar no loyalty now. Rosina felt a little sick as she uttered the next words.

'He had me abducted.'

The memory came flooding in on her, the images sharp and clear in her mind: returning the evening before last to find Brackwood Court unnaturally quiet, discovering Edgar had turned off her maid, given the rest of the servants a day's holiday and brought that awful woman, Moffat, into the house.

They had strapped her to a chair, Edgar laughing at her furious protests.

You have been a continual thorn in my flesh since our father died, dear sister. Overriding my orders, speaking out of turn. I have had enough of you and your interfering ways, madam!

She closed her eyes, trying to blot out his cruel voice.

I am the owner of Brackwood now and that is the end of it. And it is the end of you, madam. I am sending you away where you will trouble me no more. Hold her!

She remembered Moffat's strong hands keeping her head still while her brother poured the sleeping draught into her throat, the woman's warning that it would be dangerous to administer too much of the drug and Edgar's callous response.

Do you think I care? It matters not to me if she is dead when she boards the ship.

Rosina had felt the blackness closing in. Her brother's voice was getting fainter and she heard only one more thing before her world went dark.

Just as long as she never leaves it alive!

Chapter Three

Conham jumped up and caught Rosina as she toppled from her chair. Gently, he lowered her to the floor, kneeling and cradling her head and shoulders against his chest.

She regained consciousness almost immediately and began to struggle against his hold.

'No, no, don't fight me. You are safe now.'

She grew still and opened her eyes, looking up at him blankly at first, but then with recognition, and one dainty hand clutched at his coat.

'You are safe,' he repeated. 'You fainted.'

She put her free hand to her head. 'I should not have drunk the wine.'

'You should have had more to eat!' He helped her into an armchair beside the fire. 'Sit there while I order something for you.'

Rosina obeyed, if only because she did not think she could move without assistance. She sat very still and took a few deep breaths while Lord Dallamire went out. She was mortified to have lost consciousness, to have shown such weakness over something that was nothing more than a bad memory.

She said, when the earl returned, 'I beg your pardon. I am not usually such a poor creature.'

'You are in shock. I have witnessed such things in my men, after they have seen action.' He dropped his hand briefly on her shoulder before returning to his own seat. 'The landlady is bringing you something to eat, then you shall go back to bed.'

'I need to tell you what happened.'

She put her elbows on the table and rested her head on her hands. It felt important to explain, to make him understand the enormity of what Edgar had done.

He filled a glass with water from the pitcher on the tray and pushed it across to her. 'Very well. I am listening.'

Rosina sat back and stared at the glass, but did not touch it.

'Edgar drugged me and hired a woman to bring me to Bristol and put me on board a ship bound for America. Boston.' She shivered and crossed her arms. 'He was going to put it about that I had used the money Papa left me to go travelling, but in fact, he had arranged for me to meet with a…an accident at sea.'

It all sounded quite outrageous and she had no idea if the earl believed her. His countenance was inscrutable. She drank a little of the water and went on.

'I regained consciousness as I was being carried below deck, but I pretended I was still asleep. That was when I heard Moffat talking with the captain and learned what was to happen to me, once they were at sea.'

'But you escaped.'

'Yes.' Rosina cradled the water glass between her hands to stop them shaking. 'Moffat bound me, hand and foot, once we were in the cabin and away from any witnesses, but she had been imbibing gin liberally during our journey to Bristol and made a mull of it. I managed to free myself and when she fell into a drunken stupor I slipped out of the cabin. It was dark by then. Everyone on deck was busy preparing to set sail, but thankfully, the gangplank was still in place.

'No one noticed me leaving the ship, but on the quay, I was accosted by a…a man. One of the ship's crew saw us scuffling and raised the alarm. I fled.' She paused, recalling the fearful thudding of her heart, the sudden terror when she heard the shouts and knew she was being pursued. 'Then I bumped into you.'

'That is a fantastical tale, madam. You were fortunate to get away.'

'You do not believe me.'

'I *do* believe you.' He reached across the table and caught her hands, turning them palms up to expose the angry red marks on her wrists. 'I saw these marks last night when you were sleeping. If this was your brother's doing, he deserves to be flogged.'

'But he won't be. He prefers to pay others to carry out his foul deeds. He did nothing himself, save to pour the sleeping draught down my throat.' She sighed. 'It would be my word against his. Edgar will have paid his villains well to swear I went on board that ship willingly.'

'They would have little choice,' he remarked. 'For the crew to say anything else would implicate them in your abduction.'

He had been absently rubbing his thumbs gently over her skin, causing little darts of heat to flow through her. She was hardly aware of how calming, how beguiling it was until he released her hands and she had to swallow a little mewl of protest.

She was grateful that the entrance of the landlady caused a timely diversion.

'Here we are, Your Lordship, supper for the lady.' She

put down a tray with a steaming bowl of soup in front of Rosina, and drew her attention to the bread and butter and the large piece of cake. 'And if there is anything else you'd like, ma'am, all you have to do is ask.'

'Thank you. We will ring if we need you.' The earl dismissed the landlady with a smile and turned back to Rosina. 'Now, you will eat that before we continue.'

She complied, relieved not to have to look him in the face as she tried to decide just what she was feeling. She was not uncomfortable in his presence, even though he was sitting so close, drinking his wine and watching her. It was as if they had known each other forever.

When she had finished the soup and the bread she pushed the tray away.

'You have had enough?'

'Yes. Thank you.'

'Will you not try the cake?'

He broke a piece off and held it out. Rosina hesitated, then took it from him and popped it into her mouth. It was very good and she allowed him to feed her another small piece, and another. It was an unfamiliar sensation, having someone looking after her like this, but not unpleasant.

At last, she put up her hands. 'Thank you, I enjoyed the cake, very much, but I have had enough.'

He nodded. 'There is a little colour in your cheeks now. Would you like to try the wine again?'

'No, I shall drink the water.' She met his eyes across the table and returned his smile 'But thank you.'

'Very well. When you are ready to retire, the landlady will send up a maid to help you into bed.'

Rosina felt much better after her meal and not in the least tired. There was also the very real fear that the memories of her ordeal would return to haunt her dreams.

She said, 'I should like to stay here a little longer, my lord, if you do not object?'

'Not at all. Let us move to the chairs by the fire, I think they will be more comfortable. Then you can tell me how I may help you.'

She looked at him, confused.

'Do you have family or friends who will take care of you?'

She shook her head. 'There is no one. I have no family, save Edgar, and no friends apart from those who live near Brackwood. My brother has demonstrated that his violent temper knows no bounds. To contact any one of them might put them in danger.'

'Then what do you intend to do?'

Rosina had been asking herself that very question. She had never visited Bristol before; it was a strange city to her. She had no money and there was no one she could call upon. At least, not yet. She glanced at the man sitting opposite. She *thought* she could trust him, but in truth, did she really have any choice?

'First of all, I need to quit Bristol,' she said quietly. 'Then I must find a way to support myself. As a companion, or a governess, perhaps. I want to be independent and will take any honest work. But finding any respectable position will be impossible without a character reference.' She bit her lip. 'Would you... I mean, could you, perhaps, write one for me?'

'My dear Miss Brackwood, I am not married. You must know as well as I that a reference from me would hardly benefit you.'

'Oh. Yes. Of course.'

'However, there are other ways.'

'No!' Her heart plummeted and she recoiled, lifting one hand to silence him. 'Pray, say no more!'

The very thought of him suggesting that she might sell herself in exchange for his help made her want to weep, but her distress turned to anger when she saw his look of amusement.

'You have no idea what I am going to say.'

'Oh, but I do!' She pushed herself to her feet. 'That is, I can guess, and I am grateful for your help in rescuing me, my lord, but I think I should go now.'

His hand shot out and caught her arm. 'Sit down and listen to me.'

His grip was so firm she knew there was no escape. She hesitated for a moment, then sank back onto the chair.

'That's better,' he said, releasing her. 'Now, madam, listen to me. I am not proposing to make you my mistress. I am on my way to Gloucester in the morning to inspect a property. The estate has been in trust for the past five years and the steward was recently turned off for mismanagement and neglect of his duties. I have no idea what condition it is all in now, but from everything you have told me, you appear to know more about these matters than most. You could come with me to see it and give me your opinion.'

'Me?'

'Why not? It would get you out of Bristol. And if you are as experienced in land management as you say, your advice would be very helpful to me.' He sat back in his chair. 'Well, Miss Rosina Brackwood, what do you say?'

Chapter Four

Conham waited for Rosina to speak. What the devil was he doing, offering to take her to Morton Gifford? Goodness knows what the staff there would think. But if what she had told him was true, if she had indeed spent several years working with her father on his estates, then she must know something about the running of a large house and its land, and that could prove very useful.

She said, 'But surely, you must have a steward for Dallamire. Why did you not bring him with you?'

'He already has more than enough to do in Berkshire. Unlike your father, Miss Brackwood, mine did not leave his land in good heart. My intention is to sell the Gloucester properties and invest everything in restoring Dallamire, but I cannot do that until certain legal matters have been settled. That will take a few months, possibly longer, and in the meantime, I would rather not leave Morton Gifford to deteriorate even further. Naturally, the Dallamire estates must take precedence over my time, but I should like to know someone I can trust is looking after my interests here in Gloucestershire.'

'I do not understand,' she said, her blue eyes fixed upon his face. 'Are you saying you want me to work as your steward?'

He considered it. 'Why yes, I suppose I am.'

'You want to *employ* me?'

There was disbelief in the candid blue eyes she fixed upon him, and he could not blame her. It was almost unheard of, a female land steward, but somehow, now the idea had occurred to him, it was not easily dismissed. He tried to explain it to her.

'You said you wished to support yourself, but without a sponsor, or a character reference, that is not possible. I do not anticipate keeping either of the Gloucester properties any longer than necessary, but that should be long enough for my man of business, or perhaps Mrs Jameson, the housekeeper at Gifford Manor, to provide you with a suitable reference.'

'I… I do not know what to say. You would trust me to look after your lands?'

Her astonishment made him smile. 'As an officer I was accustomed to quickly summing up a man's character. Gifford Manor is not an extensive property and from what you have told me, I believe you might be capable of running it. Also—' he nodded towards the purse, which was still lying on the table '—I left four guineas in there. More than enough to take you far away from here, if you had so wished.'

'But then I would be a thief, as well as a runaway.'

'Exactly.'

He held her gaze, the candlelight reflected in his greygreen eyes, and Rosina felt something stir inside. A slight flutter of hope and excitement.

'Will you do it?' he asked. 'Will you take the position?'

'I fear people would look askance at a female steward. Unmarried, too. Some might even refuse to do business with me.'

'It is not unheard of in France for a woman to be steward, so why not here? You might pose as a widow, if you are afraid of the gossip.'

'I will not do that. I abhor pretence.'

'Then keep your own name, if you wish. We must be some thirty or more miles from Brackwood and in another county. I think it unlikely your brother would search for you here. And as for anyone not dealing with you, you could appoint an assistant to act for you, if that situation arose. One of the servants, perhaps.

'I would pay you the same as the previous steward,' he went on, naming a sum that made her eyes widen. 'And I believe he had the use of a lodge in the grounds. That would be at your disposal. I will ask Mrs Jameson to provide a maid to live there with you, to make everything perfectly respectable.'

Rosina put her hands to her temples. Only two days ago she had been at Brackwood, sitting in her favourite chair by the fire, working on her embroidery. She closed her eyes. Best not to think of that. Everything had changed now and she could not go back, only forward. She looked up at the earl.

'Will it, my lord?' she asked him. 'Will it seem perfectly respectable if I arrive at Gifford Manor, without warning and in this shabby dress? I know what *I* would think if a gentleman brought a lady to my house in such a manner.'

'You are right, of course. It would be far better for you to remain in Bristol tomorrow and purchase the necessary accoutrements of respectability. Will one day suffice?'

'Why, yes, I should think so…'

'Good, then I shall send my carriage to collect you the following morning.'

Rosina shook her head at him. 'Does nothing ever throw you off balance, Lord Dallamire?'

He grinned. 'I am a soldier, Miss Brackwood. I am accustomed to overcoming every obstacle.'

A laugh bubbled up. 'Then it is no wonder we beat the French!'

Her eyes met the earl's and something sparked between them, a moment of understanding, of connection. So strong it took her breath away and did strange things to her heart, setting it beating most erratically.

A soft knock at the door broke the spell and Rosina turned towards the fire, hoping any observer might think the heat accounted for the flush on her cheeks.

The landlord appeared. 'Beggin' your pardon, my lord, but will you be wanting dinner this evening? Only 'tis growing late…'

'What?' Lord Dallamire sounded distracted. 'Oh, yes, I must have dinner. Will you join me, Cousin, or do you still wish to retire?'

Rosina remembered she was supposed to be his unfortunate relative, involved in a carriage accident, but the events of the past half hour had set her mind buzzing, and she knew it would be hours before she could sleep.

'The soup was very good, but I do not think it will sustain me until morning. A small meal would be very welcome.'

'Then it is settled,' the earl declared. 'You may serve it in here in, say, an hour. Will that suit you, Cousin?'

She summoned up a smile.

'Yes, an hour will suit me perfectly, my lord.'

Rosina went into the bedchamber and closed the door, standing for a moment with her back pressed against it.

'What on earth am I doing?'

She wondered if she had escaped from one peril only to fall into another. Conham Mortlake, Earl of Dallamire, appeared to be a gentleman, and she felt very at ease in his company, but what were his motives in carrying her to Gloucestershire? His arguments for offering the post of land steward had sounded so logical, so reasonable at the time, but she could not believe he was serious.

And yet, he had looked and sounded perfectly serious. She shook her head. It made no sense, but then, nothing had made sense since Edgar had drugged her and sent her off to her death. Lord Dallamire had rescued her from a hideous fate and she was grateful for that. Rosina decided she would trust him for a little longer, if only because she had not fully recovered from the effects of the laudanum, and the thought of leaving his protection was too daunting to consider.

An hour later she returned to the parlour, having tidied herself as best she could. Sadly, the black silk gown was showing distinct signs of wear. The lace at the neck was torn and there was dirt on the skirts. However, she had washed her face and brushed and re-pinned her hair. That would have to do.

The table had been set for dinner but there was no sign of Lord Dallamire and she went over to the mirror and tucked a stray curl back into place. She was on edge, the assurance she had felt when she agreed to dine with him having quite disappeared.

When he came in, she summoned a smile before turning to face him. His own black evening clothes looked so immaculate that she instinctively made a little curtsy.

'No, don't do that,' he said quickly. 'You are supposed

to be my cousin. People will be suspicious if you do not treat me as an equal.'

He came to hold out a chair for her and she said, as she sat down, 'I feel very *un*equal, especially in this gown.'

'I asked Matt to speak to the landlady. Having explained that you are in a strange city, she understands that you need someone to show you the best places to quickly replenish your wardrobe. I shall provide you with the money to purchase whatever you need. You are not to worry about the cost.'

'But I do worry, my lord,' she told him, mortified. 'It goes very much against the grain to be beholden to any man. I prefer to be—'

'Independent,' he interrupted her, smiling. 'I know that. You can give me the receipts when you reach the Manor and I shall deduct what you owe me from your salary.'

'And if I do not take the position?' she asked. 'I do not know when I will be able to repay you!'

'I shall hold the debt until you can.' He looked at her, a teasing smile in his eyes. 'I shall have no need of your finery.'

Rosina felt the tension draining away. Somehow, nothing seemed quite so bad when Dallamire was teasing her.

It was almost as if she had found a friend.

They settled down to their dinner with Rosina far more at ease than she had expected. They conversed easily, and the earl was such excellent company that she accepted a second glass of wine and asked him about his plans for the future.

He sat back to consider. 'My first concern is for those who depend upon Dallamire for their existence. My father left his estates in a parlous state, barely paying their way. There are also any number of outstanding debts. He had hoped to settle those with his winnings from the gaming tables.'

'I believe it is always thus with true gamblers,' she said carefully. 'My brother is the same, always believing his bad luck is about to change, but even when he is successful, he continues to play until he has lost it all again.'

'You understand,' he said, a faint smile in his grey-green eyes. 'So you see, my first concern must be to repair the family fortunes.'

'Are they very depleted?' she asked him.

'Nothing that a prudent marriage won't resolve.'

'You mean an heiress.'

'I do. Are you shocked?'

'Not at all,' she replied. 'A rich wife would be just the thing for you.'

He smiled. 'What, no romantic notions of love?'

She pulled a face. 'I have never had any time for romance. That is for silly females who have too little occupation.'

'You are very harsh upon your sex.'

'Most young women emerge from the schoolroom with little thought except to catch a husband. And from what I have observed, most of them are disappointed, even when they achieve their dream.'

He sat back in his chair. 'And have you *never* thought of marriage, Miss Brackwood?'

'I have considered it, naturally, but I have never yet met a man I should *like* to marry. Not that I have had very many offers.' She chuckled. 'My brother says that is because I am too clever. But surely, no sensible man would be discouraged by an intelligent woman. You would not be, I am sure!'

'No, as long as she is rich.' He refilled their glasses. 'I

could not marry a woman I actively disliked, but I think it more important to have a partner one can respect. As for love, that is for fools and poets. It is an indulgence few of us can afford.'

'I agree,' said Rosina.

She raised her glass to him, happy to find herself in such accord with the earl.

They finished their dinner and Conham did not linger over his port. He bade Rosina good-night and carried the bottle and glass off to the bedchamber he was sharing with Matt Talacre. He found his friend occupying one of two armchairs placed on either side of the hearth, sitting at his ease in his shirt and waistcoat, ankles crossed and his stockinged feet stretched out towards the fire. He was sipping a glass of wine and looked up as Conham came in.

'Oho! Did she throw you out?'

'No, she did not, damn your insolence.' Conham poured himself a measure of port wine and sat down. 'I am sorry to inconvenience you, Matt, but I shall be sleeping in here tonight.'

'Then I shall have to make do with the truckle bed again. Does the lady know the inconvenience she is causing, making you share a room with your servant?'

'She does not, and I'll thank you not to tell her!' Conham retorted. 'Miss Brackwood finds herself in unfortunate circumstances and she is embarrassed enough as it is, having to accept my charity. Which reminds me, have you arranged everything for tomorrow?'

'Aye. I have ordered a carriage to be at Miss Brackwood's disposal, plus the landlady has an acquaintance who has agreed to accompany her; a retired lady's maid who knows the best places to shop in the city.'

'Excellent work.'

'I know. Surely you would not expect anything less of me?'

Conham scowled at him. 'If you had any respect for your betters, Talacre, you would be fully dressed and serving my port, not leaving me to pour my own!'

Matt Talacre was not noticeably cast down by this rebuke and merely grinned.

'Is that what you want, someone to bow and scrape to you? You chose the wrong man for that, my lord!'

'Not sure I chose you at all, Captain. I found myself saddled with you!'

'Ha, so I *asked* you to come back and search the battlefield once you had routed the French, did I, Major?'

Conham grinned. 'You had saved my life more than once, and I would have been beholden to you forever if you had died at Waterloo. Couldn't have that!'

A companionable silence fell and Conham thought back to that final battle, when they had fought together. The friendship forged in war had lasted into the peace, and once Matt Talacre's leg wound had healed sufficiently, Conham appointed him as his batman while he was with the Army of Occupation in Paris. Then, when Conham returned to England in May this year, Matt had come with him.

'I'm sorry,' he said abruptly. 'If I had known the dire state of my finances, I would never have suggested you should stay on as my aide-de-camp.'

'What else is there for me? I may be a gentleman by birth, but one with no fortune, and a cripple, too! Who else would employ me?'

There was a bitter note in Matt's voice that Conham rarely heard. His friend was generally very cheerful, but although it was seldom mentioned, Conham knew he found his lameness galling.

He said now, 'The doctors have all said you should make a full recovery, in time.'

'Aye, I know that. It's just, sometimes...' Matthew drained his wineglass and said irritably, 'Enough now, or before we know it you will be feeling sorry for me!'

'Not me, my friend. I was just wondering how much longer I must wait for you to bring the warming pan for my sheets. Damme, man, what do I pay you for?'

'To fetch and carry for you and put you to bed! Which I will do, if you can curb your impatience while I pull on my boots!'

When Rosina went downstairs the following morning Lord Dallamire was standing in the doorway, talking to a dark-haired gentleman in a black greatcoat. As she approached, the man went to move away but the earl detained him.

'No, don't go, Matthew, I must make you known to, er, my cousin.'

Rosina stopped, hoping she looked more at ease than she felt at the subterfuge.

'Mrs Alness will be following us into Gloucestershire tomorrow,' the earl went on. 'This, Cousin, is Matthew Talacre. He was a captain in my regiment and now acts as my aide-de-camp.'

'Jack-of-all-trades is what he means, ma'am. I take on everything no one else wishes to do! I have been acting as his valet, too, but thankfully, that will end once we reach Morton Gifford, where I hope the estimable Dawkins has already arrived with His Lordship's dressing coach!'

Rosina smiled politely, all the time wondering how much this man knew about her.

'Lord Dallamire explained how you had come to lose all your possessions, madam,' Mr Talacre went on, as if reading her mind. 'Very unfortunate for you, *Mrs Alness*.'

The way he said that name and the understanding in his eyes told Rosina that Matthew Talacre enjoyed the earl's confidence and she felt herself relaxing. She had two allies now in this strange adventure.

Shortly after Lord Dallamire had left for Gloucestershire, Rosina set off on her shopping trip. The retired lady's maid hired to accompany her was an excellent guide and they went first to a discreet house in King Square, where Rosina purchased a selection of evening gowns, day dresses and shoes, as well as a serviceable pelisse in dove grey and a warm cloak of blue wool for travelling. The gowns needed a few slight alterations but the helpful lady serving them assured Rosina the work could be completed in a trice, and everything would be delivered to the hotel by four o'clock. A trunk was added to their purchases and they spent the rest of the day visiting any number of milliners, haberdashers and hosiers to buy undergarments and matching accessories. By the time they returned to the Full Moon, shortly before the dinner hour, Rosina was confident she had sufficient clothes to present a decorous appearance, and that would have to do until she had the means to buy new.

It wasn't until she was alone in her room, with all the boxes, parcels and packages spread out over the bed, that Rosina was assailed by doubts. With no money of her own, she'd had no choice but to allow Lord Dallamire to pay for everything, and only women of loose virtue would accept such gifts from a man who was not her husband or a relative.

On the other hand, she told herself, one must be pragmatic. Tomorrow the earl's carriage would take her into Gloucestershire, and whether or not she remained at Morton Gifford, it was imperative that she looked as respectable as possible.

Chapter Five

It was just gone noon when Lord Dallamire's travelling carriage drew up at Gifford Manor for the second time in as many days. Conham heard its approach and hurried out to meet it.

'Miss Brackwood.' He helped her out of the carriage. 'How was your journey?'

'Excellent, my lord, thank you. Your carriage is very comfortable.'

He noted with approval her warm cloak and a poke bonnet that was very fetching, despite its modest brim.

'What a charming building,' she exclaimed, looking up at the Manor. 'Is it Jacobean?'

'Yes. Built of the local Cotswold stone. But let us go in out of the cold. Allow me to escort you to the parlour, ma'am. We can talk there.'

He led Rosina into the small porch, where an elderly butler was waiting to greet them.

'This is Jameson. He and his wife have been running this house for many years and will be an invaluable source of knowledge for you about the Manor and its lands, I am sure.' The old retainer bowed and Conham added, by way of explanation, 'I have invited Miss Brackwood to consider the post of steward here, Jameson.'

'Mr Talacre has already apprised me of the situation, my lord. I shall endeavour to be of assistance to Miss Brackwood and I have sent people down to the steward's lodge to make sure it is habitable.'

'Thank you,' said Conham.

'And wine and cakes have been set out in the green parlour, my lord,' the butler went on. 'At Mr Talacre's suggestion.'

Conham nodded.

'Matthew has not been idle,' he remarked as he guided Rosina through the screens passage and across the great hall.

'He sounds like an excellent assistant.'

'He is.' Conham ushered her into a square, wainscoted room with a blazing fire. 'I shall miss him when he is gone.'

'Oh? Is he leaving your employ?'

'No, not yet, but he will. Once his leg improves, Matt will want to make his own way in the world, not live on what he sees as my charity.'

'Talking of charity, I must thank you for loaning me the money for my purchases yesterday.'

'Think nothing of it. I hope you found everything you required?'

'Why, yes,' she said, untying her bonnet and putting it down on a side table. 'I had a very successful day. I have discarded the black gown and have moved into half mourning. It is a year since my father died. I do not think there can be any objection.'

She had removed her cloak and he glanced down at the skirts of a white muslin gown showing beneath a dove-grey pelisse.

Conham smiled. 'No objection at all, Miss Brackwood. In fact, I think—'

He stopped. He was about to say how well the military-style pelisse fitted her admirable figure. Then she looked up at him and all coherent thought had fled when he gazed into those cornflower-blue eyes.

'Yes?' Her delicate brows went up slightly. 'What were you going to say, my lord?'

'Nothing.' He turned and walked over to the side table. 'It was nothing of moment. Will you take a glass of wine?'

'Yes, if you please.'

He took his time filling the glasses, trying to work out what had just happened. She had quite taken his breath away, but that must have been the surprise of seeing her in her new clothes and with her hair properly dressed. He had not imagined the bedraggled creature he rescued from Queen Square could look so, so beguiling.

His years in the army had taught him a great deal, but very little about women. For all he knew, Rosina Brackwood might be an adventuress. He had no real proof of who she was, or if what she had told him was true, and yet he had given her money and was even proposing to trust her with the management of his property. Was that wise, when his finances were in such a perilous state? He could hardly afford to throw his money away on a whim.

And he certainly could not afford to lose his head over a pretty face!

'I hope you will keep a reckoning of everything I owe you, sir.' Her soft, determined voice broke into his thoughts. 'No more than Mr Talacre do I wish to be beholden to you.'

Taking up the two glasses, he turned back. Rosina's dainty chin was tilted up slightly and there was a stubborn look on her face. Conham's doubts vanished like smoke on a windy day. Unlike Alicia who, despite her own wealth, had taken every penny he had lavished on her as her right, he knew in his bones that Rosina Brackwood would do her utmost to repay him every last groat.

He said, gravely, 'I shall make an exact note, ma'am.'

Rosina took the proffered glass and sat down. The earl took a seat opposite, stretching out his long legs in their glossy top boots. He was wearing country dress, but the cut of his tailed topcoat and buckskin breeches was the work of a master. They fitted his lithe, muscled figure to perfection. She suddenly felt shy, and a little vulnerable, alone in this room with a man she barely knew. She sipped her wine and tried to think of something to break the silence.

'This looks an interesting house,' she said, admiring the polished wainscotting and elaborate plasterwork on the ceiling. 'It belonged to your godfather?'

'Yes, Hugo Conham.'

'You are named after him? You introduced yourself as Conham Mortlake,' she reminded him, then flushed, remembering that she had been lying in his bed at the time.

'Ah, yes. Of course. I am sure Mrs Jameson would be delighted to give you a tour of the house. As a boy I thought it a splendid place, all those suits of armour and the weapons covering the walls in the great hall.' He smiled, settling back in his chair. 'It was paradise for a young boy. Hugo taught me to shoot here, and we went riding in the park or up on the hills. In the evenings he would tell me tales of his days fighting the French.'

'And is that why you joined the army?' she asked. She had seen the way his eyes softened when he spoke of his godfather.

'In part, although I was already army-mad. My father refused to buy me a commission, and at the time I thought it was because he disapproved. Now I realise it was because he could not afford to do so. Hugo, too, said he could not support me if my father was against the idea.'

'What did you do?'

'I scraped together enough to buy myself a captaincy.' His smile was replaced by a brooding frown and he stared into the fire. 'If I had known then the true state of affairs at Dallamire I would not have joined up. I would have done my duty by my family. Not that anyone ever reproached me.'

'I should hope not,' she replied, wanting to say something to dispel the sadness that had enveloped him. 'I am sure you did your duty for your country.'

Her words had some effect. The earl's countenance lightened a little.

'I did my best. I made major before Waterloo.'

'Your family should be proud of you.'

He shrugged. 'Hugo had been dead for four years by then and my father never mentioned my promotion, although he did write to me, some weeks before Waterloo, to wish me well. That was his last letter to me. He broke his neck in a riding accident a few weeks later.'

'I am so sorry.'

They sat in silence for several moments. Then the earl finished his wine and jumped up.

'They should have set the steward's lodge to rights by now. Shall we go and see it?'

Conham escorted Rosina out of the house and to the far side of the stables and kitchen gardens, where the lodge was situated. It was of much more recent date than the Manor itself, a neat little ashlar stone building with a good view out over the park. He had never been inside before and was pleased to discover it was well appointed, with everything

Rosina might need, including the maid sent to wait upon her until such time as she hired a servant of her own.

'I hope you think it sufficiently comfortable,' he told her, when they had finished their short tour and returned to the little sitting room. 'Your office is in the Manor, and you will take your meals there, too. Unless you prefer to dine here, in private.'

'Thank you, but that would necessitate more work for everyone. I should be very happy to join the upper servants in the house.'

He frowned at that. 'I do not consider you a servant.'

'But that is what I will be, sir, if you employ me.' She laughed. 'Pray, do not look so concerned! As steward, it would be very useful to sit down to dinner and talk with those who work at the Manor.'

'Very well, but when I am in residence you will dine with me, starting with this evening,' he said firmly. 'Matthew will join us, too. He has an excellent mind for business and there are matters about your new role that we need to discuss.'

He watched her as she walked around the room, running her hand along the back of a chair, inspecting a watercolour on the wall.

'I have not yet accepted your offer,' she reminded him.

'But you will?' he pressed her. 'You would be doing me a service.'

Rosina did not answer immediately. What choice did she have? The idea of being out in the world, without money, or protection, was too alarming to contemplate.

'At least stay until Lady Day. Four months. By then I should know what I am going to do with my godfather's inheritance. And you will be in a better position to decide upon your future.'

'There is that,' she agreed. 'Very well, I will stay until March, and I thank you, my lord. I hope I will not disappoint you.'

'Oh, I doubt that,' said Conham, relieved beyond measure. She would be safe here. He could protect her.

Not that she was his primary concern. It was purely the Manor and estate that he was thinking of. Nor was he worried he might lose his heart. He had seen plenty of pretty women in his time and never yet lost his head over any of them.

He pulled out his watch. 'I shall leave you now. I expect you to present yourself in the green parlour a good half hour before dinner. Matthew will do the same. I shall stand upon no ceremony here. There are decisions to be made and at a time like this a man needs his friends around him!'

With that, he strode back to the Manor, not allowing himself to consider why he should be so pleased that Rosina Brackwood had agreed to stay on.

Rosina stared at the closed door, listening to the earl's departing footsteps. Friends! She shook her head, suppressing the burst of elation that had swept through her when the earl had said that word. He was referring to Matthew Talacre, of course, she knew that. It would be foolish to think anything else. But a tiny seed of pleasure had been planted and it refused to go away.

She crossed her arms and hugged herself. A few days ago, she had been running for her life with no one to help her. Now she was in this cosy house with a maid to wait upon her and an earl who called her his friend and who was offering her the prospect of gainful employment. She looked around the room and smiled. Suddenly, the future looked a little brighter.

Chapter Six

For dinner that evening, Rosina chose to wear the finer of the two evening gowns she had purchased in King Square. It was a grey silk, trimmed with a thin band of white lace at the neck and cuffs. A white muslin fichu fulfilled the double purpose of keeping her warm and providing a modest covering for her neck and shoulders. Five minutes before the appointed time, she took a final look in the mirror, threw her cloak about her shoulders and made her way to the Manor.

Rosina had mixed feelings about the forthcoming dinner, but any awkwardness she felt soon disappeared. Both the earl and Matt Talacre were eager to put her at ease and by the end of the meal, Rosina was far more comfortable in their company.

When the covers had been removed and dishes of nuts and sugared almonds put on the table, Rosina announced she had arranged for the housekeeper to show her over the house the following morning.

'I hope you will not be disappointed,' said the earl. 'Since my godfather's demise five years ago, only the Jamesons and a couple of servants have been living here.'

'True, but I believe Mrs Jameson has done her best to keep the house in order. From what I have seen so far everything has been very well maintained with hard work and beeswax.'

'I wish the same care had been taken with the land,' muttered the earl.

'Ah, yes, the rascally steward, Frumald.' Matthew Talacre pushed a dish of marzipan fruits towards Rosina. 'How long was he here?'

'About three years, I believe. The trustees appointed him when Hugo's steward became too old to continue. I understand that in the end Mrs Jameson wrote to the trustees to inform them Frumald was a miserly fellow, and that he was lining his own pockets rather than spending anything on maintaining the land or buildings. Once they started to investigate, it did not take them long to ascertain that she was telling the truth.'

'Damn his eyes,' declared Matthew. 'I hope they clapped him up for it!'

The earl shook his head. 'The fellow ran off as soon as the trustees began investigating. I called in at one of the farms on my way here yesterday, to see the old gamekeeper, whom I remembered from my previous visits. He gave me the word with no bark on it. Frumald was a sly dog, apparently. Slight increases in the rents, instructions for the odd wagon to be sent off to a different market. Nothing to cause an outcry, although it did raise suspicions.'

'Well, thank goodness you now have control of the place,' said Matthew, rising to his feet. 'You will soon have everything put to rights. Now, if you will excuse me, I am for my bed. Although I shall seek out Dawkins on my way, to make sure His Lordship's sheets have been warmed satisfactorily.' He winked at Rosina. 'Proper application of the warming pan is one of His Lordship's little foibles!'

'My little—! Take your sorry carcase out of here, Talacre, before I throw you out!'

Matthew went out laughing, and Rosina stifled a giggle.

'Insolent fellow,' drawled the earl. 'I should turn him off.'

But she had seen the twinkle in his eyes and knew he was not really offended. She drank the last of her sweet wine and pushed the glass away.

'I, too, should retire,' she said. 'It has been a tiring day.'

'I shall escort you back to the lodge.'

'There is no need, my lord.'

'Perhaps not, but I am going to do so.'

He picked up her cloak, which she had left across a chair at the side of the room, and put it around her shoulders before guiding her out of the house.

'You really do not need to come with me,' she repeated as they stepped out onto the drive. 'There is more than enough moonlight for me to see my way.'

He pulled her hand onto his arm before replying.

'But I want to see you safely to your door. Call it one of my, er, little foibles.'

Rosina gave in. She could not deny it would be pleasant to have his company for the short walk to the steward's lodge, although she cautioned herself not to think it anything more than gallantry. She walked beside him, feeling the strength of his arm beneath the fine woollen sleeve, breathing in the faint scent of his cologne.

He said, 'Mrs Jameson is showing you over the house tomorrow, I believe?'

'Yes. After breakfast. I believe she is vastly relieved that you are come, my lord. She thinks that now everything will be well.'

'I am very much afraid that is not the case. I hope she will not be too downcast when I sell the Manor.'

'You must, of course, do what you think best.'

'Your tone suggests I should keep it.'

'Not at all,' she said quickly. 'I understand that Dallamire must come first. It is, after all, your principal seat.'

'Yes. Although I should like the land and the house here to be in good condition before I sell. I think I owe that to my godfather.'

'And it would also increase the selling price.'

'Undoubtedly. Which is why I need a good steward for the land.'

Rosina bit her lip. 'Yes.'

'Do you think it beyond your abilities?' he asked her.

The black outline of the lodge was ahead of them, a soft glow shining from one of the windows as well as from the fanlight above the door. Brackwood Court now belonged to Edgar. There was no going back, and this small, compact little building represented a sanctuary. Suddenly, she wanted to stay here; she was eager to take on the challenge of running Morton Gifford.

'That remains to be seen,' she said briskly. 'The first thing to be done is to become acquainted with the estate. I should like to make a start as soon as possible. You said there is a gig I may use, my lord?'

'There is, but you will hardly go out alone.'

'No, I shall take one of the servants with me. One who knows the area and the people.'

'Then I suggest you take Fred Skillet, the head groom here. He was born in the village and knows everything there is to know about Morton Gifford. I will tell him to put himself at your disposal.'

'Thank you. Once I have some idea of what is required,

I shall be able to tell you if I think I can make a difference here.'

They had reached the door and as they stopped, the earl released Rosina's arm. She turned to look up at him, but with the moon behind him she could not see his expression. She had no idea if he was satisfied with her answer.

'I am confident you can do this,' he said, sweeping away her doubts. 'There is a great deal of work to be done here, and I shall be glad to know you are in charge, Rosina. Now, why do you look at me like that? What have I said?'

She hesitated. 'You used my first name.'

'Did I? I didn't notice.' He took a step away from her. 'Don't fret, I have no designs upon your virtue.'

His calmly uttered words should have been reassuring, and Rosina was surprised by her sharp response.

'I am very glad to hear it! Good night, my lord.'

And she *was* glad, she told herself firmly as she went inside and handed her cloak to the waiting maid. She had no wish to become the object of any man's desires.

Although it was very lowering to think the earl found her so unattractive.

Since the weather was dry, Rosina spent the next few days travelling around Morton Gifford. She was accompanied by Fred Skillet, who had worked on the Gifford estates since he was a boy. Not only was he knowledgeable about the estate, he was also known and trusted by everyone who lived or worked there. They might look askance at the young female calling upon them, albeit a gentlewoman with a friendly and engaging manner, but if Fred said she was Lord Dallamire's steward, come to make things right, and that they should open the budget to her, then they would do so.

When Rosina sat down to dinner with the earl and Mr Talacre three days later, she was able to explain to them just what had been going on at Morton Gifford.

'Since your godfather's death, everyone has been nervous for the future, not knowing if or when the estate was to be broken up and sold. Then Frumald, that awful steward the trustees appointed, frightened them all with threats of eviction and rent rises. Is it any wonder that your tenants had no interest in improving their homes or their businesses? The shopkeepers and millers I have spoken with see no point in expanding, while the farmers have little incentive to make changes or bring in new stock, since they will get no reward for their hard work.

'However,' she concluded, 'the land here appears to be fertile, my lord. If we can assure the farmers that they have security of tenure and bring in a fairer system of rents for everyone, it will pay dividends almost immediately. Morton Gifford need not be another drain on you, Lord Dallamire. Quite the opposite. I think it will soon be turning a small profit.'

'How soon?' Matt Talacre asked her.

'Next year, perhaps, if the harvest is a good one. Everyone agrees the weather this year has been particularly bad.'

They continued to discuss the matter while the meal progressed, and by the time the covers were removed, and the small dishes of bonbons, nuts and sweetmeats had been set on the table, Rosina had answered all their questions as honestly as she could.

'By Jove, Conham, I believe the lady really does know her business!' declared Matt Talacre, sitting back in his chair and grinning.

Rosina was pleased with the compliment, but it was the earl's verdict she needed.

At last, he nodded. 'Very well, Miss Brackwood. Leave your report on my desk, facts, figures and projections. I shall study them and then I may, perhaps, reconsider my decision to sell.'

Conham saw Rosina's look of surprise and delight and smiled to himself. She could not know that he was already minded to keep the property. He had spent some of his happiest times here as a boy and the house had quickly wrapped itself about him, just as it had done all those years ago. The furnishings might be faded and a little tired, but there was no doubting the Manor's comfort. He felt more relaxed here than he had at any time since returning to England.

'I have always felt at home here,' he admitted, when the servants had withdrawn. 'It would be somewhere to escape from the duties and grandeur of Dallamire.'

'Good idea, if you like it so much,' said Matthew. 'But what of this rich wife you intend to find? She may be like your stepmother and prefer to live in your stately pile.'

'Then she may do so.' Conham reached for the wine to refill everyone's glass. 'My wife may have parties and balls at Dallamire to her heart's content. Or in the London house, but not here. Gifford Manor is too small to accommodate more than a few friends, and that will suit me perfectly!'

'But will it suit your countess?' murmured Rosina.

The question was out before she could stop herself. The earl glanced at her in surprise.

'Damme, madam, you are growing as impertinent as Talacre!'

She blushed fierily, but Matthew came to her defence.

'No, no, Conham, don't fire up, 'tis a fair question.'

Rosina caught her breath, astonished at the informality between master and servant. She waited for Lord Dallamire to make some angry retort, but he merely grinned.

'Aye, she is, and I appreciate that.' His glance shifted to Rosina and she felt her pulse quicken at the smile warming his eyes. 'The advantage of a marriage of convenience, Miss Brackwood, is that both parties understand they will not be obliged to live in each other's pockets. I am sure my countess and I will both appreciate a little time away from one another.'

'How very civilised,' drawled Matt Talacre. 'I do not think I would want such a union.'

Conham almost retorted that he would rather not have to make such a marriage, but he didn't.

'You have always been such a romantic, Matthew. You know as well as I that many women would be only too happy to have the power and position that marriage can bestow upon them. Once they have it, they will want to go their own way.'

'Power and position?' Matt sat back, twirling the stem of his wineglass between his fingers. 'Then why did a certain rich widow in Bristol turn you down recently?'

A frosty silence met his words. Rosina felt the change and glanced at the earl, whose countenance had become stony. It was as if a sudden blast of arctic air had filled the room.

She put down her napkin. 'I think perhaps it would be best if I withdrew.'

Lord Dallamire put out his hand to stop her. 'No, no, Miss Brackwood, there is no need for you to go. It is Talacre who needs to apologise.'

'I'm damned if I will apologise! What, for challenging your absurd notion that every woman wants a man solely for his title, for his position in society? You don't really believe that, Conham.' He turned to Rosina. 'And it ain't the case, is it, ma'am?'

'Having never been to town, I do not feel qualified to answer. But for myself, I would say no, it is certainly not the case.'

'Then you are the exception, Miss Brackwood.'

'And what of Mrs Faulds?' Matthew persisted. 'She must be an exception, too, since she preferred to keep control of her own fortune rather than hand it over to you.' He gave the earl a quizzical look. 'Be honest now, man. Do you really blame her?'

Rosina waited, expecting an eruption of anger, but once again the earl surprised her. He relaxed.

'No,' he said, smiling slightly. 'I don't blame her for refusing me.'

Rosina had never experienced such a dinner before, where men spoke so freely, so openly. At Brackwood her neighbours and her father's friends had always behaved circumspectly before her. As for Edgar, he had shown nothing but contempt in her company. This free and easy banter was something new to her. It was slightly alarming, but hugely enjoyable, and she ventured a question of her own.

'Were you very disappointed, sir, when the lady refused your offer?'

She half expected him to cut her down with a withering reply. Instead, he shrugged.

'It was never a love match, but I thought we liked one another well enough. I believed we might rub along comfortably together. However, it would seem the lady prefers her independence to a title.'

After a moment's silence he lifted his glass to study the contents.

'But that is by the by,' he said lightly. 'My stepmother would never have approved of the wealthy Mrs Faulds and that could have made life very uncomfortable for everyone.

Fortunately, there are many other young ladies that *do* meet with Lady Dallamire's approval, heiresses who—whatever Matt might think—would be only too willing to become my countess. Almack's is full of 'em!'

'Well, what you lack in funds you make up for in appearance,' retorted Matt outrageously. 'You are a handsome devil, Conham. Don't you agree, Miss Brackwood?'

Rosina answered cautiously.

'Handsome is that handsome does.'

'Aye, well, Dallamire scores on that point, too. There is no one I would trust more with my life or my money, if I had any. His is chivalrous to a fault!'

'Enough, enough, damn you!' exclaimed the earl, frowning. 'Shut up and refill the glasses, Matthew!'

'Very well, my friend. But I wish you luck finding a wife who will make you happy as well as rich.'

'Oh, I don't think that will be difficult,' drawled the earl, a glint of self-derision in his eyes.

Matthew gave a shout of laughter. 'Of all the conceited—'

'No, no, Matt, just practical.' Conham grinned. 'As soon as I leave here on Tuesday, I shall start my search!'

'You are leaving Gifford Manor next week?' said Rosina. 'So soon?'

'Yes. I only ever intended staying until I could appoint a land steward to manage the estate. I have pressing matters to deal with at Dallamire and then I shall return to town.'

Conham wondered again if perhaps this was too much of a risk, leaving a woman he barely knew in charge. But he squashed his doubts. Hugo, his godfather, had always considered Fred Skillet to be an excellent judge of people, and the elderly head groom had been surprisingly complimentary when Conham had spoken to him earlier.

'Miss Brackwood knows what she's about, my lord,' Skil-

let had told him. 'She has a friendly way with her, too, that
puts people at their ease. Not like t'other bag o'wind who
was here before, all smiles to yer face but ready to take the
bread off yer plate if he thought he could get away with it.'

That was enough for him, for now.

He said, 'I do not intend to return here until the spring,
but I will expect regular reports from you, Miss Brackwood. Send everything to Dallamire and it will find me,
wherever I am.'

'Yes, my lord.'

'But what of Bellemonte?' demanded Matthew. 'Are you
not going to see that before you leave Gloucestershire?'

'No. I shall instruct my lawyers to sell it.'

Conham frowned. Matt had already mentioned Alicia, damn his eyes, and now her scathing comments about
Bellemonte came back to him. She had called it a collection of run-down buildings, and he already had enough of
those at Dallamire.

'Excuse me.' Rosina sat forward. 'What is Bellemonte?'

'Part of my inheritance from my godfather. Land and
buildings in the south of the county, close to Bristol. Hugo
bought it as a business venture but sadly he died before he
could do anything with it.' His mouth twisted. 'From the reports I have had, the buildings are dilapidated and it would
require a great deal of money to put it right.'

'But surely you should at least look at it,' she persisted.

'Putting Dallamire in order must be my priority.'

'Of course, my lord, but to sell it without even seeing it...'

She stopped and looked at Matt, who said, 'You have
to admit, Conham, Miss Brackwood has a point. We are
here for another week yet. What harm would it do to visit
Bellemonte?'

'I have not yet seen all the estate here,' he pointed out.

'That should not take more than a couple of days,' said Rosina. 'Three, at most.'

Conham found two pairs of eyes upon him and felt himself weakening. Perhaps it was the wine, but his mood had lightened. Alicia might be wrong about the state of his inheritance. After all, she had been very dismissive of Morton Gifford, calling it a few insignificant acres, and yet Rosina thought it could return a pretty profit, under the right management.

He threw up his hands. 'If you are going to unite against me, what can I say? Very well, I will send word to Bellemonte tomorrow that I will be visiting the property. But I insist you both come with me.'

'Oh.' Rosina looked startled. 'But it cannot be necessary for me to go, my lord.'

'Nonsense. I told you a man needs his friends about him at a time like this. You and Matt will accompany me and give your opinion of Bellemonte, since you both know as much about the matter as I. Besides,' he said, a mischievous smile growing inside him, 'I do not intend to be the only one wasting my time on what I have no doubt will be a wild-goose chase!'

Friends. There was that word again. Rosina turned her attention back to her meal. There was no doubt she felt valued here, in this unfamiliar house, miles from the home she had known all her life. Not only was the earl going to pay her to maintain and hopefully improve Gifford Manor, but she was also accompanying him and his aide-de-camp to Bellemonte. How long was it since someone had asked her opinion of anything?

She felt confused, dazed at the sudden change in her fortunes. Her comfortable existence had ended almost a year ago, when Papa had died. Since then, life had become ever more of a trial. Her brother had rebuffed all her attempts to help him manage Brackwood. Remembering their last, violent encounter sent a shudder down her spine.

'Are you cold, Miss Brackwood?' the earl asked her.

'No, not really.' She looked up, surprised to find the meal was over and the servants had come in to remove the covers. 'A little tired, I think. I beg your pardon, it is very late and I should retire.'

When she rose, the gentlemen stood, too, and the earl walked over to the door.

'Good night, Miss Brackwood,' he said. 'You will find a servant waiting for you in the hall. I have ordered him to escort you back to the lodge.'

Rosina stopped.

'I am five-and-twenty, Lord Dallamire. I no longer require a chaperone.'

'At your advanced age, perhaps not,' he replied gravely. 'However, I insist you allow him to light your way, through these darker months.'

She was touched by his concern and looked at him, torn between amusement and exasperation.

'Another of your little foibles, my lord?'

'Precisely.'

A smile warmed his eyes and Rosina felt the heat rising to her cheeks. Quickly, she bade both men good-night and hurried out of the room.

Chapter Seven

Two days later Lord Dallamire's carriage set off for Belle-monte just as the sun was burning off the morning mist. Winter had not yet taken hold and Rosina gazed out at the passing landscape, enchanted by the rich autumn colours of the trees on the far hills, their yellow and gold leaves glowing even in the weak sunlight. She was now familiar with the lanes immediately around the Manor, but as they drove south, she recognised very little. On her previous journey, when she had first come to Morton Gifford, she had been too anxious to take in very much at all about the landscape. Now, at least for the present, she was safe, but if Edgar should discover her whereabouts, or if the earl withdrew his support, what then?

Best not to think of that, she told herself firmly. She could not change the past and must look to the future.

In due course they arrived at a straggling village and turned down a lane past a dilapidated inn to a large cob-bled square.

Conham jumped out and gave a cursory glance around. Theirs was the only vehicle and there was no one in sight, save a ragged man, asleep against the wall of the inn. They had stopped outside a large building where a faded sign an-nounced it as The Grand Pleasure Baths. Before them was a substantial house, once a gentleman's residence, but now unoccupied, its windows shuttered and boarded. Finally, the western side of the square was defined by a set of rusty railings with large gates at the centre. On the rising land behind the gates, he could see an avenue of trees cutting through the ragged and overgrown shrubbery.

Conham was unable to keep the sarcasm from his voice as he turned back and gave his hand to Rosina.

'Welcome to Bellemonte, my grand inheritance!'

'How...how interesting.'

'Is that what you call it!' He grimaced. 'A decrepit ruin would be more accurate.'

'The park beyond the railings looks very inviting.'

'If you like neglected gardens!'

Matthew had climbed out of the far door and chuckled as he limped around to join them on the footway.

'You are determined to find fault, Conham. It is far bigger than I anticipated. Does your inheritance include the pleasure baths, too?'

Conham cast his eyes towards the large wall that had presumably been built to preserve the privacy of the bathers.

'Aye, it does, although heaven knows what state it is in,' he muttered, glancing up at the weathered sign with its peeling paint. 'Now, where is the fellow who is to meet us?' He looked around the square. 'Ah, this might be he.'

A tall individual was hurrying towards them, wiping his mouth with a large spotted handkerchief in a way that suggested he had just come from the inn. He was dressed in a puce-coloured coat with wide padded shoulders and a nipped waist. Despite the cold weather, the coat was unbuttoned to show a garishly patterned waistcoat and a cravat so intricately tied and folded that it frothed beneath his chin, while the shirt points were so high they covered his cheeks.

'Lord Dallamire. Good day to you, m'lord.' The man swaggered up, removing his hat to expose a head covered in improbably black curls as he made a low bow. 'Josiah Hackthorpe at your service!'

He gave Rosina and Matthew a perfunctory nod when Conham introduced them, but quickly turned back to the earl.

'Your Lordship will be wanting to see Bellemonte. It will be my honour to show you everything, my lord!'

Conham was inclined to resent this slight to his companions, but rather than being offended, they were exchanging looks that were brim full of amusement as the fellow made another obsequious bow. However, he was reluctant to let such rudeness pass. He wanted to make a show of offering his arm to Rosina but as if reading his thoughts, she gave a slight shake of her head and turned to Matthew, tucking her hand into the curve of his elbow.

'Aye, lead on,' said Matt cheerfully. 'We are all ready now.'

Two hours later they were back in the chaise and bowling along the Gloucester Road.

'I beg your pardon,' said Conham, feeling obliged to offer Rosina an apology. 'I should never have taken you there.'

'But why not?' she replied cheerfully. 'I thoroughly enjoyed looking around Bellemonte.'

'Hackthorpe was unconscionably rude to you.'

'Aye, and you almost added to it,' Matt said bluntly. 'Having told the fellow that we were both in your employ, if you had offered your arm to Miss Brackwood there is only one conclusion he would have drawn from that.'

'Fustian. I was merely being courteous.'

'Hackthorpe wouldn't understand that. The fellow's a tuft hunter. He'd think you had brought your—'

'Yes, yes, no need to go on!' said Conham hastily.

'Mr Talacre is correct,' added Rosina. 'The man was only interested in one opinion, my lord. Yours.'

'Then he is a fool!'

'Undoubtedly.' Matt laughed. 'But we were both amused, watching the fellow bowing and scraping to you.'

The earl grimaced. 'Not an experience I enjoy. I would rather he had told the truth, that the place is beyond repair.'

'Oh, I wouldn't say that,' said Rosina. 'Although I have to admit the old house was in very poor condition. The nails and splinters were determined to catch at my skirts.'

'It was a waste of a morning,' he declared. 'The house is nothing but a shell, stripped of all its furniture and fine panelling. The inn has become a common ale house, and as for the pleasure gardens, as they are named, it would re-quire an army of gardeners to return them to order, despite what that rascally manager said!'

'But the baths are still popular,' Rosina pointed out.

'I applaud the philanthropic idea, to provide a bathing pool that everyone may use for a penny, but it barely brings in enough to cover its costs,' he replied. 'I shall write to my lawyers immediately with instructions to sell it all off as soon as may be. The whole place is beyond redemption.'

'Do you really think so? I think it has great possibilities.'

She was regarding him, her head on one side like a little bird. He laughed.

'You sound like the fellow my grandfather brought in to landscape the grounds at Dallamire.'

'Then I think you mean *capabilities*,' she corrected him, her blue eyes twinkling. 'Capability Brown. My father often said he would have liked to have him transform the park at Brackwood. Not that Papa could afford it, but as he said, one could always dream.'

She stopped, a small sigh escaping her, and Conham noted the sudden sadness in her eyes. He sought for something to distract her.

'Very well, tell me what *possibilities* you see at Bellemonte.'

'It was more a feeling than any fixed ideas. Let me see, it is on high ground, so the air is clear. And from the top of the hill, the views over Bristol and the countryside are very good.'

'Yes,' said Matt, 'and they would be even better if the overgrown bushes were cut back and the terrace on the ridge cleared of weeds.'

Rosina nodded. 'I agree. The same applies to the rest of the gardens. I do not believe they are beyond rescue, but there would be a cost, of course.'

'And therein lies the rub,' Conham retorted. 'Dallamire Hall needs a deal of work, and the land needs investment to improve it. I might be able to justify keeping Gifford Manor, if it pays its way, but Bellemonte must be sold.'

'Yes, of course, my lord.'

'But you will not be making any final decisions just yet,' said Matthew.

'No, not immediately, but I have the ledgers now,' he said, patting the heavy books piled on the seat beside him. I mean to take them with me to London next week. I shall have to take advice on the market price of such a property, but I hope it will provide something towards the restoring of Dallamire.'

Chapter Eight

Rosina spent the next two days exploring Morton Gifford with Lord Dallamire. He told her it was ten years since he had stayed here for any length of time, but when they drove around the estate in the gig, she was surprised how many of the people he already knew. From the conversations that followed it was clear they remembered him fondly and she began to build up a picture of Conham as a schoolboy. Polite and friendly, interested in people and eager to please.

Then there were the tenants who had come to Morton Gifford in more recent years, to whom she could introduce *him*. They were naturally cautious of meeting such a grand personage as the Earl of Dallamire, but his easy manners soon won them over.

'You have made excellent progress in little more than a week,' he said as she drove the gig back to the Manor on the second day. 'I expected a great deal more resistance to the new ideas you have proposed.'

Rosina flushed, pleased and gratified by his words.

'It was not difficult to persuade them that change has to come, especially since they will benefit, as well as the estate.'

'I think you underrate yourself, ma'am. Local people are notoriously suspicious of newcomers.'

She laughed and shook her head. 'The previous steward made himself so odious that almost anyone would be welcome!'

'I don't agree, but let us not argue. Suffice to say that I am confident I am leaving the Manor in good hands.'

'Thank you. I only wish there was more time to show you some of the hill farms and hamlets further afield.'

'Yes, we would have covered more ground if we had been riding. What a pity there is no lady's mount in my godfather's stable.'

'Well, even if there had been, I have no riding habit.'

'Then that must be remedied before my next visit. Get yourself a habit and ask Skillet to seek out a suitable mount for you. Charge everything to the accounts.'

'Oh, no, I could not do that!'

'You can and you will.'

'But you are paying me so well. Far, far more than I would earn as a governess or a companion.'

'It is no more than Frumald was being paid, and now he is not here to cream off the profits from the estate, I hope to see far more going back into the coffers! And trust me, your salary will not go far once you have employed someone to look after the lodge for you.'

She bit her lip. 'My lord, I cannot thank you enough for giving me this opportunity.'

'Then don't,' he interrupted her, adding roughly, 'I needed a steward and if Edgar Brackwood could not see your worth then he is a fool as well as a villain.'

Rosina's thoughts had been far away from her brother, but her heart began to race with panic as the memory of his betrayal came rushing back. How he had sent her off to Bristol, to certain death. The horse jibbed as her hands tightened on the reins.

'I beg your pardon,' said the earl quickly. 'I did not mean to upset you.'

'No, no. I was not… That is…' She steadied herself and the horse. 'I was surprised by the recollections. I am so busy now, I rarely think of Edgar.'

'I am glad. He doesn't deserve that you should think of him.'

He reached out and briefly squeezed one of her hands. Rosina froze, her heart thudding so hard again that it was suddenly difficult to breathe. She kept her eyes fixed on the road, fighting for calm. What she was feeling now was nothing like her revulsion at the thought of her brother. This was entirely different. Her whole body felt alive with a sudden, blinding awareness of the man sitting beside her.

They had been driving together all day, chatting companionably, his shoulder sometimes rubbing against hers when the gig bumped over the uneven roads. It had been relaxed, enjoyable, but now she was almost overcome by unexpected sensations. A sudden tension inside her, a powerful yearning for him to pull her into his arms and kiss her, as he had done on their very first meeting. She had never felt such strong, primal feelings before and they frightened her.

'Are you ill, Rosina? Would you like me to drive?'

'No. Thank you, I can manage now.'

It took a supreme effort to drag her thoughts away from the desire pooling inside her but somehow, she succeeded. The earl had employed her as his land steward, a role normally performed by a man. To betray weakness, instability, would be disastrous. She could not afford to lose this position now. From somewhere deep inside she hauled up a smile.

'I was feeling a little homesick for Brackwood, that is all. I am quite well now, my lord.'

It was not true, but the earl would be leaving Morton Gifford in a few days. She would do her best to avoid his company and regain control of these foolish and unruly desires. They had no place in her new life. In fact, they could prove disastrous.

Rosina was a little quiet and withdrawn at dinner but Conham did not remark upon it. He blamed himself for mentioning her brother while they were out in the gig. It had brought back a host of painful memories for her. She had hidden it well and drove back to the Manor without incident, but Conham had been aware of a certain restraint afterwards, as if Rosina had withdrawn a little. She retired early, pleading fatigue, and on Sunday morning, as he waited in the hall for the carriage to take them all to church, he hoped she would not cry off.

In fact, it was Matthew who did that, joining him in the hall to explain why he would not be going.

'I have not attended a service for years and I'm damned if I will start now.'

'Well, most likely you are,' Conham replied. 'Damned, that is.'

A soft laugh made him look up. Rosina was coming down the stairs, dressed for the short journey in her grey pelisse and with the ribbons of her bonnet tied at a jaunty angle beneath her chin. His pleasure in seeing that she had quite recovered her spirits made him forget all about Matthew until he felt a quick dig in the ribs.

'That is not the sort of language to use in front of a lady, Conham!'

'I have heard far worse, from both of you,' she retorted, smiling as she came across to join them.

'My apologies, all the same,' said Matt. He gave a little bow. 'I shall leave you both to do your duty, and hope the sermon is neither too long nor too dull!'

Rosina's eyes twinkled merrily as she thanked him. 'And I shall say a prayer for your redemption.'

'I fear it will take more than one prayer for that rogue!' said Conham, watching Matthew limp away.

'Very likely,' said Rosina, a laugh in her voice. 'But I like him, all the same. The carriage is at the door now, my lord. Shall we go?'

After the service, there were any number of parishioners wishing to make themselves known to the earl, or to remind him of their acquaintance. As everyone milled around the churchyard in the weak sunshine, Conham noticed that Rosina, too, was busily engaged. She chatted with tenants and their wives, farmers and neighbours, always friendly, but with a quiet dignity that he thought could not fail to please. There was a rosy glow to her cheeks and he barely recognised the bedraggled waif he had rescued in Bristol.

'So she is your replacement for that rogue Frumald!'

The gravelly voice jolted Conham from his muse and he turned to find a portly, bewhiskered gentleman in a brown coat and bagwig standing beside him. It was Sir John Rissington, the squire.

'Yes, that is Miss Brackwood, Sir John.' He bowed, lower than necessary perhaps, but the last time they had met, he himself had been little more than a grubby school-boy. 'Have you been introduced?'

'Aye. That is, she went out of her way to make herself known to me, when we met by chance. All very right and proper,' he added quickly, shooting a glance at Conham. 'She was with Skillet and he performed the introductions.'

This was an opportunity to spread word of Rosina's eligibility for the post of land steward, and Conham knew he must make the most of it.

'Miss Brackwood is highly experienced in land management, Sir John. She was running her father's estates in Somerset until he died last year.'

'Ah, that explains why she is so assured.' The squire nodded. 'Pity, though. A handsome gel like that should be married.'

'Perhaps she will be, one day. But for now, I have gained an excellent steward.'

The older man regarded Rosina, his bushy eyebrows drawn together. 'You know what everyone will think.'

'I am aware it is somewhat…irregular,' Conham replied calmly. 'However, she has her own staff in the steward's lodge, and until I decide what to do with the property, I need someone to manage the land.'

'And anyone would be better than that scoundrel the trustees put in charge! Well, well. She seems a very capable young woman. Has a good head on her shoulders, too. She asked if she might call on me for advice, if she needs it. I said yes, of course, but I'd be grateful if you will make sure she knows I meant it. Hugo Conham was a good friend. It has pained me to see his property so misused.'

With that, the squire walked off, leaving the earl to the mercy of another neighbour wishing to make himself known. By the time Conham had extricated himself from everyone who wanted a word, Rosina was already sitting in the carriage.

'I beg your pardon for keeping you waiting,' he said as he climbed in. 'I thought I would never get away!'

'Are you surprised?' she asked him. 'Everyone is eager to speak with the new owner of Gifford Manor.'

'And its steward,' he retorted, grinning at her.

'Well, yes, although I know a good number of your tenants now, and this is an excellent way to become acquainted with their families. It is early days, but I think most of them are happy to accept me as steward.'

'They are. Although one or two came to me with their problems today.'

'Oh, I am sorry.'

'No need for that. I instructed them to talk to you. Told them you have my full confidence. It is true, you know,' he told her, when she flushed. 'From what I have seen and heard thus far, I am happy to leave everything in your hands until Lady Day.'

'Thank you, my lord.'

He paused. 'And Squire Rissington tells me he will be happy to give you the benefit of his advice, which could be useful. He owns most of the land around Morton Gifford.'

'I know. That is why I thought it would be wise to make the acquaintance of Sir John and his lady.'

She turned to gaze out the window and Conham sat back, content to watch her. She had the most delightful profile, with its straight little nose and that dainty chin. How long would it be, he wondered, before someone paid court to her? She had insisted that she valued her independence, but that could change, if a suitor came along who was sufficiently rich and charming. He did not like the idea, but it was no business of his. Rosina had said she would stay until Lady Day, but after that... If he was going to sell the place it would not matter, but if he kept it, he might need to find a new steward.

When they reached the Manor Rosina went off to her

office, saying she had unfinished business that required attention, and Conham was left standing in the hall. He felt restless, unable to settle to anything indoors. He glanced out the window then set off at a run up the stairs. There were still a good few hours of daylight left, enough time for a brisk walk to clear his head.

Having walked further than intended, Conham did not go down to the drawing room until shortly before dinner. He found Matt Talacre and Rosina already there and deep in conversation.

They broke off when he came in, Matt handing him a glass of wine and quizzing him for being late.

'How little faith you have in me,' Conham scoffed. 'And in my valet.'

'Oh, I have complete faith in Dawkins,' Matt retorted. 'The man is a saint, and can turn you out in style in the blink of an eye. Once you are present!'

He winked at Rosina, who chuckled, but since dinner was announced at that moment there was no time for more teasing exchanges. They went into the dining room, where conversation rambled over politics before touching on Conham's appearance at church that morning.

'I've no doubt that caused a flutter in the dovecot,' Matthew remarked.

'Not unexpected, but it proved useful.' Conham reached for the buttered parsnips and added some to his plate. 'Many of those I spoke with were glad I had taken possession at last.'

He passed the dish to Matthew, who said, 'But do they know you are looking to sell?'

'I am hoping now it need not come to that, if the new plans Rosina has in mind show progress by Lady Day.'

She looked up at that. 'You have read them already?'

'I have read enough to instruct you to make a start,' he replied.

'And what of Bellemonte?' asked Matt.

'The sooner that is off my hands the better.' Conham saw him exchange a glance with Rosina and put down his knife and fork.

'What?' he demanded. 'What have you two been plotting?'

Rosina shook her head. 'Not plotting, my lord. But Matthew and I have been *discussing* Bellemonte's future.'

'Oh, is that why you had your heads together when I came in? I call that plotting.'

'We had to talk of something, since you were so damnably late,' retorted Matt. 'Rosina thinks something might be done to improve the pleasure grounds at relatively little cost.'

Matthew? Rosina? Conham frowned. They hardly knew each other and were already on first-name terms.

He said, more sharply than he intended, 'I have already looked at the ledgers. The gardens are barely breaking even.'

'That is because they are so sadly run-down,' observed Rosina.

'As are the buildings. Everything at Bellemonte is beyond redemption.'

When she did not reply, Conham looked up and noticed the stubborn tilt to her chin.

'But you are not convinced.'

'No,' she said. 'I, too, have looked at the accounts, my lord. The baths are already breaking even and with a little improvement the income can be increased. I also think it is possible to revive the gardens.'

'You need to look into it, man,' said Matthew. 'Here, Rosina, let me help you to a little more of the fricasseed rabbit. It is exceedingly good.'

Conham frowned. 'I do not need to look into it. Belle-monte requires investment. Money that I don't have.'

'We should pay Bellemonte another visit, Matthew,' Rosina suggested as if he had not spoken. 'We need to look at it again, more closely. Mr Hackthorpe said they have a concert every Monday evening in the tea rooms. With supper, and all for the princely sum of threepence!'

Matt snorted. 'No wonder they are not making a profit.'

'It is so shabby that even threepence is probably too much!' muttered Conham.

'Yes, but that could be remedied, my lord.'

'Enough now, madam. Cease your funning and let's say no more about it.'

He frowned at Rosina, but Matt Talacre was not so easily silenced.

'Actually, I think it would be a very good thing to visit the gardens tomorrow night, Conham. To see just what it is you have inherited.' He grinned. 'And I am intrigued by the idea of your owning a pleasure gardens!'

'Well, you need not be, because I won't be their owner for long!'

'We shall go as paying customers,' Matt went on, ignoring him. 'What say you, Rosina? Supper and a concert, and perhaps a stroll about the gardens after.'

'In November?' protested Conham.

'Mr Hackthorpe said the gardens by lamplight are very popular,' Rosina reminded him.

'Aye, with the riff-raff from the surrounding villages! It would not be safe for you, madam.'

Her brows went up. 'How can you know that? Besides, I have no intention of wandering around the dark avenues *alone*, my lord.' She gave him a sunny smile. 'I shall not feel nervous with you and Matthew to escort me. Besides, as the owner of the gardens, my lord, you really should be aware of what the people are getting for their money.'

Conham found his resolution crumbling.

'Rosina's right,' Matt told him. 'Nothing like surveying the ground before taking action, my friend. You told me that, when we were in the army.'

Two pairs of eyes were fixed upon him and Conham capitulated.

'Very well,' he said with just the suggestion of gritted teeth. 'We shall go, but I shall not inform Hackthorpe. I do not want him fawning over us all evening!'

Chapter Nine

They arrived at Bellemonte to find only a few vehicles in the square, but any number of people were making their way into the gardens on foot. The earl surveyed the crowds through his eyeglass.

'A distinctly dubious assortment of customers,' he remarked. 'Are you sure you want to go in?'

Matthew was already opening the door.

'We are here now, we should at least take a look,' he said, climbing out.

They left the carriage and joined the throng filing through the gates.

'There is one of the reasons the receipts are so poor,' remarked Matt, glancing along the broken railings. 'People are slipping in through the gaps.'

The Pavilion was a large building that had clearly seen better days, and Josiah Hackthorpe had not taken them inside on their earlier visit. Now they went into the concert room. It was a large, airy space, in need of decoration but otherwise perfectly acceptable. The orchestra, when it began, was woefully under-rehearsed. After sitting through half an hour of poorly played chamber music, Conham could stand no more. He escorted his companions away to the supper room. There were large fireplaces at each end of this ornate chamber, but only one fire was burning and the air felt damp. They each took a glass of wine from a hovering waiter and made their way to where a cold collation was set out on long tables at one side of the room. The food was plentiful, but it all looked dry and unappetising.

'Oh, dear,' murmured Rosina, a laugh trembling in her voice. 'Mr Hackthorpe told us his suppers would rival the finest you could find in Bath.'

Matthew scoffed. 'He clearly did not expect us to come and see for ourselves.'

'No.' Conham had put aside his wine after only one sip. Now he raised his quizzing glass and surveyed the table. 'Mrs Jameson can provide us with a far superior meal. I think we should forego supper and take a stroll in the gardens before returning to Gifford Manor.'

His suggestion was readily accepted by his companions. They collected their outdoor clothes and went out to explore the gardens.

'It will be quicker if we split up,' said Matt as they moved away from the buildings. 'I am going to look at the boundary fencing. I want to see if it is all as bad as those railings at the entrance. Rosina, perhaps you and the earl can see if the lighted paths are as good as Hackthorpe said they would be.'

'Very well, although I do not hold out much hope of it.' Conham took out his watch. 'We shall meet back here in, say, an hour.'

'That will hardly give me time to walk the boundary,' Matt objected. 'Let's make it two.'

Conham was about to say he would be damned if he'd spend two hours wandering around the neglected gardens, but Rosina spoke first.

'I agree, Matthew. We need to spend a little time looking

at everything we can. Lord Dallamire will not have another opportunity before he leaves Gloucestershire.'

'Confound it, I have already told you my opinion!'

'You have indeed, my lord,' she replied, 'But since we are here we might as well make a thorough inspection, don't you agree?'

He wanted to say no, he did not agree, but she was smiling up at him in a way that dissolved his rising temper. He contented himself with a scowl, which only made her laugh.

'Come along, then, my lord, let us make a start!'

Matthew limped away into the shrubbery and Rosina set off with the earl along the main walk, which was illuminated by numerous coloured lamps hanging from the trees.

'This is very pretty,' she observed. The earl did not reply and she glanced at him. 'I do believe you are sulking.'

'Nonsense!'

'You would rather be anywhere than this. Pray, do not be afraid to say so, Lord Dallamire.' She hesitated then added in a mournful tone, 'It would be the most savage blow to my self-esteem, but I shall bear it.'

'Witch!'

She laughed. 'No, no, merely trying to coax you out of the sullens, as any friend would do.'

'Ha, with friends such as you and Matt Talacre—'

'Yes, you are very fortunate, are you not, my lord?'

'That is not how I would put it. Quiet now. If we have to explore these damned gardens the least you can do is spare me your teasing.'

Having succeeded in coaxing him out of his bad mood, Rosina fell silent. For a short time.

'I have never visited Vauxhall Gardens, my lord. Is this very like?'

'Not much.' A small group of revellers came towards them and the earl pulled her quickly to one side.

'I suppose people there are better behaved,' she said, watching the little party continue unsteadily on its way.

'Not at all. Despite the higher ticket prices, and extortionate sums for what passes as supper, Vauxhall can be riotous, especially when everyone is masked.' He pulled her hand back onto his arm and set off again. 'However, it is in far better condition than this! For one thing, the Grand Walk is much wider, and has many more lamps.'

'I agree the foliage has seriously encroached on this path, but I think this has a certain charm.'

'If you say so, madam. *I'd* say it is beyond saving.'

'I noticed when we were here in daylight that there are recesses and alcoves on either side of the path.' She began to look around. 'They are all overgrown now, but I remember seeing a few stone figures…yes, there is one. I can see the head and shoulders rising above the shrubs. And on the other side there is a small colonnade. Look, you can just see the tops of the columns.'

'Yes, you are right. I think there are even more, up here.'

They continued to peer into the shadows at the side of the meandering main path, and even if Dallamire was not quite as eager as Rosina, at least she thought he was now showing more interest in the gardens. The ground had been rising steadily but soon they reached a bend, where the main route curved away and downwards, leaving only a narrow track leading up into the darkness.

Rosina stopped. 'Why, that is the way to the viewing terrace! Do you remember, Conham? We walked up there and looked out over Bristol.'

'Yes, I remember.' He pretended not to notice that in her excitement she had used his name. 'What of it?'

'We should walk up and look at the same view at night.'

'There is no moon.'

'There is a crescent,' she said. 'From the viewing point we should be able to pick out the river and the city.'

'But why would we want to do that?'

'Having looked out over Bristol by day, I should like to see the same view at night.'

She had turned to look up at him, the lamplight showing her hopeful expression. He sighed.

'Very well, if that is what you want.'

'I do,' she said. 'Who knows if I shall ever have the chance to do so again?'

'And I would by no means curtail any pleasure of yours,' he said politely.

She gave him a sunny smile. 'Thank you!'

She turned and headed towards the upward track. Conham followed, but they had gone no more than a few steps along the path before she stopped. He could see why. After the lamplight of the main walk there was nothing but impenetrable shadow beneath the close, overhanging branches. He remembered how they had pushed aside the untended plants on either side of the track when they had walked there in daylight. In the dark it would be almost impossible to negotiate.

More than enough reason to turn back, he thought. A perfect excuse to cut short this pointless exercise.

Instead, he reached up and unhooked one of the lamps from the nearest tree. Then, taking her hand, he set off into the darkness.

The single lamp gave them barely enough light to see their way, and Conham kept Rosina behind him to protect her from the worst of the overgrown foliage. Mostly it was just leaves, or stray tendrils of ivy, but the occasional small branch caught at their clothes. He stopped again.

'This is not sensible, Rosina.'

'Pho,' she answered him. 'It is only a few twigs. Besides, it cannot be far now, I can see the night sky. Look.'

It was true; there was a definite lightness ahead of them and in a very short time they stepped out of the constricting darkness of the trees to see the sliver of moon suspended high above them.

'There, you see?' she declared, moving ahead of him. 'It is light as day out here.'

It was a gross exaggeration, but Conham said nothing. He followed her up the winding path until they had reached the long terrace that marked the northernmost boundary of the grounds. Beyond was nothing but fields and a large wood, but Rosina had turned to look back over the gardens and towards the city.

'There.' She clasped her hands before her. 'I *said* it would be worth the effort!'

Conham gazed out at the view. Over the treetops he could see the pale outline of the lower gardens and the Pavilion. Beyond that, in the distance, were the roofs and spires of Bristol and the river winding in and around everything like a silver ribbon. He glanced at Rosina. Her eyes, her whole attention, was fixed on the distant city and something contracted inside him, like an iron band around his chest.

His years in the army had taken him to many countries. He had stood on hills and mountain ridges in Portugal and Spain, gazing down on cities far grander than Bristol, but here, now, sharing this moment with Rosina and witnessing her innocent pleasure, he thought this must be the most memorable of them all.

A sudden gust of wind raced across the terrace, icy and biting. It flung Rosina's blue cloak back from her shoulders. As if waking from a dream she started, her hands fumbling to reach the cape that was fluttering away behind her.

'Here, let me help you.'

Conham put down the lamp and caught the flapping material, stepping close to wrap the warm woollen folds about her. For a moment they stood thus, her back pressed against his chest and his arms around her. The strong wind had teased free several curls from beneath her close-fitting jockey cap, and the tendrils brushed his chin. His pulse quickened. He closed his eyes, imagining how it would be to turn her about, to feel her heart beating against his as he captured those soft lips beneath his own. To explore her mouth with his tongue and kiss her until she was moaning with pleasure...

'Thank you, Lord Dallamire.' She was gently pulling the mantle from his fingers. 'I have it now.'

He stepped back smartly, breathing in the cold air, fighting down the desire raging through him. What the devil was he doing? He picked up the lamp.

'We should get back.'

'Yes.'

She turned, avoiding his eyes and clutching her cloak around her as if it could defend her from far more than the weather. Confound it, had she guessed what was in his mind? It was not his way to tamper with innocents. Or to promise more than he could give. Conham reminded himself sharply that he needed to marry a fortune.

A flurry of snow whirled in from one of the small clouds scudding across the sky and he said, trying to lighten the mood, 'We are going just in time, I think.' He put out his

hand but she did not move. He felt rather than saw her re-
luctance and let it fall again. 'Stay close behind me.'

They set off back down the path, Conham going ahead
and holding the lamp high. Even so, he knew Rosina would
be walking in his shadow. He could protect her from ob-
truding branches but she would not be able to see the rough,
uneven path beneath her feet. He stopped.

'I'd be happier if I knew you hadn't tripped or slipped,'
he said, without turning around. 'Take hold of my coat.'

He thought she might refuse, then he felt a slight tug as
she clutched at his greatcoat. They set off again, Conham
shortening his stride to make sure he did not outpace her.

By the time they reached the main path again, Rosina
had regained her composure. Not that she would have lost
it, if her cape had not flown open. If Dallamire had not
stepped up so close. He had enveloped her, his broad chest
against her back, his strong arms wrapped around her. Su-
premely warm and comforting yet oh, so very dangerous!

While the earl replaced the lamp on a branch of the nearest tree, she fidgeted, refastening her cloak. She needed to
rid herself of the wicked thoughts and images crowding her
head. They were turning her insides to water. For someone
who prided herself on her common sense, she had shown
a sad lack of it this evening.

Nothing to do with the earl's presence, of course. It was
merely the moonlight and the dark sky with its scattering
of stars. And the night air, she thought, a touch wistfully.
It had been calm, almost balmy, before that wintry breeze
blew in and whipped away her cloak. Heaven knew what
might have happened if they had stayed there any longer,

the earl with his arms about her, his breath on her cheek and her whole body crying out for him to kiss her.

Just the thought of what might have followed sent another delicious shiver down her spine and she was obliged to give herself a mental scolding. Conham had made her land steward of Morton Gifford with a salary she could never attain in more conventional female roles. She must never forget that. If she made a success of this and could keep her good name, then it might be possible to find a similar post elsewhere, to secure an independent future for herself.

When Dallamire offered her his arm she took it, head up, breathing steadily as they set off back towards the Pavilion. Being alone in the moonlight with a handsome man might be construed by many females as incredibly romantic, but Rosina had no time for such silliness.

The main path was far busier than when they set out, and Rosina guessed supper in the Pavilion was now over. She also suspected that many of those they passed were intoxicated. With Dallamire at her side Rosina felt perfectly safe, but it was clear that Bellemonte's visitors were far from respectable, as she observed to her companions once they were all safely in the carriage and on their way back to Gifford Manor.

'Precisely,' said the earl. 'I have neither the time nor the funds to turn the gardens around. Hackthorpe's contract runs out on Christmas Day, then Bellemonte will be put up for sale to the highest bidder, and that's an end to it!'

No more was said on the subject for the remainder of the journey. Rosina settled back in one corner, content to listen to Conham and Matthew talking in a desultory manner. It was clear to her now that they were more than just master and servant. There was a strong bond between them. She remembered Conham's words to her at the lodge, about having friends around him. With the loss of her father and Edgar's treachery still raw, it was no small comfort to think that these men regarded her as a friend.

And that, she told herself, was another reason to be thankful she had not made a fool of herself upon the viewing terrace tonight.

The carriage made good time returning to Morton Gifford, and when they reached the Manor, Rosina declared she had no appetite for supper, but would retire immediately.

'Then I will walk you to the lodge,' said the earl.

'Thank you, my lord, but your footman is already here and waiting to do so.'

'Then he can go away again.' He dismissed the man with a wave. 'I shall accompany you.'

Rosina gazed at him helplessly. He might call her a friend, but he was still her employer. How could she refuse?

'Besides,' he continued, 'it will give Matthew time to arrange for our supper to be brought to the library, and to make sure there is a good fire burning.'

'I should have known he would not let me rest,' declared Matt, grinning. 'I shall bid you good-night, then, Rosina. Sleep well.'

He lounged away and the earl turned to Rosina. 'Shall we go?'

She fell into step beside him on the drive, taking care not to walk so close that their arms might brush.

'Matthew and I are leaving in the morning,' he reminded her. 'I hope you will join us for breakfast. We can go over any last-minute details that might arise. About the estate.'

Rosina felt a ripple of apprehension at the prospect of being here alone, without the earl's presence. What if her brother found her? He had tried to do away with her once; next time she might not escape. She quickly shook off her fears. She was not alone here, there were any number of servants and she was well-known in the area. Edgar could not drag her away from Morton Gifford against her will.

'A good idea, my lord,' she said now. 'I will be there.'

'Good. And if you use the carriage while I am away, you must instruct the driver to bring you to your door.'

'Indeed I shall not,' she replied, indignant. 'I am not a guest here but land steward, at least until Lady Day.'

'I would have thought seeing Bellemonte tonight might have discouraged you from staying even that long!'

'But I have very little to do with Bellemonte, which is fortunate, since I shall be busy enough looking after Gifford Manor and its land. I do not want to let you down.'

'Somehow, I don't think you will do that.'

His smile and the warm tone he used sent a little flutter through Rosina, a warm mixture of pride and pleasure, and she was grateful for the darkness to hide the telltale blush upon her cheek.

It took only a few minutes to reach the lodge. Not long enough, thought Conham, as they approached the small building. He stopped and turned to Rosina.

'Good night, Miss Brackwood.'

'Thank you.'

His brows went up. 'What, for escorting you here?'

'No, not just that. For including me in your visit to Bellemonte tonight. For asking my opinion, even if you have already made up your mind to sell.'

He looked up to the night sky and sighed. 'I am not selling it through choice, Rosina. Heaven knows Bellemonte is in such a parlous state it will fetch little enough, but there is

no alternative. Dallamire must be my priority. I need every
penny I have to keep it in order. And more.'

'Yes, of course.'

The stars were twinkling above them, just as they had
done at Bellemonte. He took a deep breath.

'That's why I must find a rich wife. You do understand
that, Rosina?'

He dragged his eyes away from the stars and fixed them
on her face. She nodded.

'To quote from one of Papa's favourite books, "Handsome young men must have something to live on, as well
as the plain."'

She was looking up at him, her eyes reflecting the star-
light, and he could not tear his gaze away. The air around
them was thick and charged with electricity, like the pre-
lude to a thunderstorm. One word, one touch, and he knew
the storm would break. He felt suddenly awkward, off balance, but there was something he must tell her.

'Rosina—'

The lodge door opened with a creak and lamplight
spilled out around the black outline of the maid. Conham
could no longer see Rosina's expression, but he caught the
slight lift of her shoulders and heard a murmured 'good-
night' before she disappeared into the house.

He turned away, balling his hands into tight fists as he
began to walk swiftly back to the Manor. Confound it, was
the lady's position not precarious enough without his trying to take advantage of her at every opportunity? He was
a damned rogue. She was in his employ, and she was also
fiercely independent. Despite the strong attraction, he could
not afford to marry her. He needed a bride with a substantial dowry. A great many people, including his stepmother

and half-sisters, were depending upon him to repair the fortune his father had gambled away.

Reaching the house, he strode inside, but instead of making his way to the library he went up to his room, telling the butler, whom he met on the stairs, to make his apologies to Mr Talacre and say he would see him in the morning.

Chapter Ten

The earl went down to breakfast to find Matt Talacre alone at the table.

'My apologies for last night,' he said before Matt could speak. 'I found I was not hungry after all, just dog-tired.'

'Aye, so Jameson informed me.'

Conham saw the speculative gleam in his friend's eyes but willed himself not to react.

'Once I had handed Miss Brackwood over to her maid, I went straight to bed.'

Matt shrugged. 'No matter. I had plenty to occupy me.'

'Oh?'

'Yes. I sat down and wrote out my thoughts about Belle-monte.'

'Would you like to share them?' Anything, as long as it stopped Matt from talking of Rosina.

'Very well.'

Matthew paused while he selected another bread roll from the basket on the table.

'After I had inspected the boundary fencing last night, I went back to take another look at the Pavilion. It is not in such poor repair as I first thought. Nothing that a little paint and minor refurbishment would not remedy.

'So, before I went to bed, I fetched the ledgers and went

over them. I think, no, I am sure, that with a little investment and some hard work, Bellemonte could begin turning a better profit by next summer.'

Matt stopped and looked at Conham, who nodded.

'Go on.'

'All the ticket prices need to be increased, of course.
That would instantly bring more in from the baths, which
could remain open for the present. As for the gardens, the
bushes and trees require some attention, as do all the paths.
And I think the main walks would be improved with new
coloured lamps. All that could be done during the winter,
ready for a grand reopening in May.'

'But at what cost?' asked Conham. 'As I told you, I have
no money to invest in Bellemonte.'

'That is the point.' Matthew sat forward, his eyes shining. 'I am not asking you to put more money in. I would
like to invest mine.'

'Yours!'

'The money I received when I sold my commission. I
haven't needed it, since you are paying me a salary. I have
checked all the figures and I think it will be enough to get
things started.'

He broke off as Rosina came in. She greeted both men
in her usual calm, friendly way, and Conham felt an in-
tense relief that she was not offended or upset by anything
he had said last night.

'Good morning,' he said. 'Did you know about this hare-
brained idea of Matthew's?'

'To invest in Bellemonte? Yes. Matthew came to my office before breakfast and we looked at the figures together.
I believe it might work.'

He narrowed his eyes at her. 'And you told me you
weren't plotting.'

'Not at all, my lord. Merely trying to help.'

'Conham, you have told me often enough that I would one day find something that interests me,' said Matthew. 'This does. With your permission, I would like to remain in Gloucestershire, oversee Hackthorpe's removal at the end of December—it is only a few weeks, after all—and manage the renovations myself. The public house will need a new landlord. I have no objection to locals drinking in the taproom, but the place was once a thriving inn for travellers and I think it could be again.'

'Yes,' added Rosina, 'and do not forget there are the gardens, too. The basic ground plan is still in evidence and that would be an excellent starting point for our improvements.'

'*Our* improvements?' Conham interrupted her.

She nodded. 'Why, yes. You will still be the owner, so it is in everyone's interests for this project to be a success.'

'I want to improve the path up to the viewpoint,' said Matt. 'Rosina has suggested we build a small circle of columns up there and call it the temple of… Which goddess was it, Rosina? What did you call her?'

'Selene, Greek goddess of the full moon.'

There was a slight blush on her cheek and she avoided his eyes, which made Conham wonder if she was thinking of that moment on the terrace. The midnight madness that had brought him dangerously close to doing something they would both regret. He had not forgotten it, his fitful, dream-filled sleep was proof of that.

'Yes, and in the summer we might have someone up there selling refreshments for those who make the climb.' Matt's voice interrupted his thoughts. 'Most of these ideas can be carried out at very little cost.'

'And quickly, too,' added Rosina, who had regained her composure. 'Matthew's idea is to have the gardens open again by the summer. More improvements can follow, when funds allow.'

Matt raised his coffee cup and regarded Conham over its rim. 'If you can hold fire on selling Bellemonte until Lady Day, I hope to show you some improvement in Bellemonte's fortunes.'

'You and Rosina appear to have thought it all out.' He paused. 'I suppose you would continue to live at Gifford Manor?'

'No, no. I shall put up at the inn until I can make a few rooms habitable in the big house.' He laughed. 'We learned how to make ourselves comfortable in veritable *ruins* when we were in the Peninsula, do you remember, Conham? In time, I want to renovate the whole place and turn it into an hotel, keeping the top floor for my own use. One of the first things I want to do, though, is to make the area more respectable. I plan to employ two or three watchmen, and to build a charley box.'

Conham looked up. 'A what?'

'A lock-up, where those intent on trouble can be left to cool their heels overnight. Once we have cleared the worst of the scoundrels from the area and increased the prices, the customers will come flocking in.' Matt went on, warming to his theme, 'There are plenty of rich merchants in Bristol willing to pay handsomely for their entertainment. And Bellemonte is only a couple of miles from the Hotwells and Clifton Village. Oh, I know the hot baths there are superior, but apart from the theatre and the assembly rooms, there is very little in the way of entertainment for those in residence.'

Conham sat back, considering, while the others waited expectantly.

'This is utter madness,' he said slowly. 'But it might just work.'

'It *will* work,' Matt was adamant. 'Of course, it is only the beginning. We shall need more investment in the future, but I thought we might sell shares—only in small amounts. I do not want to risk losing control of the project.'

Conham frowned at him.

'And just what do you want from me?' he demanded. 'Apart from my not selling Bellemonte, that is.'

'Your name. Once it is known the gardens enjoy the patronage of the Earl of Dallamire I have no doubt the crowds will come.'

Conham's fingers tapped on the table. 'We would need legal documents.'

'Of course, we will draw up an agreement for rents, and the division of profits. I want it to be watertight, Conham. As they say in these parts, shipshape and Bristol fashion. I will consult with Rosina regularly. She can act as your agent while you are away and keep you informed of progress.'

'You are already agreed on this?' Conham looked at Rosina.

'Yes, we discussed it earlier this morning. I know there is a risk but believe me, my lord, I would not lend my support to such a scheme if I did not think it could benefit you.'

Matthew leaned forward. 'Well, man, what do you say?'

Conham gave his attention to his breakfast, but his brain was working furiously. It was years since he had seen Matt looking so eager and enthusiastic about anything. He knew the man had a good head on his shoulders and he trusted him not to make a mull of it. Eventually, he pushed away his plate.

'Very well. If you think you can do this with no extra funds from me, I am willing to let you put your scheme into action. Hackthorpe's contract on the gardens and the inn expires on the December Quarter Day, but he has no legal hold over the old house or the baths, so you may do what you will with that now.'

'Thank you, I shall make a start, then.' Matt beamed at him across the table. 'I won't let you down, Conham!'

An hour later all three of them walked to the door, where the earl's travelling chariot was waiting on the drive. Conham turned to Matthew.

'We will look at this again when I return at the end of March, but until then any expenditure must come from your own funds.'

'Agreed!' Matt gripped his hand and pumped it. 'I think, between us, Rosina and I can make a success of this for you!'

Conham nodded and climbed into the coach. He looked back, his last view being of Matt and Rosina standing together on the drive, watching his departure. They were already very friendly. Who was to say where that would lead over the next few months, if they were working closely together? It was very likely that they would fall in love but that was no business of his. He hoped they would be very happy.

He shrugged himself into the corner and looked out at the bleak, wintry landscape. He must find himself a rich bride, that much was certain, and he had no right to be a dog in the manger where Rosina was concerned.

Chapter Eleven

Spring was bursting into bloom in the London parks. New leaf buds were appearing on the trees but it was still early March and the warm, sunny days gave way to icy nights. Consequently, the long windows of the ballroom overlooking Green Park had been firmly closed.

Conham stood by one of the windows, staring out into the darkness. It was near midnight and behind him, the dancing was continuing. He could hear the scrape of fiddles mixing with the chatter and laughter that filled the room.

By heaven, he was bored! He longed to be out of London. He would much prefer to be at Gifford Manor, sitting quietly by the fire in the drawing room and sharing a glass of wine with Matt Talacre. Perhaps they might even persuade Rosina to join them for a business dinner. Only it never felt like business when she was present. It was always far more pleasurable than that. They would sit at the dining table talking late into the night, and even if they disagreed it was never serious, they always found some common ground, something to smile about.

He tore his thoughts away from Rosina. She was his land steward and as unattainable as ever. By heaven, if only he had paid as much attention to his own land as she had to Brackwood, perhaps he would not be in this mess now!

'Dallamire, what are you doing, standing here all alone?' His stepmother's voice interrupted his thoughts. 'You must come and dance.'

'I have partnered more than enough young ladies for one evening, ma'am.'

'And did none of them take your fancy? If there is anyone in particular you would like to stand up with for the waltz, I am sure our hostess would oblige...'

'For heaven's sake don't suggest it,' he interrupted her. 'To dance the waltz with anyone would be as good as announcing our betrothal!'

'Well, that is what you are here for,' she told him. 'Dallamire, you have been dithering all winter! You need to find a bride, sir, and a rich one. You appeared to be getting on well with Miss Hewick. She's a very pretty behaved girl, she would make you a good wife.'

'Yes, if you like someone who agrees with your every utterance!'

The countess gave his arm a sharp tap with her closed fan. 'Pray, do not be so disagreeable, Dallamire. She has a fortune as well as birth and breeding.'

'But no brain!'

His stepmother's eyes snapped.

'I vow you are being odiously provoking this evening! If you had not stayed away in France for so long, if you had returned to Dallamire earlier, this might not have been necessary, but you know we are all depending upon you to restore the family fortunes.' She stepped closer. 'If you will not think of me, consider your poor half-sisters, reduced to penury by our unfortunate circumstances. If you do not stir yourself, Dallamire, they will end up old maids!'

Conham almost ground his teeth. 'Since they are still in the schoolroom, I cannot see the urgency!' He took a breath, fighting down his irritation. 'I have told you, madam, when the time comes the girls will be presented at court in a fitting manner.'

'And you will need to marry a fortune to make that happen,' she argued. 'Now. If Miss Hewick does not please you, there is another young lady here who might do so. Come along, I shall introduce you to Miss Skelton.' She tucked her hand in his arm and gave a little tug. 'Dallamire, will you come and do your duty?'

Conham looked down into the countess's lined, determined face and swallowed a sigh. There was no escaping his duty, so he had best get it over with.

'Yes, of course, ma'am. Lead on.'

He went back into the fray, smiling outwardly, while inside he felt all the enthusiasm of a man heading for the scaffold.

The sight of the blackthorn flowers in the hedgerows and primroses pushing up in the grassy banks cheered Rosina as she rode back to Gifford Manor. It was almost four months since she had arrived in Gloucestershire, and she had thrown herself into the work of the estate. She had blotted out her old life so successfully that now she rarely thought of Brackwood, or her brother. She had been accepted surprisingly well by her neighbours and the estate's tenants, in part because the squire's wife, Lady Rissington, had befriended her, but it also helped that the previous steward had been such a rogue that almost any replacement would have been welcomed.

However, the hard winter had seriously impeded Rosina's plans to improve the estate. She had made some progress, but not as much as she would have liked, and Lady Day was now only weeks away, when Lord Dallamire would return to judge her progress.

Conham was never far from her thoughts. She had written to him several times, reporting on estate matters and informing him of any changes she wished to make. The replies were always brief and often written by his secretary or the steward at Dallamire.

Did he ever think of her?

Rosina doubted it. Not only was he busy with affairs at Dallamire, he had also said he intended to find himself a wife, something she did not think would prove very difficult. She was forced to agree with Matt that, despite his lack of fortune, Conham was a handsome devil, with his auburn hair that fell across his wide brow, the crooked grin and strong jawline. Then there were those grey-green eyes that could light up with laughter in an instant. It was more than enough to send any lady's pulse racing. He was also tall, with broad shoulders that looked as if they could bear all one's problems.

No, she had no doubt there were any number of heiresses ready to snap up the Earl of Dallamire, and Rosina lived in daily expectation of hearing that he had contracted a brilliant alliance. Not that she could bear to read the society pages in the London newspaper that Squire Rissington insisted on bringing over to her, once he had read it, but Jameson scanned it eagerly, and she was sure the butler would waste no time in passing on the happy news, when it came.

Gifford Manor was in sight, rising above its surrounding trees, the honey-coloured stone warm and glowing in the sunshine. If Dallamire did find himself a bride, it was entirely possible she would persuade him to sell the estate at Morton Gifford. If that happened, Rosina could only hope she had done enough to convince the earl to provide her with a reference, and recommend to the new owner that she continue in the post.

As she trotted through the gates she saw a carriage pulled up at the door. A second glance and she saw the earl was standing on the drive, giving instructions to his driver. He looked up as she drew nearer and Rosina felt a wave of happiness surge through her body.

'We did not expect you for a week yet!'

'You have acquired a pony!'

They spoke at the same time, and both smiled self-consciously.

'Yes, this is Bramble.' Rosina leaned forward to run her hand along the mare's brown neck. 'Welsh-bred and chosen for her stamina and steady nature. Fred Skillet went to Painswick to buy her for me. She can carry me all day with never a stumble.'

'She is certainly a sturdy beast,' remarked the earl, rubbing the mare's nose. 'Although clearly not chosen for her looks.'

Rosina laughed. 'Hush now, I will not allow you to abuse her! She is proving very useful to me, since she is equally at home pulling the gig.'

'Then I will happily allow her space in the stables,' replied the earl, grinning. 'Is that where you are going now? I will have someone take the pony away and you can come into the house.'

He signalled to a hovering servant to take the mare's head and he stepped around to lift Rosina from the saddle. For a moment her heart took flight. She was suspended in his arms and her stomach flipped at the sudden feeling of helplessness, the sensation of being at the earl's mercy, totally dependent upon him. It should have been unpleasant, but it wasn't. In fact, she felt a definite disappointment when he put her down and she quickly busied herself, shaking out her skirts to hide her confusion.

Conham, too, was struggling to remain calm. His pleasure at seeing her and the easy way they spoke to one another—it was as if they had been acquainted for years. It had seemed the most natural thing in the world to lift her down from the saddle.

Until he was actually holding her, that is. A light but heady fragrance assailed his senses, summer flowers with just a hint of lemon, clean and fresh, and she was surprisingly light in his arms. Surprisingly *precious*. He did not want to let her go. The urge to kiss her was so strong that it shocked him, and it had taken every ounce of his self-control to set her on her feet. Now Conham looked about him, at the retreating carriage, at the house, across to the far hills. Anywhere but at Rosina.

He cleared his throat. One of them would have to break this awkward silence.

'Yes, well. Come into the house,' he repeated. 'I did not send word that I was coming today and nothing has been prepared. Mrs Jameson is making ready my room and then Dawkins will need to unpack. In the meantime you can tell me how you have gone on.'

'Then I suggest we go to my office,' said Rosina. 'If you were not expected there will be no fires burning in any of the other rooms.'

'Good point. Come along, then!'

Conham escorted Rosina into the house and held open the door for her to precede him into the office. It looked much as it had done when he had last seen it in November, dark wood cupboards lining the walls, a large desk in the centre of the room, yet something was different. It took him a few moments to notice the changes: a jug of early

spring flowers on a table by the window and extra cush-
ions on the steward's desk chair as well as the armchair in
the corner. How odd that such tiny changes could make a
room feel so much more welcoming.

'We will be more comfortable over here,' he said, pushing the armchair closer to the hearth and indicating that
Rosina should sit down. She hesitated, watching him pull
up a plain wooden chair for himself.

'Would you not prefer to use my desk chair?'

'No, no, you sit down, I shall do very well here.' He
grinned as he settled himself on the hard seat. 'I want to
know how my tenants feel when they come in here to see
you!'

She smiled at that. 'They rarely come to the house. I prefer to visit them.'

'And how are you received? Answer me truthfully now.'

'In the main, my reception here has been very good.'

'And has there been any talk?'

'Talk?'

'Any gossip that you are my mistress?'

She blushed a little but answered him with equal frankness.

'Of course, at first. But the squire and his lady acknowledge me, which has helped a great deal.'

She could not help adding, with a touch of pride, 'I believe, however, my reputation as an experienced land steward is spreading. I have had more than a few letters now,
asking for my advice.'

'That is a great compliment.'

'Yes, it is, although I hope word does not spread south
as far as Somerset.'

'You are concerned your brother might hear of it?'

She shook her head. 'Not seriously concerned. I think it

is the novelty of a female land steward that has engendered a little gossip within the area. It will die down soon enough.'

'And the tenant farmers, the local tradesmen—is anyone proving especially difficult?'

'No. That is, one or two tried to bully me at first, but I learned very early at Brackwood how to deal with that! I understand that it hurts the pride of some men to answer to a woman, but I have dealt with that problem, too.'

'Oh, how?'

'I have taken on a young man from the village. Davy Redmond, the vicar's son. He was at Oxford but has finished his studies now and is come home. Having been born and raised here, he is familiar with the life of a rural parish and is acquainted with everyone in the area.'

'That seems like an excellent plan. When will I meet this young man?'

'Tomorrow. He is taking several of the tenant farmers to Home Farm today, to show them the new drainage we have put in there. We are trying to persuade them that it is worth the effort to drain at least some of their lower meadows. My father did something similar at Brackwood, to very good effect. I have spoken to the squire and he agrees with me that these farms in particular would benefit from the investment.'

'And how much will it cost *me*?' Conham enquired.

'Very little.' She went across to the desk and pulled out a sheaf of papers from one of the drawers. 'These particular leases are due for renewal on Lady Day and I am hoping you will agree to maintaining the present rents and guarantee the farmers a full year's lease if they will undertake the improvements we have suggested.'

He took the papers she was holding out to him and glanced at them.

'I will need to study all this a little more before I can agree.'

'But of course. I would not expect anything else, Lord Dallamire.'

'Very well. Have all the ledgers and accounts brought to my study tomorrow and I will look at them.' He rose. 'I had best go and change. Will I see you at dinner?'

'I think not. I shall dine with the Jamesons, as I usually do.'

'We might continue discussing these new plans of yours.'

She smiled but shook her head. 'Tempting, but it will not do, my lord, and you know it.'

'I know nothing of the sort!' He frowned at her. 'I thought we were friends, Rosina. Why are you being so formal?'

'I have no choice. Can you not see that it must be this way? You made me steward here and I would like to remain in the post for some time yet. I am in your employ and cannot compromise my position by dining alone with you, even though a lady might risk it.'

Conham growled. 'You *are* a lady!'

'Thank you.' She smiled a little, but he could tell from her mulish look that she was not to be moved. He sighed.

'So be it. I know your reasoning is sound, but when we are alone you will call me Conham, do you understand? That is an order.'

'Yes my—Conham.'

Their eyes met and a giggle escaped her. The tension eased immediately and Conham went up to his room, still smiling, albeit a little rueful. He would miss her presence at dinner but he knew she was right. Any hint of scandal and it would be impossible for her to remain at Morton Gifford as land steward. And he really did not want her to leave.

* * *

Rosina carried all the accounts and papers to the earl's office very early the next morning, still unsettled by the see-saw of emotions she had felt when she had first seen him yesterday. She was pleased he was at the Manor and yet she knew she must be on her guard. It would be very easy to be too familiar, to tease him or touch his arm, or call him Conham in front of the servants. Just one slip would be enough to set tongues wagging. Not that she thought any of the servants would deliberately set out to destroy her reputation, but it would only take an ill-judged word and her position here would be untenable.

She was back in her own office before the earl had left the breakfast room and it was there that he found her some hours later. He came in just as she and Davy were poring over a large map of the estate, and she lost no time in presenting her assistant.

'I know your father, of course,' said Conham, giving the young man a friendly smile. 'I sat through any number of his sermons with my godfather as a schoolboy. You had no desire to go into the church?'

Davy shook his head. 'Alas, no, much to my father's disappointment, although he is far too good to mention it. He sends his regards, by the way.'

They chatted for a little longer before Conham turned to the subject of drainage on the tenant farms.

'I have read Miss Brackwood's report and looked at the plans this morning. And I believe you spoke with the farmers yesterday, Mr Redmond?'

Rosina was content to let them talk, knowing Conham wanted to discover if her assistant understood the matter in hand. Davy acquitted himself well, he was deferential and polite, but in no way intimidated. She thought Con-

ham would like that and she was right, for he told her as
much when she went with him to his study to collect up
all the documents.

'I am glad you like him,' she said. 'He is already proving an asset to the estate, and keen to learn more.'

The earl was standing behind his desk, looking down
at an open ledger.

'When exactly did you take him on?'

'At Christmas. Squire Rissington knew I was looking
for someone and suggested Davy Redmond might be just
the person.'

'And you have been paying him monthly.'

'Yes.'

Conham ran his finger down the entries in the ledger. He
had already looked at them once, but he wanted to be sure.

'There is no mention here of any wages for an assistant.'
He glanced up, and saw that Rosina was looking a little
self-conscious.

She said, 'I was not sure the estate could bear the cost.
I have been paying him myself.'

'How much?'

When she told him, he frowned. 'It will not do, Rosina.'

'But my salary is more than generous. Far more than I
could earn as a governess or a teacher.' She raised her chin.
'And if, as a *woman*, I am not capable of fulfilling my role
here, surely I should be responsible for employing someone to assist me.'

'We agreed a fair wage for the post, but it is not an ex-
cessive one. Frumald was a scoundrel and he was lining
his pockets at the estate's expense with far more than you
are paying Redmond.

'You will add the young man to the wages roll with immediate effect, do you understand?' He saw the stubborn

look on her face and said again, more forcefully, 'Do you understand, madam?'

'Yes, my lord.'

'Oho! So we are back to being formal when we are alone.'

'*You* addressed me as madam.'

'That was because I was angry with you!'

She gazed at him, brows raised, and he laughed. 'What's sauce for the goose, eh?'

'I would not be so impolite as to suggest such a thing, my lord.'

She spoke coolly, but a twinkle lurked in those blue eyes. He grinned at her.

'Witch! No, no, do not fire up again. Here.' He closed the ledger and handed it to her. 'Take this away now. I have seen enough to know the estate is in safe hands.'

'Thank you, my—' She stopped when he threw a warning look at her. 'Thank you, Conham.'

There was a decided smile in her eyes now and he liked that, just as he liked the becoming flush that mantled her cheeks. He imagined himself moving around the desk and taking her in his arms, kissing her until they both forgot all about drains and ditches and debts. If only that were possible.

He turned his sigh into a cough and said brusquely, 'Very well. Off you go now. But you will dine with me tomorrow. A working dinner,' he added. 'I sent word to Matt Talacre and he is joining us. To discuss Bellemonte.'

He did not fail to miss the lightening of her countenance, or the sudden smile that curved her lips.

'Have you seen much of Matthew?' He was careful to keep his tone light, and held back from adding *while I have been away*.

'No, he has not called, although we have exchanged correspondence about Bellemonte. His letters and copies of my replies are here, somewhere...' She glanced down at the books and papers cradled in her arms.

'Ah yes, of course. I saw them. They make interesting reading.' The little demon of jealousy subsided. 'We can discuss everything tomorrow evening.'

She nodded. 'I shall look forward to it.'

'As will I.'

Their eyes met and held, as if neither of them wanted to move. Then Rosina hurried from the room and Conham was left standing by the desk, breathing in the fading traces of her scent.

Chapter Twelve

The sun was already climbing in the clear sky when Rosina left the steward's lodge the following morning. It was not only the prospect of a bright warm day that accounted for her sunny mood. The earl was back at Morton Gifford, and even the sight of him riding away across the park as she walked to the Manor did not dishearten her. Just the fact that he was in residence was enough to lift her spirits.

She spent an hour with Davy Redmond before he went off to see the gamekeeper, who had reported a spate of poaching in the home wood. After that she settled down to read through the new tenancy agreements Davy had prepared.

It was midday before she finally put them aside and rubbed her eyes, wondering what to do next. The sun was still shining, and she was tempted to take a walk. Then she noticed the large pile of books on the table by the window. They were in the main local histories, plus instructive tomes on farming practices and animal husbandry purchased by Hugo Conham. She had been studying them during her first weeks at Gifford, but now decided it was time they were returned to the library shelves.

Rosina collected up all the books and set off for the library. It was situated at the back of the house, with large windows that looked out over the rolling hills. It was a glorious spring day and she promised herself that as soon as she had put the books back in their proper place, she would collect her shawl and enjoy a brisk walk in the sunshine.

She had just pushed two accounts of local history back amongst their fellows when she heard the door open. She turned, thinking it must be a servant, but she gasped, her clutch tightening on the books in her arms, when she saw her brother's stocky frame filling the doorway.

'You!'

'Surprised, Sister?'

Edgar closed the door and stood with his back to it, his lip curled in a smile that chilled her blood.

'Who let you in here?' she demanded, trying to keep a tremor out of her voice.

'Some fool of a footman. I told him I was your brother and not to bother announcing me.'

The last time Rosina had seen Edgar he had been forcing laudanum down her throat while the hard-faced woman, Moffat, held her prisoner. She told herself he could not do that here. There were servants in the house, if only she could alert them. She glanced towards the fireplace and immediately he took a few steps forward. There was no way she could reach the door or the bellpull without his intercepting her.

Rosina fought down her panic. If she screamed there was a slight possibility someone would hear her, but she could not be certain and it might push Edgar into violence. All she could do for now was play for time.

'How did you find me?'

'Sheer chance. You will remember my good friend Alfred Tumby. He was an admirer of yours.'

'He was an odious villain,' she retorted. 'He tried to seduce me, and with Papa lying ill above-stairs!'

'Nonsense. If you hadn't been so starched up, he would have made you a fine husband. Not that any of that matters now. The thing is, he was visiting friends in Wales and stopped at Chepstow, where he heard a group of farmers talking of an estate in Gloucestershire that has employed a female land steward. Name of Brackwood.' His lips parted in another leering smile. 'That was very foolish of you, my dear. Should have called yourself something different.'

She put up her chin. 'Why should I? *I* have nothing to be ashamed of.'

'Instead, you would drag our name into the gutter.'

'It is you who has done that,' she shot back at him. She curbed her anger and went on, trying to sound nonchalant, 'But I am curious to know: did you think your plan had worked, that I had perished at sea?'

'I could not be sure. Moffat wrote to tell me she had fulfilled her part and left you on board the ship, but then I heard nothing. I thought the captain might have decided it was safer not to commit anything to paper, or that his letter had gone astray. I should have preferred to be able to announce you had perished at sea but that was a small matter. You were gone, out of my way.' He uttered a string of vicious curses that made her wince. 'Or so I thought, until I heard Tumby's story. Naturally, I had to investigate. And now I have found you.'

'Well, you can go away again,' she told him, trying to ignore the fearful thudding of her heart. 'I am no threat to you. I want merely to live my own life.'

His face darkened. 'Oh, no, dear sister, I cannot allow that. Not now.'

He came towards her, menace in every line. Rosina took a

step back, but even as she was deciding if her energies were best used to scream or retreat, the door opened.

Conham had seen a gentleman's hat and gloves on the side table as soon as he walked into the Manor and did not stop to divest himself of his own, once he learned the visitor's identity. He rushed to the library and, stepping into the room, he summed up the scene at a glance.

Edgar Brackwood swung around to see who had entered and now glared at Conham. Rosina looked pale and defiant. She was clutching an armful of books like a shield, and Conham was relieved he had arrived in time to protect her. There was no longer any doubt in his mind about Brackwood's part in Rosina's abduction.

Beneath a thatch of fair hair, the young man's face was blotched an angry red. His fury was almost tangible, and Conham knew the situation was volatile. He must tread carefully.

'Sir Edgar.' Conham put his hat and crop on the side table and slowly drew off his gloves. 'To what do we owe the pleasure of this visit?'

His icily polite manner had the desired effect. Brackwood's fists were balled tight but he contained his anger and even managed a small bow.

'My lord. I wish to talk to my sister. Alone.'

'Ah, but does Miss Brackwood wish to talk to *you*?' drawled Conham, moving forward.

Rosina answered swiftly, her voice clipped and angry. 'We have nothing to say to one another.'

'There, Sir Edgar. You have your answer.'

'I will not leave without my sister. She must come home with me.'

'So that you can try to murder her again?' Conham saw

the man's look of surprise and continued in a voice as smooth as silk. 'Oh, yes. Miss Brackwood has told me all about that.'

'She is lying!' Brackwood took a step closer. 'You cannot prove a thing against me.'

'Perhaps not, but I prefer to believe the lady.'

'Please, Edgar.' Rosina put down the books. 'I do not want to quarrel with you. I only want to be left alone to live my own life. Please go.'

'Not without you, madam!'

Brackwood lunged towards her but Conham was quicker. He stepped between them.

'You are not welcome in my house, Brackwood. It is time for you to leave.'

'Very well. If you are content to be a laughing stock, installing your whore as steward here, that is no business of mi—'

His last words were lost as Conham brought his fist crashing into Brackwood's jaw. The blow sent the man sprawling to the floor, where he remained, cringing in fear of a further onslaught.

'No, Conham!' Rosina rushed up and caught his arm. 'No more, please!'

'Don't worry, I am done. The man's a bully, and not worth the effort.'

He went across to the bell pull, where his violent tugging on the sash resulted in Jameson and one of the footmen hurrying into the room. They stopped and goggled at the figure cowering on the floor.

'Get him out of the house and into his carriage,' Conham ordered. 'Send a rider with him, to make sure he leaves my land. And Jameson, make it known that this man is not to be allowed on my property again. Is that understood?'

He waited while the men helped Brackwood to his feet

and escorted him out of the room before turning to Rosina.
Her eyes were fixed on the closed door, hands clasped in
front of her as she tried to control their shaking.

'Well, that was diverting,' he remarked, strolling across
the room to her.

'I b-beg your p-pardon.' She struggled to speak. 'I n-never
thought he w-would f-find me.'

Conham pulled her gently into his arms as she dissolved
into tears.

'Hush now. It was inevitable. I only wish we'd had the
forethought to warn the servants to be on guard against
the fellow. How did he discover you were here?' he asked,
handing her his handkerchief.

'Farmers. T-talking of me in Ch-Chepstow.'

'Chepstow! By heaven, your fame has spread far and
wide!'

'Pray, do not laugh. I should have known better than to
come here! A female land steward was bound to cause a
great deal of gossip.' She pushed herself away from him
and wiped her eyes. 'It reflects ill on you, too. It was wrong
of me to accept the post.'

'Fustian! No one here believes you are my mistress.'

'If they did, they would not dare tell you.'

He caught her arms and turned her to face him. 'That
is beyond foolish, Rosina. Your brother was goading you.
Goading *us*. There was always going to be talk at first but
that has died down now. You have earned your place here
and I am content to have you remain, as land steward, for
as long as you wish.'

'That is very kind, sir, but—'

'I am not being kind!' He gave her a little shake. 'You
have a way with people, Rosina. At a time when many stewards are feared and even hated, *you* are respected and ad-

mired. I have heard nothing but good reports of you from everyone I have met since I returned. The job is yours. As long as you want it.'

Conham desperately wanted to kiss away the last of her tears, but that would not help the situation at all. He released her and stepped away.

'Now, dry your eyes, madam, and let's have no more of this nonsense. Matthew will be here soon for dinner and I would still like you to join us, if you feel well enough.'

'Yes, of course,' muttered Rosina, giving her nose a final wipe.

She said, with a fair assumption of calm, 'I had best go and change, if you will excuse me.'

She went to hand the mangled handkerchief back to him, then thought better of it and walked to the door, where she turned back.

'Will you tell Matthew about Edgar's visit?'

'He is likely to hear something of it from the servants, and if he does, I will explain. But you need not make yourself uneasy. Matt would not be surprised to learn I drove the villain from the house. He does know something of your story, after all.'

'Ah yes, of course.' She hesitated, wanting to apologise for all the trouble she had caused, for weeping over him like some feeble-minded female in a silly gothic romance. In the end she settled for a simple *thank you* before whisking herself out of the room.

Chapter Thirteen

Rosina had purchased a new evening gown from the local dressmaker, a celestial blue crape over a white satin slip, but after what had occurred, she decided to wear the grey silk she bought in Bristol for her dinner with the earl and Matt Talacre. She asked Mrs Goddard to dress her hair simply with a parting in the centre and pulled back into a Grecian knot, and then picked up her new shawl, a rose-pink cashmere she had found by chance in the village, on a market stall selling not-so-old clothes. She studied herself in the mirror and, once she was satisfied that she looked the very model of propriety, and that her dress could not be in any way construed as frivolous, she set off to walk to the Manor.

Conham was crossing the great hall when he heard voices in the screen passage. He grinned when Matthew Talacre walked in.

Conham stopped. 'Matt! It is good to see you. Come along into the drawing room.'

'Welcome back to Gloucestershire, my lord.' Matt followed him across the hall and remarked, once they were alone in the drawing room, 'I had not expected you for a week or two yet.'

'I had concluded my business in town. There was no reason for me to stay longer.'

'What, could none of the beauties there tempt you to stay? I have been in daily expectation of seeing your betrothal announced in the London newspaper.'

'Then I am sorry to disappoint you.'

'Damnation, man, you told me you were going to London with the sole purpose of finding a rich wife.'

'I did. Sadly, I could not find a lady to suit.'

'What, not one?'

'No.' Conham shifted uncomfortably under his friend's scrutiny.

'Coming it too brown, my friend!' Matt exclaimed, with brutal frankness. 'I have it on good authority—my cousin Mildred, companion to Viscountess Wodington and an avid reader of the society pages!—that there were at least six very eligible females on the market this winter.'

'Confound it, Matthew, have you been discussing me with your cousin?'

'No, no, my friend, your name was never mentioned, so you can put down those hackles! Lady Wodington is in Hotwells to take the waters and I went over to call upon Mildy.'

'And you just happened to hit upon the subject of heiresses.'

Conham's sarcastic tone had no effect at all upon his old friend, who merely grinned.

'It came up, amongst other things. Let me see, did you meet Miss Throckley?'

'Yes. She has a squint.'

'Miss Jessop? My cousin told me she is the talk of the town. The family is from Yorkshire. Halifax, or Bradford, I believe. Rich as Croesus.'

'Aye, and very full of themselves. The father is aiming higher than a mere earl for his daughter.'

'Then what about Julia Hewick? Related to the Duke of Chandos.'

'Yes, I stood up with her a couple of times.'

'And?'

'No conversation.'

'And the celebrated Miss Kingston? Mildy wrote to tell me she is very pretty.'

'Perhaps, if you can ignore her constant giggles.'

Matt laughed. 'By heaven, my friend, you are very hard to please!'

'I am looking for a *wife*,' retorted Conham. 'I need to know that we can at least be comfortable together. And besides, I have no idea what these females really think of *me*. My impression is they would all of them marry an ogre just to become a countess.'

Matt sobered. 'I can tell your heart isn't in this, my friend.'

His pitying tone caught Conham on the raw.

He burst out, 'Damn it all, Matt, the Mortlakes have owned Dallamire Hall and its estates for centuries. It is my duty, as head of the family, to save the house if I can. I *must* marry money, if I am to restore Dallamire.'

Rosina's entrance put an end to their discussion, much to Conham's relief. After a few moments exchanging greetings, he shifted the conversation away from himself by asking Matthew to tell them how matters were progressing at Bellemonte.

'Very well. There is a great deal to do, but I am making good progress. My leg is healing, too, so I am now able to tackle much of the work myself.' He held up his hands, displaying the roughened skin. 'Although I can no longer pretend to be a gentleman!'

'One should never decry honest toil,' Rosina told him, smiling.

Conham agreed. 'Indeed not. I have read your letters, Matt. You are making good progress. An interesting idea of yours, bringing in some of your old regimental comrades to help you clear the pleasure gardens.'

'Many of them have been unable to find work since returning to England and are eager for the chance to prove themselves. They work hard, which pleases the gardener I have hired. He is confident now that we will be ready for reopening in May. I hope you and Rosina will both be able to attend?'

'I will do my best, but I cannot promise,' said Conham. He saw that Rosina was regarding him with a slight frown and he put up his brows. 'Is that not good enough?'

'No, my lord. Your presence will be necessary to ensure the opening is a success.'

'And I will need your support if I am to raise more funds for the next phase of the project,' added Matt. 'My reason for going to Hotwells was not only to see Cousin Mildred. I went to look at the spa. I talked to some of those taking the waters, and the doctors, too. Bellemonte cannot boast of hot baths, so it is not a direct rival, but we have the swimming pool and the cold bath, which are already gaining popularity, especially since I opened a private bath for the ladies and employed watchmen to ensure the streets are safe for visitors.'

Rosina turned to Conham. 'Did you note that the watchmen, too, are former soldiers?' she asked him. 'Trustworthy men, in need of employment.'

'Yes, I did. Since the end of the war I have seen far too many good men unable to find work to support themselves and their families. I am delighted that Matt is able to help some of them.'

'Aye,' put in Matt, grinning. 'Because of their regular

patrols, Bellemonte is a positive haven of respectability these days.'

'What, even the tavern?' asked Conham, surprised.

'Not yet. It closed when the current lease expired, but I have a new landlord in mind, a captain of the footguards who is willing to use what is left of his funds to improve the inn. He is an honest fellow and his wife an excellent cook, so between them they will make a big difference, but I need to assure them they will be able to rent the inn from you for at least a year.' Matthew laughed. 'It is all part of my plans for Bellemonte, Conham. We need to talk about it.'

'Aye, but later,' said Conham. 'Here is Jameson come to tell us dinner is ready.'

They walked across to the dining room and no more was said of Bellemonte until the meal was finished.

'I should withdraw now,' murmured Rosina as the last of the dishes were removed.

But Matthew would not hear of it.

'We have not finished discussing Bellemonte yet.' He turned to the earl. 'Tell her she must stay, my lord!'

Conham was enjoying the evening. It was everything he had hoped for. He was far more at ease here than in town, where he was constantly on his guard against raising false hopes in matchmaking parents or their daughters. Even Dallamire felt cold and inhospitable without Matt's cheerful companionship. As for Rosina, he very much wanted her to stay a little longer, although he refused to think too much about why that should be.

'Yes, you must remain,' he said to her now. 'To discuss Bellemonte. I should value your opinion.'

That becoming blush touched her creamy cheeks and she said, 'Then I should very much like to stay.'

Masking his inordinate pleasure at her answer, Conham turned to Jameson, the only servant left in the room.

'Bring an extra glass for Miss Brackwood, if you please.'

'And will Miss Brackwood drink *brandy*, my lord?' the butler asked him in repressive accents.

'I have no idea.' Conham's lips twitched. He looked at Rosina. 'Will you, ma'am?'

'No, not brandy,' she replied, trying not to laugh. 'Perhaps a glass of madeira?'

Mollified, the butler bowed and went out. Rosina shook her head, chuckling.

'Poor Jameson, I am sure he thinks we will be carousing late into the night.'

Carousing. The word sent Conham's mind careering away from business. He imagined himself dining alone with Rosina, sitting beside her and drinking sweet wines, offering up tiny slices of peach or pineapple and then leaning close to kiss the juice from her lips…

'Well, he would be wrong,' declared Matt. 'We are talking business and it would not be right to exclude you from that. You have been involved in the planning of this from the beginning. Besides, I shall need your help persuading the earl to lend me his support.'

Conham sighed and dragged his thoughts away from a very pleasant daydream.

'Very well, Matthew, tell me what it is you want of me. I will consider anything, except spending more money. You know all my unentailed land is mortgaged to the hilt.'

'Hardly your fault, my friend,' said Matt quietly. 'If you had been informed at the outset, you could have come home directly after Waterloo.'

'I have thought that myself, but it is too late now for regrets.' Conham shrugged. 'The countess acted as she thought best in my absence. If I had not joined the army, if I had remained at Dallamire and shown more interest in the estates, then I might have seen how things stood. I might have been able to do something about it.'

'But you weren't,' growled Matt. 'You have been over that ground before, Major, and it does no good to fret over it.'

'I agree, you cannot change the past,' Rosina said, gently. 'It is what happens now that is important.'

'Yes, and I must decide what to do for the best.'

'Your stepmama and half-sisters,' she asked. 'Are they provided for?'

When Conham hesitated, Matt spoke up.

'He is too generous to say it, so I will. Lady Dallamire and the girls *are* provided for. The countess *could* move to the Dower House and live very comfortably within her means, but she prefers to remain at Dallamire, living in the grand manner, and expects Conham to resolve everything.'

'Oh, dear.'

'Selling my godfather's estates would not cover all my debts,' explained Conham, observing the anxious look on Rosina's face. 'Don't worry, I intend to keep Morton Gifford, if I can.'

'And Bellemonte?' she asked.

'Matt's plans have a fair chance of making money.'

And providing his friend with a much-needed boost to his funds and his confidence. Conham did not say this, but he knew from the look Matthew gave him that he understood.

'I believe it could do very well for both of us, but I need you to put your name to my proposals.' Matt leaned forward, elbows on the table. 'My plan is to open up the stables again. The yard and outbuildings are still there but derelict. They would service both the inn and the hotel, when it is finished. The project needs more funds but I believe I already know several possible investors, all trustworthy men. I want to keep their share of the business small, in order that the project is not at risk if any one of them should suddenly pull out.'

He paused as Jameson came in with the decanters. Once they each had a full glass, Conham waved away the butler and waited until they were alone again before inviting Matthew to continue.

Rosina sipped at her wine and listened attentively while Matt Talacre outlined his ideas. The earl interrupted him occasionally to ask a question, but it was clear that Matthew had calculated the final costings quite rigorously.

'So you see, Conham,' he concluded, 'before I can do anything more, I need your assurance that you will not sell Bellemonte, at least for the next twelve months. After that I believe we may well begin to see a return on the investment.'

'I think I can give you that assurance, Matt. From your reports and what you have told me it is clear that you have considered this matter very thoroughly. I am also impressed with what you have managed to achieve in just a few months.' He turned to Rosina to refill her glass and added, 'What you have both achieved. Well done.'

It was his warm smile as much as the praise that sent a rush of pleasure coursing through Rosina. It was encouraging to have him acknowledge her hard work.

'All we need to do now is raise the funds to develop Bellemonte,' said Matthew. 'I do not think it will prove too difficult.'

'I wonder.' She swallowed nervously before posing her question. 'Would I be able to invest?'

Two pairs of eyes turned towards her. She took a deep breath and continued.

'The idea came to me this evening, while Matthew was outlining his plans. There is no longer any need for secrecy, now my brother knows I am here, so—'

'Wait!' Matt put up his hand. 'Your brother found you? When was this?'

'He came here today,' said Conham. 'Having heard of a Miss Brackwood making a name for herself as a land agent in Gloucestershire.'

'The devil he did!'

'I threw him out, and told him not to set foot on my land again.'

'Can you trust him to do that?'

'The servants know not to let him in the house again. Also, I made him aware that I know of his part in Rosina's abduction, even if I cannot prove it. I hope that will be enough to keep him away.'

'I hope so, too, but that is not the point,' Rosina interrupted them impatiently. 'Now that Edgar knows I am alive, there is no longer any reason for me to hide. I can write to my family's attorney. Papa entrusted him with the jewels my mother left for me and I am going to ask him to release them. Not that I intend to wear them. I want to sell them.' She hesitated. 'I have no idea how much they will realise. I do not suppose it will be enough to make me a rich woman, but it should be sufficient to invest in Bellemonte.'

Silence greeted her announcement. Both gentlemen were staring at her.

Matt Talacre cleared his throat. 'I am honoured by your trust, Rosina, but are you sure about this?'

'Very sure.'

'Investments are always a risk, Rosina,' the earl cautioned her.

'I am well aware of that, but I have no need of the money, at least not yet. And I truly believe this can succeed. From what Matthew has said, the returns could be far better than investing in the Funds.'

Matthew laughed. 'By Jove, then I shall be very glad to welcome you as an investor, Rosina. Let us shake hands upon it!'

Smiling, Rosina reached out to take his hand.

'I shall wait to hear what your jewels will raise,' Matthew told her, sitting back again. 'If it is sufficient, we may be able to restore Bellemonte without the need for any other investors at present. Would that not be an excellent solution?' He lifted his glass. 'I propose a toast to our new adventure!'

Rosina raised her wineglass. Inside she was giddy with excitement, feeling there was now some real hope for the future.

'To Bellemonte,' she cried gaily.

'Aye, to Bellemonte,' said Matthew. He tapped sharply on the table. 'Conham? Come along, man, will you not join us?'

The earl was distracted, frowning slightly, but he looked up quickly.

'What? Oh, yes.' He saluted his companions. 'To Bellemonte.'

The toast drunk, they all repaired to the drawing room, but it was not long before Matthew announced it was time for him to ride back to Bellemonte.

'I want to make an early start in the morning,' he said. 'I am grateful for your faith in me, Rosina, and for yours, Conham, my old friend. Truly.'

He went out. In the silence that followed his departure, Rosina heard Matthew's footsteps fading away, and shortly after that the soft chimes of the hall clock filtered through the door. She counted them.

'Midnight,' she said. 'It grows late.'

Conham pushed back his chair. 'I will walk you to the lodge.'

Rosina did not demure as he draped the cashmere shawl around her shoulders. They stepped outside to make the short journey by the light of the moon, which was making fitful appearances between scudding clouds. Conham did not proffer his arm, and she thought he seemed a little distracted, but she was still fizzing with excitement and was content just to walk beside him in silence.

'I need to ask you something, sir,' said Rosina, when they were halfway to the lodge.

'Oh?'

'I shall need assistance to sell the jewels. I think it would be best done in London and I had hoped you would be willing to sell them for me. Or rather, to ask your man of business to do so. I believe that is the surest way to obtain the best price, if you have no objection?'

He did not answer immediately and she turned her head to look up at him, but it was impossible to read his expression in the dim light.

'It must be your decision, of course,' he said at last. 'But to put everything you have into Bellemonte... Is that wise, Rosina?'

'Why not? *You* have decided it is a sound enough investment.'

'Yes, but that is different.'

'Why?'

They walked several steps more before he replied.

'If Matt's plans fail, you could lose all your money.'

She laughed. 'But I do not believe he will fail. I have every faith in Matthew.'

'Ha! *That* is only too clear!'

The harsh response shocked her and she stopped.

'What do you mean? I thought you trusted him implicitly.'

'I do, but I also recognise that every investment carries a risk.' He hissed out a breath and began to walk on again. 'I suppose it is not my place to interfere.'

'Wait, wait.' She caught up with him and touched his arm. 'Conham, what is it? What is wrong with you?'

He swung around to face her.

'I do not want you to be hurt, that is all. Hell and damnation, Rosina, I care about you!'

'Then why are you so against me trying to secure my future?'

'I am not, I just…'

'Do you think it so very unwise for me to throw my lot in with Matthew's plans?'

Conham raked a hand through his hair.

'I think it would be better for the two of you to marry and have done with it!'

'What?'

She clutched at her shawl, her head spinning. She felt dizzy, uncertain. As if the very ground beneath her was crumbling away.

'Matt's a good fellow, Rosina. He'd make an excellent husband. In fact, it would be an obvious choice for you. You are already as thick as thieves together! He would always be on hand to protect you from your brother, too, which must be an advantage.'

Rosina stared at him. Her earlier elation had quite gone,

replaced by a raging disappointment, which turned to anger as the meaning of his words became clear. How dare he suggest such a thing! She considered telling Conham that she could never marry a man she did not love. Or even better, scratching his eyes out.

In the end she settled for an angry laugh.

'I am well aware that *you* must marry, my lord, but *I* am not trammelled by any such necessity! I can assure you that I have no thoughts of marriage.' She drew in a breath and announced grandly, 'Now I have found my freedom, not even a man as rich as Croesus could persuade me to give it up!'

She turned on her heel and strode off towards the lodge, seething with indignation.

Conham fell into step beside her and they walked on in stony silence. He cursed himself, knowing he had erred, and badly, in speaking to Rosina of marriage and Matt in the same breath. He had been unable to help himself, unable to control the demon of jealousy that had been unleashed as he watched them throughout dinner, noting how friendly they were, how easy in each other's company.

He decided it was best not to risk saying anything further tonight. He might only make things worse. The demon was still there, subdued now but ready to roar into life again at the slightest provocation.

At the lodge door she bade him a frosty good-night and Conham turned and walked away. A good night's sleep, and then he must find some way to repair their friendship.

Chapter Fourteen

Rosina woke with a thumping headache. She ascribed it to the wine she had drunk, but in her heart she knew it was more likely caused by a lack of sleep. She had tossed and turned for most of the night, thinking that Conham would rather see her married to Matt Talacre than have her remain here as his land steward.

Did he not understand her at all? Did he not know that she had no interest in marrying a man merely for the protection of his name? That he could think she would even consider such a thing angered her and, having no wish to see or speak with the earl, she sent a message to Davy to say she would meet him at Burntwood Farm and went off to the stables to collect her pony.

A gallop across the park, followed by an absorbing day discussing with tenants the improvements she had in mind for the farms did much to restore her spirits. However, she was still too angry with Conham to want to talk to him. She took an early dinner alone at the lodge and spent the remainder of the evening writing letters.

Her attempts to avoid the earl the next morning were foiled when she heard him call her name as she hurried to the stables. She was obliged to stop and wait for him to come up to her.

'I am on my way to meet Davy, can this wait?' She hoped she sounded businesslike rather than angry.

'It will not take long. In case I did not make myself clear, I wanted to confirm that I will help you to sell your jewels. Of course I will. If that is what you wish.'

No contrition, no apology. She said coolly, 'I do wish it. I have written to Mr Shipton, my family's attorney, and I am awaiting his reply.'

'Very well. When you hear from him let me know. I will come with you to collect them.'

'Thank you, but there is no need. Mrs Goddard can accompany me.' She saw him frown and added, 'Mr Goddard, too, if you think I need more protection.'

'I will not allow you to make the journey without me.' He raised one hand to silence any further objection. 'I insist. It is not just the valuable items you will be carrying. I should not rest until I knew you were back here safely.'

With that, he turned and strode away, leaving Rosina to continue to the stables. As an apology it left a lot to be desired. But as an olive branch...well. A little smile was unfurling inside her. It would suffice.

It was a week before Rosina heard from Mr Shipton and another four days before she set off for his office to collect her jewels. The earl had insisted on coming with her, putting at her disposal his travelling chariot with postilions at the front and a guard sitting on the rumble seat.

'I want to leave nothing to chance,' he said as he handed her into the carriage. 'From what you have told me of your brother, I would not be surprised if he tried to waylay us.'

'If he hears of it,' she agreed. 'However, Mr Shipton has known for years that Edgar and I are not on the best of terms. I can only hope he did not feel himself obliged to tell my brother of our appointment.'

'Well, we shall see,' he replied, climbing in after her. 'Drive on, Robert!'

The chariot bounded forward and soon they were bowling along the lanes away from the Manor. Conham took out his watch.

'We should be at our destination by noon. What time is Shipton expecting you?'

'I told him I would call around two.'

'Then we have time to eat before we call upon Mr Shipton.' He grinned. 'Never wise to go into battle on an empty stomach.'

The journey into Somerset was uneventful. Once they had passed Bath they stopped at the Crown, a posting inn some two miles from Brackwood, which Rosina knew by reputation. They were shown into a private parlour and after removing her cloak, Rosina went over to the hearth to warm her hands at the cheerful fire.

'You have been very quiet this past hour,' Conham remarked. 'Are you anxious at returning to Brackwood?'

'A little,' she confessed. 'I have no idea what lies Edgar has spread about me. I admit I half expected to learn that he had somehow prised Mama's jewels away from the attorney.'

'But Shipton has confirmed that is not the case.'

'True. Or at least, not at the time of writing to me. In his letter, he merely said he was relieved to know that I was safely back in England, although he was sorry I was no longer living at Brackwood.' She smiled a little. 'One can have very few secrets from one's lawyer, and Mr Shipton was well aware that Edgar and I disagreed over how the estate should be run, so his answer was extremely circumspect. As for Mama's jewels, I can only hope that they are still safe.'

'We shall soon find out,' said Conham, pulling out a chair for her. 'Come and sit down.'

The meal put new heart into Rosina and when they resumed their journey, she looked with interest at the familiar landscape.

'I have always loved Somerset, especially in the spring,' she said, gazing out the window.

'Do you miss it?'

'Of course. I grew up here, I have so many happy memories of my life here. This is bringing it all back.'

She gave him a little smile before turning her attention back to the view outside the window. As they drew closer to the village, she could see changes that disturbed her. Farm buildings looking dilapidated, the remains of one barn standing stark against the sky, its roof torn off during the winter and never replaced. On the edge of Brackwood itself she noted with dismay that the labourers' cottages looked neglected. One or two, that she recalled had housed young families, were now standing empty.

'I am sorry, did you speak?' asked the earl.

'Only to myself.' She sighed. 'The village is looking very run-down.'

'Only to be expected after a harsh winter.'

'Yes, but…' She stopped, closing her lips on any criticism of her brother. Brackwood was no longer her concern.

At precisely two o'clock, the earl escorted Rosina into Mr Shipton's small office. The lawyer was a tall, spare man with thinning hair and a gaunt face, but his eyes, behind the spectacles, were kindly as he greeted Rosina.

'I am pleased to see you looking so well, Miss Brackwood.'

He turned his attention to Conham, bowing to him before fixing the earl with a mildly enquiring gaze. Rosina quickly introduced them.

'Lord Dallamire was good enough to escort me,' she explained. 'You were no doubt surprised when I wrote to tell you I was land steward at Morton Gifford.'

Conham did not miss the faint note of defiance in her voice. She had lifted her chin, challenging the attorney to think there was anything improper in this extraordinary news. The old man merely nodded.

'I cannot deny it, although I am sure the task is well within your capabilities.' He smiled slightly. 'I know I speak for many when I say that your talents are sadly missed here at Brackwood, ma'am, sadly missed indeed. Shall we all sit down?'

An hour later, Rosina stepped out onto the High Street. A leather box was clutched in her hands, but the success in obtaining her mother's jewels was overshadowed by the news Mr Shipton had imparted to her.

'Edgar, married! I cannot take it in,' she uttered as they waited for the earl's travelling chariot to come up. 'I know Mr Shipton thought it was a kindness to keep the news until he could tell me in person, but it is still a shock.'

'I am sure it is,' said Conham. 'What would you like to do now?'

'I hardly know. I feel a little dazed.'

The chariot had come to a stop beside them, but Conham ignored it and looked about him.

'We could walk to the Red Lion and order coffee, or wine if you prefer?'

'No,' she said quickly. 'Thank you, but no. I do not want to see the landlord or anyone else in Brackwood today.'

'I can understand that.' He gave her fingers a slight squeeze before handing her up into the carriage. 'We will head back to Morton Gifford.'

'Except…'

'Except?' He was about to follow her but stopped, one foot on the step. 'Tell me what you would like to do, Rosina.'

'Papa's old valet. He lives with his widowed sister at the edge of the village. I *should* like to see them, and explain what has happened. Not everything, of course. Merely what I told Mr Shipton, that I changed my mind about going abroad and remained in England, and I am estranged from my brother.'

'Very well.' He gave his orders to the coachman and jumped in beside her. 'But why not tell everyone the truth? Brackwood deserves no loyalty from you now.'

'Perhaps not, but if Edgar will leave me to live in peace then I will do the same for him.'

'The world should know how badly he has behaved to you.'

'But there is no proof. Even if I were to tell the world, not everyone would believe me. There would still be doubts, questions.' The chariot slowed and she looked out the window. 'We have reached the Paxbys' house. May I ask you to take care of my jewel box, sir?'

'Of course, if you trust me to keep it safe for you,' he replied lightly.

She smiled, but when she responded, he heard the slight tremor in her voice.

'My friend, I have already trusted you with my life and my reputation. I am not anxious about a few little gems.'

He met her eyes, his heart contracting as he gazed into the blue depths. She had forgiven him; that silly quarrel was forgotten. It was only the trust she had just spoken of that prevented him from taking her in his arms and kissing her.

She called you her friend, man. You cannot let her down!

'Of course I will take care of it.' He took the box she was holding out to him and hid it in the small space behind one of the squabs. 'There. When do you want me to call back for you?'

Rosina knocked on the cottage door and it was opened by a plump, homely woman dressed neatly in a grey gown and snowy apron.

'Mrs Jones, good day to you.'

'Miss Brackwood! Well, bless me! Come in, ma'am, come in!'

She stood back, holding the door wide, and Rosina heard the carriage drive off as she stepped over the threshold.

'Good heavens, Jem will be that pleased to see you!'

At the sound of their voices, a querulous voice called, 'Martha, who is it, who's there?'

'It is I, Mr Paxby. Rosina Brackwood.' She moved further into the room and crossed to the fireplace, where her father's aged valet was sitting in an armchair, a patchwork blanket wrapped around his knees. 'No, no, sir, don't get up.'

She placed a hand on his shoulder before turning back to accept the offer of tea from his sister, then she pulled a chair closer to the old man's and sat down.

'I thought you had left us,' he exclaimed, his rheumy eyes fixed on her face. 'They said you was gone off to America.'

'I decided to stay in England, after all.'

'But not with Sir Edgar.'

'No. Not with him.'

'Can't say I'm surprised,' said Martha, bustling up with the tea tray. 'But it was a sad day when you left us, Miss. You know your brother's married now?'

'Yes, I had heard.'

'It is rumoured the lady's family had no choice,' she added, placing the tray down on a nearby table. 'It being what you would call a hasty wedding.'

'You mean...?'

'I do, Miss.' Martha rested her hands on her stomach and gave Rosina a darkling look.

'Seen her at church a couple of times,' muttered Mr Paxby. 'Poor little dab of a woman. Didn't look to be happy, but that's no wonder. Everyone knows he married her for her dowry.'

'Now then, Jem. We've no reason to think she's unhappy.'

Martha chided the old man as she handed him a cup of tea, but the look he gave Rosina was eloquent. He knew Edgar's temper as well as she did, although the valet had always been too loyal to Papa to speak ill of his son.

Rosina sipped her tea and encouraged the valet to talk about the old days. She was content to listen to his stories of Brackwood Court when she was a child and he and Sir Thomas had both been hale and hearty. She was conscious of the time, and did not wish to tire the old man. At length, she finished her tea and took her leave, promising to call again.

'Thank you, ma'am. Your visit's done Jem the world of good,' Martha told her as she escorted Rosina to the door. 'He misses life at Brackwood Court something fierce and although he don't speak of it, I know he frets over what the new master is doing. Or rather,' she added, her homely face adopting an uncharacteristic frown, 'what he is *not* doing. It's been a tonic for him to see you, though, and to know you are well.'

Rosina heard the faint doubtful note in the widow's voice as she said this, her eyes on the handsome travelling chariot that had drawn up. She had explained that she was land steward at Morton Gifford, but she was well aware that many, including Mr Paxby and his sister, would find it hard to believe that a woman could hold down such a position.

Conham waited until Rosina had waved to Martha as the chariot pulled away from the little house, then he asked her what she would like to do next.

'There is still time to visit Brackwood Court, if you would like to see it?'

'Thank you, but no, I do not wish to see it,' she said emphatically. 'There is nothing for me there. I should like to go home, if you please.'

It cheered him to hear her refer to Morton Gifford as home, but the sadness in her countenance concerned him.

'Did your meeting with your father's valet bring back painful memories?'

'No indeed. We talked of happier times. But what I have seen here and what I have learned from Mr Paxby and Mr Shipton today suggest things are not being managed as they ought.' She stopped and shook her head. 'I keep saying Brackwood is no longer my concern, but it is so very hard not to care. But who knows, things may not be so bad as they seem. My brother is still learning how to go on here. Perhaps he will settle down, now he has a wife.'

'Perhaps he will.' Conham spoke more in hope than expectation.

'I had forgotten quite how many of Mama's jewels Papa

had put aside for me,' said Rosina, changing the subject. 'Diamonds, too. I should be able to invest a useful sum in Bellemonte.'

'Yes.' He hesitated, not wishing to stir up their previous argument. 'I shall not try to dissuade you, but I hope you will consider putting some of it in the Funds. For a little security.'

'I believe Bellemonte is secure enough, is it not?'

'I hope so, but I am no expert. Far from it. In fact, you would do well to ignore any advice I may give. I know far less than you about these matters!' He turned to stare out the window, saying bitterly, 'Unlike your excellent father, mine did not always make the wisest choices where money was concerned.'

'Would you like to talk about it?'

Her voice, gentle, sympathetic, broke into his dark thoughts. Conham closed his eyes for a moment. He desperately wanted to tell her. Rosina already knew something of his debts, but would it sink him still lower in her estimation? He felt the gentle touch of her fingers on his arm.

'I am very willing to listen, if it would help. In confidence. We are friends, are we not?'

'Matt knows the whole sorry tale, so you may as well know it, too. My stepmother is an excellent woman in many ways. She gave my father two delightful daughters, whom he loved very much. When she wrote to me to tell me of my father's demise in a riding accident, she assured me there was no need for me to sell out immediately. She and the lawyers would deal with everything.

'However, she kept from me the fact that six years ago my father mortgaged all the unentailed lands at Dallamire. He was a gambling man, and not content with running up huge debts at the gaming tables, he speculated wildly with the money he borrowed, believing he could pay off all his debts and the mortgages, too. Of course, that never happened. Somehow, when he died, the lawyers managed to keep the creditors at bay while I was away. I was never informed of any of this. It was only when I came home that I discovered the true state of affairs. That I am now responsible for the repayments. I could sell some of the land, but even that will not be enough to cover all my commitments.'

'And would leave you with even less income.'

'Precisely.' His mouth twisted. 'I knew next to nothing about the responsibilities and obligations of my new position and I have had to learn very quickly.'

'Oh, Conham!'

'Aye. If Bellemonte does prove successful then the profit will help pay off the mortgages. However, if my business acumen is as poor as my father's…'

He trailed off, grimacing.

'But your father was following a gambler's instincts rather than any sound business plan,' she said, tucking her hand into his arm. 'Besides, this is not based on your judgement alone. Matthew and I also believe it will work. Which is why I want to invest in it. But I need not decide anything until the jewels are sold. Will you write to your man in London, and ask him to arrange it for me?'

Conham nodded. Somehow, just talking with Rosina, having her in his life, made the future seem a little less dark.

'Better than that. I will take them myself.'

'Oh, I would not want to put you to any trouble!' She removed her hand from his sleeve and rearranged the folds of her cloak. 'Although you will have to go back to London, will you not? To continue your search for a wife.'

'Yes.'

Her words were like a sudden drenching with icy water, but he could not deny the truth of them. He could not neglect his duty or Dallamire by staying any longer at Morton Gifford.

Chapter Fifteen

The day being far advanced, they decided to dine at the Crown and arrived at the hostelry just as the sun was setting. The travelling chariot came to a halt behind another vehicle and as Conham helped Rosina to alight, he saw a footman jump down from the larger carriage and open the door while gazing expectantly towards the inn.

'That augurs well,' he murmured. 'If the owner of that smart equipage is leaving, I have high hopes of there being a private parlour for us.'

Even as he spoke, a couple stepped out of the building. Conham felt Rosina clutch his sleeve as the gentleman glanced idly in their direction then stopped, glaring at them. She uttered one shocked, breathless word.

'Edgar!'

They were but yards away; there could be no avoiding a meeting, with the landlord and any number of interested servants looking on. Conham knew what must be done.

He nodded. 'Brackwood.'

He said it with a degree of hauteur that he hoped would evoke a polite response from the man, if nothing more cordial. Brackwood inclined his head.

'Lord Dallamire.'

'I believe I am to congratulate you, Edgar,' said Rosina, recovering a little.

'Yes. This is my wife. Harriet, my sister Rosina and her...' He met Conham's steely gaze and went on with only the faintest sneer. 'Her *employer*, the Earl of Dallamire.'

Conham watched the ladies exchange curtsies before he made an elegant bow.

'Your servant, Lady Brackwood.'

Edgar Brackwood clearly had no time for such civility and he scowled.

'What were you doing in Brackwood, Sister?'

'I called upon Mr Shipton.'

Rosina spoke calmly enough although her fingers clutched tightly at Conham's sleeve. He thought Brackwood would ask her reason for visiting the attorney but, glancing down, he saw that her chin was raised and he smiled inwardly. He was familiar with that rebellious tilt, and he could imagine the defiant look in her blue eyes. By heaven, she had challenged him with it often enough! He was not surprised that Brackwood remained silent.

'But let us not stand any longer in this chill wind,' she went on. 'I bid you good day, Edgar. Lady Brackwood.'

Conham felt the squeeze on his arm. He touched his hat and escorted Rosina past her brother and his wife and into the inn without another glance.

'Goodness, how, how unfortunate,' declared Rosina, once they were alone in a private parlour. She untied her cloak with hands that were not quite steady. 'I do not know which of us was most surprised, Edgar or me!'

'I thought he would have a fit of apoplexy,' remarked Conham.

'He certainly looked most put out! I felt sorry for his

poor wife. I thought she might faint off at any moment, which would not be surprising, if she is indeed with child.' Rosina sighed. 'She is just as Mr Paxby described her. Small and mouselike. I am very much afraid Edgar will bully her. After all, we can be very sure it is not a love match, at least on his part.'

'I am in no position to criticise him for that,' said Conham, drily.

'No, but *you* will do all in your power to make your wife happy.'

Rosina uttered the words without thinking, but her heart took off at a gallop when she saw the look in Conham's hard eyes. They positively blazed, expressing feelings, passions that she recognised. That she shared.

Her heart was pounding, her whole body tingling with a sense of danger, as if the very air around them could ignite at any moment. She was painfully aware that they were alone. One gesture, one wrong word, and she knew, with devastating certainty, that he would cross the small space between them and drag her into his arms.

And oh, how she wanted him to do just that!

It would not stop at kisses. Rosina knew the emotions whirling about them were far too powerful. Conham filled her dreams, he was never far from her thoughts, and if he touched her now her fragile defences would crumble. She would throw herself at him and do everything she could to satisfy the aching desire she felt for this man. And that would be disastrous. She would face ruin in the eyes of the world, all hopes of respectable employment would be wiped out.

Or he would feel obliged to marry her, which would destroy all his family's hopes of restoring their name and house to former glory.

Quickly, she turned away, desperate to recover the situation.

She said, 'Seeing the new Lady Brackwood today has convinced me that marriage is a prison for women. I am right to make my own way in the world.'

She waited, half hoping that Conham would contradict her, but he said nothing and she went on with false cheerfulness.

'I hope they will not be long in bringing us something to eat. I am very eager to drive on to Morton Gifford and get back to my work. As I am sure you must be, my lord.'

Conham listened to Rosina with growing dismay. He had thought himself well under control but he knew that he had given himself away. Rosina had read in his eyes that he wanted her. Did she realise he would give up his life to make her happy?

Because that was what he must do. She was telling him, with awful, gut-wrenching clarity, that they could never have anything more than friendship.

They completed the journey in what could best be described as an awkward politeness, each sitting close to their corner, trying to avoid touching within the close confines of the travelling chariot.

Rosina wanted to weep, but she dared not risk Conham turning to comfort her. With a supreme effort she maintained her composure until they reached Morton Gifford, where the driver had orders to drive on to the lodge. When they left the main road and passed through the gates, Conham broke the silence.

'I would suggest you allow me to lock your jewel box in my strong room at the Manor.'

'Yes, thank you. It will be safe there until you can take the jewels to town.'

'Are you sure there are no pieces you wish to keep for your own use?'

'Perfectly sure. I have my pearls and a few trinkets.' She managed a small laugh. 'When would I ever wear diamonds or emeralds?'

To hear her talking like this was too much for Conham. She was trying so hard to be cheerful and her bravery tore at his heart. Something between a growl and a moan escaped him and he reached out, dragging her into his arms.

'Oh, don't…don't.'

But her protest was half-hearted and she clung to him as he covered her face with kisses.

'You *should* wear them,' he muttered. 'You deserve to be dressed in the finest silks and wearing a king's ransom in jewels. Every day!'

He captured her lips and Rosina gave herself up to his kiss. It was ruthless, demanding. Her skin tingled, her body was on fire with all the yearning desires she had so rigorously suppressed since he had first kissed her on that dark, wintry night in Bristol.

But it was the thought of that first encounter that now intruded and a renewed sense of self-preservation brought her to her senses. However much Conham might want her, she knew they could never be happy together.

'Ah, no, we cannot. We must not do this,' she muttered, somehow finding the strength to push against him.

Conham released her just as the travelling chariot stopped outside the lodge. The blood was pounding through him; his breathing was ragged, painful. The new lanterns outside the lodge door sent a faint glow into the carriage, enough for him to see the tears gleaming in Rosina's eyes. The sight tore at his heart.

'What else can we do? I lo—'

'No!' She put her fingers to his lips. 'No. Please don't say it, Conham. That would only make things worse.'

'But I want to marry you, Rosina!'

'That can never be.' She drew in a breath, as unsteady as his own. 'You must marry well, for the sake of your family. I could sell my jewels and invest the money safely in government funds, but even with the money Papa settled upon me it would only bring in, what…a hundred pounds a year at most.' She pushed herself out of his arms. 'You need *thousands* to restore Dallamire and live as an earl should.'

'Dallamire be damned,' he said savagely. 'What is to prevent us going abroad?'

'Conscience.' She uttered the word flatly. 'Can you in all honesty tell me you could abandon your stepmother and your half-sisters, give up Dallamire and your good name? Could you truly do all that and still be happy?'

He wanted to say yes, that with her beside him he would think the world well lost, but something stopped him.

'You see?' She reached up and cupped his cheek. 'You are far too good, too kind, to turn your back on everyone who depends upon you.'

'Then be my mistress!' He caught her hand and pressed a kiss into the palm. 'I could set you up in your own establishment—'

'Paid for by your rich wife!' A bitter laugh escaped her and she pulled herself free. 'None of us would be happy with that arrangement.'

With a groan he sat back, rubbing one hand across his eyes. 'Confound it, what a damned tangle!'

There was an agonising silence. Then.

'I should leave. Go away somewhere...'

'No, that will not do!' Conham reached out for her, this time catching both her hands. 'I cannot bear to lose you. I have grown accustomed to having you here, to seeing you every day. I could not bear it if I did not know where you were. If I did not know you were safe.'

'Nor I you.' Her words were so quiet he almost missed them.

She pushed him away and sat up straight, folding her hands in her lap.

'There *is* an alternative, my lord. We can forget this moment, and carry on as we had planned. You will sell my jewels for me and I will invest in Bellemonte. It would be painful, but it is the only way.'

For a long time they sat there, side by side, saying nothing and staring into the darkness.

'You would stay on here, as land steward?'

'Having worked so hard to overcome everyone's initial doubts and prove myself, I should very much like to continue.'

'Another twelve months, then. Until Lady Day next year.' He uttered the words, even though it would be agony to have her so close, yet so unattainable.

'Yes, I will stay. Heaven knows I have nowhere else to go. Brackwood is lost to me now.' She spoke so softly he hardly heard those last words, then she seemed to pull herself together and said in a stronger voice, 'However, if Bellemonte is a success, my investment might provide me with sufficient funds to set up my own establishment.'

But that was a long way in the future, thought Conham. For now, she would be under his eye, somewhere he could look after her. Even if not in the way he would like.

He said, almost to himself, 'Do you think we could do this?'

'It will be easier when you are not here.'

Her frankness almost made him laugh, even as it sliced into his heart.

'Of course.' He closed his eyes, gathering himself. 'I bid you good-night, then, Rosina.'

He jumped out of the carriage and held his hand out to help her down.

'I plan to leave very early tomorrow. I shall not see you before I go. Write to me, if there are any matters that you cannot deal with yourself.'

She nodded. Her eyes were downcast and he caught the glint of tears on her lashes. Leaving her there and ordering the driver to take him back to the Manor was the hardest thing he had ever done in his life.

Chapter Sixteen

It was May. Rosina stood in the square at Bellemonte and gazed at the entrance to the gardens. The ironwork had all been repaired and the lettering in the metal arch that curved above the gates was freshly picked out in gold.

'Grand Pleasure Gardens.' There was no mistaking the pride in Matt's voice as he read the words aloud. 'It is only a week until the opening ceremony, Rosina! I admit, there were times I thought we would not be ready.'

She squeezed his arm. 'I never doubted you would succeed.'

'I could not have done it without you,' he told her. 'Your investment was most timely. I cannot thank you enough for that.'

'I am glad my small sum could be of use.'

'Two thousand pounds!' He laughed. 'A handsome sum, by anyone's reckoning. It meant we could begin on the renovations for the Pavilion without having to wait for new investors. By heaven, Rosina, everything has progressed a great deal quicker than I imagined it could! But are you sure this is what you want?' He turned to look at her. 'If you had invested elsewhere, in the Funds, for example, you could set yourself up in your own house, quite comfortably.'

'I know that, but I do not need the money at present,

and Bellemonte's returns should prove far more lucrative, in the long term.'

'You have no wish to move away from Gloucestershire?'

She had known Matt Talacre long enough to understand the concern in his eyes.

She shook her head. 'No, I cannot bring myself to leave Morton Gifford. Not yet.'

She had never told him how she felt about Conham, but somehow he knew, and it was a comfort.

'Then I am very grateful to you for your trust in me, Rosina. I hope it will be repaid a thousandfold!'

'Then we shall all be rich!' She laughed. His exaggeration had lightened the mood. She added with a smile, 'I have no doubt Bellemonte will be a success, my friend, although it might take a little while and I am glad for you. Truly.'

Rosina knew Matt had thrown himself into the work with a will, taking on physical challenges as well as dealing with the management of the project, and the change in him was noticeable. The exercise had helped to strengthen his wounded leg, so that his lameness was barely perceptible. His spare frame had filled out a little, too, and he carried himself more proudly. He looked like a different man and she could not wait to know what Conham made of the transformation in his friend.

Conham. It was six weeks since he had left for London and since then she had heard no word from him. His secretary had conducted all correspondence concerning the sale of her jewels, and the proceeds had duly been forwarded without any word from the earl himself.

Giving herself a little shake, she turned to look at what had once been the run-down tavern. It was freshly painted, the front step scrubbed and a new sign swung proudly above the door, proclaiming this was now The Dallamire Arms.

'And the inn, too, looks very grand, Matthew.'

'Aye. My new landlord is a very good fellow. It was his idea to ask the earl if he might change the name. By the by, talking of Conham, when do you expect him?'

'I know no more than you,' said Rosina. 'Mrs Jameson has had no word telling her to prepare his rooms.'

'And he has not written to you?'

'No. Why should he?' She forced herself to smile.

'No reason. I just thought…' Matt glanced at her again, then shrugged. 'Conham was never one for letter writing.'

It was not what he had been about to say, but Rosina let it go.

'You promised me a full tour of the gardens,' she reminded him, taking his arm.

'So I did! Come along, then. We only closed off sections of the grounds during the renovations, to keep interest alive, and I think it has worked. Tickets for the reopening are selling well. Once I have shown you around, then we will go into the inn. There is a very respectable private parlour in there now and I will treat you to cakes and wine before you leave. I shall introduce you to the landlord and his wife as my business partner!'

Rosina drove back to Morton Gifford late that afternoon, cheered by the progress at Bellemonte. It had helped to divert her mind from Conham, for a few hours at least. He was her first thought each morning, and last one each night. She did not admit to anyone how much she missed him, but it was a constant ache, almost physical at times.

Thus it was that when she reached the Manor, her heart began to beat just a little faster when she noticed signs of an arrival. She hurried into the house to find the earl himself standing in the hall, talking to Jameson while servants struggled up the stairs with several large trunks.

'You are here!' Even his frowning look as he turned towards her could not prevent the smile spreading over her face. 'Welcome back to Gifford Manor, my lord.'

'Thank you.'

'We had no idea when you would be returning,' she went on, peeling off her gloves. 'If I had known I could have postponed my visit to Bellemonte.'

'It was all arranged last minute.' It was hard to read the expression in his hooded eyes, but despite his polite tone, Rosina sensed he was ill at ease. 'I sent a rider on ahead of us early this morning, when we stopped to change horses at Bath. To prepare rooms for my visitors.'

Visitors! Rosina forced herself to keep smiling, conscious that Jameson was still in the hall and a footman was hovering, waiting to relieve her of her outdoor clothes.

'You have guests, my lord?'

A sense of foreboding was growing inside her.

'Yes. My stepmother, the Countess of Dallamire, is with me. And Lady Skelton and her daughter.'

'Ah.' Not by the flicker of an eyelid did Rosina show her dismay. What could this be but the visit of a prospective bride? 'Then I will not detain you, my lord. Excuse me.'

She handed her bonnet and pelisse to the waiting servant and hurried away to her office. Wild thoughts chased through her mind and she told herself not to jump to conclusions. It would be foolish to read anything into this. Why should Conham not invite his stepmama to stay? Or anyone else, for that matter. Lady Skelton might turn out to be an aged crone, and her daughter an elderly spinster. Although she could not bring herself to believe that.

Rosina closed the door and sat down at her desk, feeling a little faint. She dropped her head in her hands, berating herself for her weakness. She had known Conham was looking for a rich bride; why was she so surprised?

Because she had expected to read of his betrothal in the London paper. Or he could have stirred himself to write to her on estate business and added the information as a postscript. Instead, he had brought the lady here, to Morton Gifford, where she would be forced to witness their courtship. After all they had said at their last meeting, would Conham really be that cruel?

She pulled a ledger towards her and opened it, trying to concentrate on the figures, but the question kept forcing its way into her mind. It took every ounce of resolve not to go in search of Mrs Jameson to glean more information, but she hated the thought of listening to gossip and was determined not to leave her office until it was time to join the upper servants for dinner.

The time dragged. She wrote up a report on Bellemonte and made a note of questions and suggestions to discuss with Matthew at their next meeting. Then she set to work on her accounts until the chimes of the hall clock told her it was nearing the dinner hour.

She was just blotting the last row of figures when there was a knock at the door. Conham came into the room and she looked up, trying to ignore how handsome he looked in his evening clothes, the black coat fitting without a crease across his broad shoulders, his auburn hair gleaming red in the early-evening sunlight that blazed into the study at that time of day.

'I hope I am not disturbing you?'

'Not at all, my lord.'

'I wanted to explain. I had no intention of bringing anyone with me, but when my stepmother suggested it, I could hardly refuse. I should have written. I am sorry.' He was pacing the small room, reminding her of a caged animal. 'The countess is keen that I should marry as soon as possible. Miss Skelton comes from a good family. Excellent credentials.'

'Including a generous dowry?'

Heavens, how could she sound so calm, so practical?

'A *very* generous dowry.'

'Then you should offer for her with all speed.'

'Yes.'

He came to a stand before the desk and looked down at her, his eyes troubled. She looked away before he glimpsed in her countenance the seething mass of jealousy, rage and misery she felt inside.

Rosina closed the ledger. 'Thank you for informing me, my lord. Now, if you will excuse me, it is nearly time for dinner.'

He did not move. She added pointedly, 'Your guests will be waiting for you.'

She kept her eyes lowered and tidied the desk while the silence lengthened between them. Then, just when she thought she could bear it no longer, she heard him turn and leave the room.

Rosina exhaled, long and slow. He had apologised, removing her reason to be angry with him. The jealousy and unhappiness she must deal with herself. And now that first meeting was over, they could continue as master and steward. It would be difficult, but surely not impossible. She had thought herself prepared. She had known that at some point Conham would marry, but she had not realised the depths of despair that would engulf her when the idea became a possibility. If only she had known how painful it would be, then she would have taken the money she received for her jewels and run far away from Morton Gifford. From Conham.

She closed her eyes. The salary he was paying her was far higher than anything she could command elsewhere, and she had sunk all her money into Bellemonte now. She could not withdraw without jeopardising Matthew's plans, as well as the earl's. She had no choice but to continue.

Her spirits sank even lower when she joined the Jamesons for dinner that evening. She knew it was likely that the subject of the earl's visitors would come up, but when she learned that Mr Dawkins would not be joining them, it was inevitable. Mrs Jameson's housekeeping skills had not been tested very much over recent years and she was now relishing the challenge of having ladies in the house.

'This has always been a bachelor household,' she explained. 'Lady Dallamire has never been here before and not for the world would I have her find anything wanting. Thankfully, we only recently turned the house upside down. There is nothing like spring sunshine for showing up every speck of dust, is there, Miss Brackwood? As soon as Lord Dallamire's message arrived, I inspected every nook and cranny and was relieved to find them spotless. I have brought in two more girls from the village, though, just in case. With three ladies in the house there will be far more fetching and carrying to be done, I am sure.'

'I believe the earl has two half-sisters,' offered Rosina, trying to avoid mentioning Miss Skelton. 'Did the countess include them in the party?'

'Oh, no. They are still in the schoolroom at Dallamire, I believe, which is fortunate, since the house is now as full as it can hold. No, *this* visit has another reason altogether.' The housekeeper lowered her voice a little. 'Her Ladyship is matchmaking!'

'Now, now,' said her husband, frowning a little. 'We should not be gossiping about these matters.'

'Oh, pish, Mr Jameson, you are as bad as Mr Dawkins, not wanting to talk about the master, but this is not gossip, for none of us would say anything outside these walls. And this may be our only opportunity. The ladies' maids are all so busy, I have had to send their meals up to them tonight, but tomorrow I shall invite them to dine with us. Very ladylike they are, too,' she added. 'The countess's maid is French, and inclined to turn her nose up at our country ways, which is not surprising, I suppose, if they are more accustomed to a grand house like Dallamire. However, Lady Skelton's and her daughter's maids are very pleasant and agreeable.'

'And did they say how long their visit is likely to be?' asked Rosina, curiosity getting the better of her.

'Only two weeks. Miss Skelton's maid told me they had planned to stay in London for the season, only then Lady Dallamire invited them to make a short visit here.' She chuckled. 'Well, we can all guess what *that* means!'

Mr Jameson looked up from his dinner to say firmly, 'Enough now, madam.'

His spouse, thus admonished, turned her attention to her dinner and Rosina was left to her own thoughts. With the reopening of Bellemonte's Grand Pleasure Gardens only a week away, did that mean Conham had changed his mind about going, or did he intend to bring his visitors? She could not decide which she would prefer.

When dinner was over, Rosina went to the great hall to put on her pelisse before walking back to the lodge. Jameson was carrying a tray of decanters to the drawing room, and as the butler passed through the open door, the sound of animated chatter flowed out. She heard Conham's deep voice, then the sweet, bell-like sound of a lady's laugh.

Matt would lose a significant opportunity to puff off his new project to his investors if Conham decided to stay away from Bellemonte. But she thought it most likely he would attend, accompanied by his guests. Rosina followed the footman with his lantern out into the darkness. Either way, her pleasure in the event was now sadly diminished.

Chapter Seventeen

Rosina kept herself busy for the rest of the week, the good weather giving her an excuse to spend more time out of doors, but she knew she could not avoid the earl and his guests forever.

The inevitable meeting occurred when she was riding back to the stables one afternoon. She saw the open carriage on the drive, Conham riding beside it on his black hunter. Her heart sank when they all stopped and waited for her to come up to them. Bramble was nothing like the beautiful horses she had ridden at Brackwood, and today's ride had been particularly muddy. She had taken a short cut across the meadows to reach one of the farms and she knew it wasn't just the pony's sturdy legs that were spattered with dirt. However, there was no avoiding the meeting so she squared her shoulders and approached, bidding the earl a calm good day.

Conham touched his hat to Rosina before presenting her to the occupants of the carriage. They responded, eyeing her with varying degrees of curiosity. She knew some of her hair had escaped around the edges of her riding hat, and that her skirts were liberally splashed with mud, but there was nothing to do but smile and brave it out.

'I have been visiting Valley Farm,' she told Conham, by way of explanation. 'Stratton has been reroofing his barn.'

'Ah yes, you wrote to tell me.' He nodded. 'I must go down and see it for myself. Although not today. I am about to accompany the ladies on a short tour of the park.'

'So, you are the new land steward here.'

Lady Dallamire's voice cut across them, thick with disapproval. She was a tall, thin woman, dressed in widow's weeds and with her dark hair sprinkled with grey. Before Rosina could respond, she turned away and addressed Conham.

'It is most irregular. I have never heard of such a thing.'

'Perhaps not, but Miss Brackwood has proved herself to be an excellent choice.'

'But surely you do not ride out unaccompanied, Miss Brackwood?' remarked Lady Skelton, a stern-faced matron in a walking dress and pelisse whose colour exactly matched her iron-grey hair. 'Is that wise?'

'There is little danger riding about the estate, or in the village.' Rosina answered her cheerfully. 'I used to do so on my father's estate, when he was too ill to go out himself.'

The youngest member of the party, Miss Skelton, was staring at Rosina with a look of awed fascination. She was a young lady of no more than one-and-twenty, her willowy figure clothed in a fashionable deep rose pelisse and with a matching bonnet, beneath which a mass of glossy black curls peeped out to frame a very pretty face. When Rosina gave her a friendly smile, she blushed rosily and looked away.

'I cannot think it a suitable occupation for a lady,' declared Lady Dallamire in repressive accents.

'It is, however, a *respectable* occupation, ma'am,' Rosina

countered, more sharply than perhaps she should. 'And there are precious few of those open to ladies.'

'Miss Brackwood knows more about land management than anyone else who came forward for the position,' said Conham. He turned to Rosina and touched his hat to her again. 'But unlike those of us idling our day away in pleasure, I know you have work to do, ma'am. We will not keep you from it any longer.'

His smile took the sting out of the dismissal, and Rosina was grateful.

'Thank you, my lord.'

She nodded to the ladies and urged Bramble to walk on, feeling their eyes upon her as she rode away. She sat up very straight in the saddle, conscious that the Welsh pony was by no means an elegant beast. Rosina had no doubt she would be compared very unfavourably with the graceful Miss Skelton.

Rosina was dismayed but not surprised when Conham informed her he was taking his guests to Bellemonte's grand reopening.

They were in her office and had just spent an hour on estate business, which, he had told her, was all he could spare.

'I understand,' she replied. 'You have guests, after all.'

'Yes.' He paused. 'I have invited them to come with us tomorrow evening.'

She nodded. 'Then if you will allow me to use the chariot, I shall go on ahead.'

'No, *I* will use the chariot. You will be more comfortable travelling in the landau with the other ladies.'

'Very well.'

She thought there would be nothing comfortable about sitting with the countess and Lady Skelton. Since that first introduction, whenever Rosina encountered the ladies in the house or grounds, they ignored her.

As befitted a servant.

Rosina presented herself in the hall at the appointed time the next evening, wearing her white cambric muslin, trimmed at the hem with a single flounce. Over this she wore a new pelisse of dark red velvet. It fitted snugly to the high waist, where it was confined with a narrow band of matching satin before falling down to her ankles in soft folds. She had trimmed a straw bonnet with red ribbons to match and, knowing the other ladies would disapprove of her presence whatever she wore, she had secured the bonnet with a defiantly jaunty bow beneath one ear.

The earl politely handed them all into the carriage and the ladies set off, travelling in a chilly silence that was finally broken by the countess.

'Really, I do not know why Dallamire should insist you should come along this evening, Miss Brackwood. Surely there is no need for his steward to attend.'

'You are quite right, ma'am. I am not here in my capacity as the earl's land steward. I am an investor.'

'What!'

'Lord Dallamire owns the land, but Mr Talacre and I have invested in the development of Bellemonte.' Rosina could not suppress a smile at the look of shock and surprise on the faces of her auditors. 'You might say we are all, er, business partners.'

'Well, a lady involved in *business*!' exclaimed Lady Skelton. 'How extraordinary. I have never known such a thing.'

'Oh, I am sure you have, ma'am,' said Rosina. 'Think of the milliners and modistes you use, I am sure at least some of them are in charge of their own business. And my father often talked of Mrs Coade, who manufactures the excellent Coade Stone. He even purchased two of her sculptures for the gardens at Brackwood Court.'

Lady Skelton gave a little titter of disdain. 'Milliners, tradespeople,' she declared. 'Not the *haute ton*, at all.'

Rosina went on as if she had not heard her.

'And of course there is Lady Jersey, who has been a senior partner of Child's Bank for the past ten years.' She smiled. 'She is a patroness of Almack's, and I am sure you would be delighted to accept vouchers from her for Miss Skelton, would you not, ma'am?'

Lady Skelton looked nonplussed, but the countess gave a little snort of laughter.

'Very well, Miss Brackwood, you have made your point. But as for this business venture, well. Time will tell if my stepson was wise to keep Bellemonte.'

'It will indeed, ma'am.'

Rosina settled back in her corner, pleased that she had not allowed herself to be browbeaten, and satisfied that Lady Dallamire, at least, was looking a little less disapproving.

Matthew was waiting at the gates to meet them. He tenderly handed the countess out of the carriage, declaring what a pleasure it was to see her again.

'It has been too long, ma'am. And may I say you are looking as radiant as ever!'

'Enough of your insolence,' she scolded, although it was clear she was not displeased with Matt's form of address.

'No, no, I mean every word, Lady Dallamire. You cannot conceive how delighted I am to have you grace our celebrations with your presence.'

'Yes, well, I hope I shall not be disappointed,' she retorted sharply.

Rosina moved away a little and watched as the countess presented him to Lady Skelton and her daughter.

'I see Matt is working his charm on my stepmother and her guests.'

She turned to find the earl beside her. 'Yes, he is. Very much at his ease, and so confident! Have you noticed how well he is looking? He appears to be perfectly at home here.'

'Yes, I have.' Conham smiled as he observed his friend chatting to the ladies in such an animated fashion. 'This could be the making of him.'

There was no time for more. Lady Dallamire commanded his attention and he went off to give her his arm.

Matthew guided them all to the Pavilion, which was now resplendent with fresh paint.

'You see the card and tea rooms have been furnished in the very latest style,' he said, ushering the party through the building. 'Then we have the supper room, and the ballroom, which is also an ideal place to promenade during the day, if the weather is inclement.'

Conham had to admit he was impressed. Compared to his last visit, everything now looked new and elegant. Chandeliers blazed in every room, picking out the gilding on the plastered ceilings and casting a warm glow over the guests. Matthew suggested they should enjoy a light repast before venturing out into the gardens.

'I shall not be able to accompany you, alas,' he informed them. 'However, Dallamire has been here before. I hope he will tell you how much everything is improved.'

Conham grinned and waved him away. 'Yes, yes, you have given us enough of your time. Off you go and do the pretty by your other guests.'

When Matt had gone, Conham escorted his party back to the supper room, where an impressive array of refreshments had been laid out on long tables covered with snowy white cloths. They found an empty table and the countess took charge of seating everyone. Conham found himself sitting between Lady Skelton and her daughter, and since his stepmother dominated the conversation, he had no opportunity to speak to Rosina until they were back in the vestibule.

She was the first to join him after the ladies had gone off to collect their cloaks, prior to visiting the lamplit garden walks, and he spoke without preamble.

'I am sorry, I hope my guests have not spoiled your enjoyment of the evening. It was never my intention—'

'You could hardly leave them at the Manor,' she replied. 'And it cannot be a bad thing that they are present. There are few people here with whom you are acquainted, but it will be widely reported that both the Earl *and* the Countess of Dallamire were in attendance.'

'Aye, Matt will make sure of it!'

'And why not? He wishes it to be known that Bellemonte is a very fashionable place.' She looked about her. 'Judging by those I have seen here tonight, I believe it has every chance of succeeding.'

'And that will benefit all of us.'

'Yes, although nothing compared to what you need to restore Dallamire's fortunes.'

'But it could make a real difference for you, as well as Matthew.' He paused, then added quietly, 'I hope it does, Rosina. I hope, eventually, you will achieve the independence you desire.'

'What are you saying, Dallamire? What are you and Miss Brackwood discussing?'

His stepmother came up and Conham reluctantly turned away from Rosina. It was time to do his duty.

'Nothing of moment, ma'am.' He smiled at Miss Skelton and her mother, who had now joined them. 'Shall we go and explore the gardens?'

The countess agreed, but insisted that Conham accompany Amelia. 'And you must escort Lady Skelton, too, Dallamire. I wish to talk with Miss Brackwood.'

Rosina hid her alarm at this news and fell into step beside the countess as they set off along the path, following the earl, who strolled ahead of them with a lady on each arm.

'Dallamire has told me of your background, Miss Brackwood. He says your father owned an estate in Somerset. I believe that is where you learned about land management.'

'Yes, ma'am, it is.'

'My stepson has been singing your praises.'

'Has he?' Rosina hoped she was not blushing. 'The earl is very kind, ma'am.'

'He is, but you must not expect anything to come of it.'

'I do not know what Your Ladyship means.'

'Oh, I think you do, Miss Brackwood. You are a clever woman, after all.' The countess waited, possibly expecting a modest disclaimer, and when nothing was forthcoming, she continued. 'Let me be frank. My stepson may be very impressed with your intellect but he will never marry you.'

'I do not expect him to do so,' replied Rosina, bristling.

'I am glad. I would not wish to see you disappointed. The Dallamires can trace their history back to the Conqueror. You may entice him into bed, but he will not forget himself so far as to marry a servant.'

'I am his *land steward*, madam, not his servant,' said Rosina, holding on to her temper.

'Which is even worse!' declared Lady Dallamire. 'You are associating with men of all ranks, sullying your hands with *commerce*. If he forgot what was owed to his name and married you, he would become a laughing stock. His peers would despise him for ignoring his duty to his family!'

Rosina drew herself up. 'The earl is not one to forget his responsibilities, my lady. It is not in his nature. He is the most honourable man I know.'

'Precisely.' The countess gave Rosina a pitying look, then she reached across to pat her hand. 'You may be a lady who has fallen upon hard times, but Conham is not your knight in shining armour, my dear. He knows it is his duty to take a rich wife. He has been bred to it.'

'Has he?' Rosina hid her anger beneath a derisive smile. 'You make him sound like a prize stallion.'

The countess's eyes narrowed, but then she laughed gently.

'Why, perhaps that is what he is,' she said. 'He certainly knows what is due to his rank and his name. His pride, his *conscience*, will not let him do other than provide for those of us who are dependent upon him. I shall say no more, Miss Brackwood. You are a sensible woman; I trust you will not make Conham's life more difficult than it already is.'

With that, she set off again and Rosina followed, curbing a sudden desire to storm off in the opposite direction. They soon caught up with Conham and the other ladies, who had stopped at a fork in the path to wait for them.

A short conversation ensued before the party moved again, strolling along the main path that Rosina recalled would take them back to the Pavilion. The earl and Miss Skelton were still leading the way, but Lady Skelton was now walking with the countess, and as they were both ignoring Rosina, she dropped back. She had no desire to listen to them discussing the best warehouses for bridal silks, as if a marriage between Lord Dallamire and Miss Skelton was as good as decided.

Which it probably was, she thought miserably. The countess had not told her anything she did not already know. She had merely confirmed that Rosina was wholly ineligible, compared to the rich Miss Skelton. Conham himself was aware of it, too. She had watched him earlier, doing his best to set Amelia Skelton at her ease. Even now, he was bending his head to catch her words, giving her one of his encouraging smiles.

Resolutely pushing her unhappiness aside, Rosina forced her mind to more practical matters. She had invested in these gardens; it was in her interests to look out for anything that might be improved. It would also be useful to note whether the majority of visitors were members of the gentry or well-to-do tradespeople.

Matt's voice broke into her thoughts: 'Have the fearsome matrons cut you out?'

She jumped and looked around. Smiling, he offered her his arm.

'Well, have they?'

'I chose to fall behind.' She slipped her hand onto his sleeve. 'I have been observing your customers.'

'That does not answer my question. Oh, no need to throw me that warning look, we are sufficiently far behind now that they will not hear us.'

She hesitated. 'They are intent on promoting a match for the earl. With Miss Skelton.'

He gave her a searching look. 'Would you mind that?'

Rosina laughed, pleased she could sound so carefree, so genuinely amused.

'Good heavens, no! Conham needs to marry well, we all

know that. And Amelia Skelton is a sweet, biddable little thing. He could do far worse.'

'Damned with faint praise, then!'

She flushed a little. 'Truly, Matthew, it is not our concern, so let us not waste time on the matter. Tell me instead how you have gone on tonight. I must say there appears to be hundreds of people in the gardens.'

'There are, and they are still coming in! The notices in the newspapers, and the bills I posted around the hotels and shops have proved worthwhile. There are any number of people who have come to see what Bellemonte has to offer before committing themselves to a season ticket.' He stopped and took her hands, saying eagerly, 'I really think we can make a success of this, Rosina! There is a great hunger for more entertainment than the city can presently offer, and being only a mile or so from Clifton and the Hotwells, we are ideally placed to provide it.'

The excitement in his voice was unmistakeable and his eyes glowed in the lamplight. Rosina could not help but smile at his enthusiasm.

'I think you are right, Matt, but have a care,' she warned, squeezing his fingers. 'You must not overstretch your resources.'

'*Our* resources, m'dear. You have invested in Bellemonte, too. And don't forget it was you who thought to buy Mr Matthews's Directory and Guide,' he added, pulling her hand back onto his arm and resuming their walk. 'That has proved very useful in knowing where best to direct our advertisements.'

Ahead of them, Conham noted that the arbours to the side of the path had been cleared of foliage and new lamps hung within, so that the stone benches and figures could now be seen in all their glory. He turned to point out one particularly fine sculpture to his stepmother and as he did so he noticed Matthew standing with Rosina. They were holding hands and she was laughing up at him. Conham felt an unexpected stab of jealousy so strong that he stopped talking, midsentence. Until he heard the countess's sharp voice addressing him.

'Well, Dallamire, did you say something about a Rysbrack? Pray, continue!'

'What?' He dragged his wandering thoughts back to the ladies looking up at him expectantly. 'Ah, yes. Rysbrack.' He cleared his throat, hoping it would also clear his head. 'The goddess in the arbour over there, Matthew is confident it is by the sculptor. Of course he needs to have that confirmed, but it seems very likely, because there are any number of Rysbrack's works in and around Bristol...'

They moved on, Conham searching his memory to find things of interest to say about the gardens. His struggle was made harder because he could not stop thinking about Matt and Rosina. Were they still following? He kept his eyes resolutely on the path ahead, afraid that if he looked back he might discover they had disappeared, that Matt had whisked Rosina into one of the romantic arbours and was now making love to her.

Chapter Eighteen

For Rosina, the evening at Bellemonte was bittersweet. Watching Conham paying court to Miss Skelton was not easy, and the other ladies in the party didn't welcome her presence. She would have liked to wander off and explore the gardens alone but without a companion she knew that would have been most improper, not to say foolhardy. Matthew had other guests to attend and after he had left her, she trailed along at the back of the group, excluded from the matrons' conversation and trying not to heed the smiles that passed between Conham and Amelia Skelton.

By the time the carriage deposited them all at the door to Gifford Manor, she had a pounding headache and was glad of the short walk back to the lodge, accompanied by a footman who neither wanted nor expected her to talk to him.

Conham saw Rosina walk away. He wanted to stand there and watch her until the bend in the path hid her from sight, but it could not be. His attention was quickly claimed by the countess and he escorted his guests into the house. Lady Skelton carried her daughter away up the stairs, declaring they were both exhausted, and Conham was left to join his stepmother for her customary glass of claret in the drawing room.

'An interesting evening,' she declared, when they had been served with wine. 'I hope the venture will prove a success for you.'

'Thank you.' Her tone indicated that she did not believe this, but he let that go.

'However, I still believe you would have done better to sell Bellemonte and put the money into Dallamire. The roof on the west wing is leaking again.'

'I am aware of that, ma'am. The lead guttering has failed. I have already set men to work on it, as well as several other problems that need urgent attention.'

'The whole house needs urgent attention,' she snapped. 'Dallamire Hall is hardly likely to impress a future bride in its present condition.'

He smiled slightly. 'Is it too much to hope that a woman might like me for myself, rather than my houses?'

'Do not be so tiresome, Conham, this is not about you. I am thinking of the future of the family! Mortlakes have lived at Dallamire for generations.'

'And will continue to do so,' said Conham, refilling their glasses. 'My keeping Bellemonte makes no difference to that.'

'It delays refurbishment of your principal seat,' she retorted. 'I brought the Skeltons here to see you because I could not risk Lady Skelton discovering just how badly run-down Dallamire has become.'

She saw the flash of irritation in his eyes and had the grace to flush. 'I know it is not entirely your fault,' she conceded. 'Your father did nothing to the house. And he was far too complacent, believing he could restore our fortunes with a few successful nights at the card tables.'

'Then borrowing even more to cover his losses.'

'It was always a point of honour with your father to pay

his gaming debts.' She pulled out her handkerchief. 'You cannot blame him for breaking his neck when he did!'

Conham watched her dabbing at her eyes. He had long ago given up arguing with his stepmother. What was done was done. It was his duty to put it right.

The countess and her guests remained at the Manor for another three full days, during which time Conham saw nothing of Rosina. Whenever he spoke with Davy, the young man told him that she was busy. One day she was visiting several farms, another riding out to inspect a new barn, and on the third she was in the village, helping the vicar to organise a widows and orphans fund.

The countess demanded Conham's full attention and he did his best to put Rosina to the back of his mind while he threw himself into playing host to his guests, until at last the travelling carriage was at the door, loaded and ready to carry them away to London.

'I trust we shall see you in town very soon,' said Lady Skelton as he handed her into the carriage.

Conham murmured something noncommittal and turned to take his leave of the countess. She, however, was not so easily dismissed.

'You must come as soon as you can,' she commanded. 'I had hoped to hear that there was a firm understanding between you and Miss Skelton by now.'

'I am sorry to disappoint you, ma'am.'

She said, bluntly, 'I can hold off the other suitors for a few weeks, perhaps, but a pretty girl with such a large fortune will not remain single for long.' Her fingers curled around his hand like claws. 'And you *need* a large fortune, if you are to rescue Dallamire. Remember that!'

'I can hardly forget it,' he replied, feeling the web of obligation tightening around him.

With his visitors gone, Conham needed an outlet for his frustration. He ordered his horse to be saddled and rode off cross-country to the high ground north of Morton Gifford. He rode for miles, soothed by the exercise but knowing he could not outrun the problems that beset him.

He returned to the stables, tired and muddy, with barely enough time to change for dinner, and had just handed his horse over to a groom when he heard a carriage. He looked around in time to see Rosina turning the gig into the yard.

He stopped to watch, drinking in the sight of her. She was dressed in her riding habit, the mannish jacket fitting snugly over curves that were anything but masculine, and she looked completely at home as she manoeuvred the vehicle through the narrow arched entrance. By heaven, he thought, as she drew up beside him, she was everything he wanted in a partner. Kind, intelligent and resourceful.

And out of your reach.

'You have been out riding,' she greeted him as he helped her alight.

'Yes.' He glanced down at his mud-spattered boots and breeches. 'My guests left early and it being such a fine day, I took the opportunity to ride to Gifford Hill.'

'How delightful that must have been! I have been to Bellemonte.' She pulled a small leather bag from the footrest. 'These ledgers need to go back into the office.'

'Then I will walk with you.' He fell into step beside her as they took a shortcut across the grass. 'How is Matt?'

'In high good humour,' she told him. 'We have been going over the receipts. The grand opening was a triumph.

Ticket sales were excellent and he has already had more than a hundred requests for season tickets!'

'A good start.'

'Yes, very good. The baths, too, have become more popular, even though Matthew increased the price a little. And the wardens he employed are very successful at keeping out the less…er…*respectable* customers.'

Conham heard the laughter in her voice and swiped his riding crop at a thistle that had escaped the gardener's scythe. He knew he should be happy to find her in such good spirits, but for some illogical reason it irked him, and his irritation grew as she chattered on, describing the progress that had been made at Bellemonte and the success of its opening night.

'It helped a great deal that you were in attendance,' she told him, leading the way into her office. She laughed. 'One can never have too many earls at these events, you know!'

'I am glad an earl can be useful for something!'

'I beg your pardon,' she said quickly. 'I did not mean to be disparaging.'

She put the bag onto the desk and dropped her gloves on top of it before turning to him, smiling.

'Oh, Conham, Matthew is in alt about the prospects for Bellemonte, and so full of plans for the future! I have never seen him so happy. I wish you could have been there.'

'I don't believe that.'

'I beg your pardon?'

He felt a stab of guilt for his ill temper, but he could not stop himself from continuing.

'My presence would have sadly curtailed your chance to flirt with him!'

Her eyes widened in horror, which flayed his conscience

even more, but the demon jealousy had not finished with him yet.

'Well,' he demanded savagely, 'has he kissed you? Is that why you are blushing?'

She slapped him, hard.

Conham reeled back, the shock of knowing he deserved it hurting far more than his stinging cheek.

'How dare you!' Rosina glared at him, her face as white as the cravat tied so neatly beneath her chin. 'How dare you even *think* I would… Matthew and I are friends, nothing more.'

Having done its work, the demon slunk away, leaving Conham full of remorse.

'Yes. Of course. I beg your pardon.' He added, as she walked to the door, 'Rosina, forgive me!'

She turned, her eyes stormy, and delivered a parting shot that hit him squarely in the gut.

'And if we were anything more than that, it would be no concern of yours, my lord!'

Rosina strode out of the Manor and hurried away to the lodge. Tears were not far away and she wanted to be alone when they fell. How could he think that she would flirt with Matthew? How could he say such things to her? But even before she reached the lodge door, she knew exactly why he had lashed out at her. Had she not felt the same illogical rage when she had seen him with Amelia Skelton? Had she not wanted to spit and scratch and tear?

By the time she had washed and dressed for the evening her temper had cooled, replaced by a dull ache of unhappiness. She could not face company, and sent word to the housekeeper she would take supper at the lodge. She was somewhat surprised when Mrs Goddard returned from her errand not carrying a tray, but a letter.

'An express has come for you, madam,' she said, holding out the sealed message. 'I thought I should bring it over to you directly rather than wait for Cook to put your supper together. I'll go back and fetch that now.'

'Yes, yes, thank you,' said Rosina, quickly breaking the seal.

She scanned the letter, barely noticing the servant's departure, nor Conham's entrance moments later.

'You have received an urgent message. Is it bad news?'

'Papa's old valet, Mr Paxby.' She did not raise her eyes from the paper. 'He has had a fall and taken to his bed. He wants to see me.'

She looked up, as if suddenly aware of his presence. 'Why have you come?'

'I thought you might need help.'

Of course. The earlier confrontation was forgotten. It was the most natural thing in the world that he should be here.

She turned again to the letter. 'It is from Martha, Mr Paxby's sister. She says he is asking for me and declares he will not rest until we have spoken. I fear he must be very ill. Excuse me, I must go to Brackwood.'

'I will come with you.' He caught her arm as she went to walk past him. 'But not tonight, there is no moon. We can leave as soon as it is light and be at Brackwood almost as quickly.'

'Yes. Thank you.'

When he had gone, Rosina sat down, still clutching the letter. She needed to pack, but not immediately. Conham would call for her in the morning. All she had to do was be ready to go with him.

Conham. He had offered his help and she had accepted, without a second thought. She closed her eyes. Their friendship was too deep, too strong, to be broken by a few hasty words. But when he married, as he must do, what would happen then?

Chapter Nineteen

They set off at dawn and by late morning, the earl's travelling chariot was bowling through Brackwood village. It pulled up at the small neat house and Conham accompanied Rosina to the door, prepared to support her if the worst had happened and they had arrived too late.

She knocked and was greeting the woman even before the door was fully opened.

'Mrs Jones, I received your letter and came as quickly as I could!'

'Oh, bless you, Miss Brackwood, Jem will be so pleased. He is recovering well from his fall, but he's been fretting so much about seeing you that he can't be easy. Come along in, ma'am. And you, too, my lord,' she said, when Rosina had introduced him.

'Thank you, ma'am, but I think it best if I do not.'

Rosina looked up at him. 'Please, stay. I have no secrets from you.'

Her words warmed his heart but he shook his head. 'Mr Paxby may want to talk privately with you. A stranger's presence could unsettle him. I will call back within the hour, will that do?'

Her answer was a smile and a nod. Conham touched his hat and went back to the chariot.

Rosina watched him go before stepping into the house. She remembered the one large room from her previous visit. It sufficed as a kitchen and sitting room, but now she saw that in the far corner a bed had been made up for Mr Paxby, who was propped up against the pillows.

'He's not so bad, ma'am. It's just a sprained ankle and a few bruises,' said Martha, a note of apology in her voice. 'But when I first put him to bed he wouldn't lie still until I had written to you. Making himself ill with it, he was.'

'And I am glad you did write to me, Mrs Jones.' Rosina gave her a reassuring smile before hurrying across to the bed. 'My dear Mr Paxby, I am sorry to see you like this. Is there anything I can do for you?'

'Ah, 'tis good of you to come, Miss Brackwood. There is something I need to tell you, while I still can. My memory isn't what it was, you see. I didn't even remember this until I was laid up here, in bed, and fearing I might not leave it again.'

'Now, now,' she chided him gently. 'You must not think like that. Your sister is taking the very best care of you.'

'She is, bless her, but when the Lord calls me, it will be too late, so I must tell you this now.' His thin hand plucked at the cheerful patchwork coverlet. 'You will remember when Sir Thomas sent you off to the north, to attend your aunt's funeral.'

'How could I forget? If I had known Papa would be taken ill while I was away I would never have gone.'

The old man wiped away a tear. 'Aye, ma'am, it was very sad, but he was adamant someone should go in his stead. It should have been your brother, of course, but he couldn't be persuaded.' The old man scowled. 'Not that he was much company for your father, even though he told you he'd look after him! But that's by the by, and Sir Thomas was content enough, while you were away.

'He spent every day in his study, working. Putting his affairs in order, he told me. It was as if he knew the end was near. And he was heartened, the day you left, by a letter from two old friends. They were visiting Bath and as they were little more than ten miles from Brackwood, they proposed to call.'

'Yes, I remember you told me. You said their visit had cheered him enormously.'

'Yes, it did. But I have been thinking on it since you last called and I wonder now, from something Sir Thomas said to me at the time, if they helped him to write a new will.'

Rosina froze. 'A…a new will?'

'Yes, ma'am. It was when I was helping your father into bed that night, after his visitors had left us, and he says to me, "I can rest easy now, Paxby, knowing Brackwood's future is secure." I thought no more of it, especially since he had that seizure the very next day, and we was all at sixes and sevens, but it's come back to me now.'

'But there was no new will, Mr Paxby,' said Rosina. 'The one Mr Shipton read out after the funeral was dated some four years earlier.' She paused, then, 'Did you ask him about it?'

'No. I did not think it important at the time, because the estate is entailed, so Brackwood is already secure. But then, the day after you came to visit, Sir Edgar called on me.'

'I'd gone shopping,' put in Martha, from the other side of the room. 'If I'd been here, he'd never have troubled Jem so. I'd have given him short shrift, baronet or no baronet!'

'I am sure you would,' said Rosina, smiling. 'Go on, Mr Paxby.'

'He demanded I tell him what we had discussed. I

couldn't rightly say, because it was nothing of consequence, was it?'

'It was purely a social call, Mr Paxby. I came to see how you went on, as befits an old friend.'

'He wouldn't believe that, miss, no matter how many times I told him. He threatened me with dire consequences if I was to speak out of turn and I told him straight I would never do such a thing! Then, out of the blue, he asked me about your father's visitors. He demanded to know who they were, but I could tell him nothing, bar that Sir Thomas had mentioned one of them was groomsman at his wedding. Then Sir Edgar lost his temper,' said the old man, his voice rising. 'He suggested I had been gossiping about your sainted father's last days, and that I had told you he'd destroyed his father's new will, but I didn't, Miss Brackwood, did I? I hadn't even considered the idea of a new will until he mentioned it!'

'Ooh, if that isn't Edgar all over!' declared Rosina. She reached over to take the old man's agitated hands between her own. 'Hush now, Mr Paxby, you must not upset yourself. You know as well as I that when Edgar is in a rage he quite loses his head and says the most foolish things. Now, I shall ask Martha to bring you some fresh tea.'

'It's already done, miss.'

Mrs Jones appeared at her elbow with a cup and together they calmed the invalid, plumping up his pillows and smoothing the coverlet before Martha helped him to drink his tea.

The cup emptied, the old valet lay back against the pillows and smiled at Rosina.

'Thank you for coming, Miss Brackwood. The matter's been troubling me ever since Sir Edgar came here. Perhaps I had it wrong and Sir Thomas wasn't talking about a new will, but whatever it was I feel sure now it must have been important to him. Do you not think so?'

Rosina hesitated, then she said quietly 'I do, Mr Paxby. I do indeed.'

Conham returned at the appointed time and Mrs Jones opened the door wide.

'Do, pray, step in, my lord. Miss Brackwood is just saying goodbye to my brother and won't be above ten minutes, I am sure. And I have tea brewing already, for it's all I can get Jem to drink now. But there is some of my cowslip wine, if Your Lordship would prefer?'

His Lordship did prefer, not trusting tea that might have been stewing for an hour, but knowing that to refuse everything would cause offence. Once his eyes had accustomed to the dim light, he could see Rosina talking quietly with an old, white-haired man lying in the bed at the far end of the room. He sat down and allowed his hostess to bustle about him, bringing his wine, which he pronounced excellent, but he refused a slice of cake, saying he was about to carry Miss Brackwood off to partake of a nuncheon before they returned to Morton Gifford.

Mrs Jones nodded sagely. 'Very wise, when you have a long journey ahead. It was very kind of you both to come today. Jem is tired now but Miss Brackwood's visit has done him the world of good. He thinks a great deal of her, my lord. He says she has a way of winning people's hearts.'

'Yes.' Conham watched Rosina taking her leave of Mr Paxby. 'She has a very rare gift for that.'

Not long after, they were in the travelling chariot and bowling back along the Bath Road. It was clear to Conham that Rosina was labouring under strong emotions and it took little prompting for her to tell him all that Mr Paxby had relayed to her.

'My brother has always been a hothead, and to frighten a poor, sick old man almost out of his wits was unforgiveable!' she said, when she had come to the end of her tale.

'And to mention destroying a will was downright foolish,' added Conham. 'It smacks of a guilty conscience.'

'Yes, I thought that,' said Rosina, frowning. 'But there is no denying that my brother often speaks without thinking.'

'You were not present when your father's friends called to see him?'

'No. Papa was too ill to travel to his sister's funeral but he was very anxious someone should represent him.' She hesitated. 'I know that might seem a little unusual…'

His lips twitched. 'But you are a most unusual lady, Rosina.' He noted the gleam in her eye. It was a moment of shared amusement, something to be cherished. He said lightly, 'But tell me, why did your brother not go?'

'Papa asked him, but Edgar had come home on a repairing lease and claimed he needed complete rest.'

He did not miss the scathing note in her voice.

She went on, 'However, he promised to look after Papa while I was away. When I got back, I discovered he had spent most of his time gambling and…and worse, at the local inns. Thankfully, my father had Paxby to look after him.'

'The important thing now is to ascertain if there is, or was, a new will,' said Conham. 'First, we will need to find your father's friends.'

'Mr Paxby did not know them, although he did say that one of them had been Papa's groomsman,' she replied, frowning a little. 'If so, that would be his great friend James MacDowell. Papa sometimes talked of him. He was a professor at Edinburgh, I believe.' A sudden smile smoothed the crease from her brow. 'I shall write to the university, and hopefully they will forward my letter on to him.'

The earl was crossing the hall the next day when he saw Rosina adding a letter to the notes already on the silver tray, ready to be taken to the post later that day.

'It is written, then?'

'Yes.' She did not pretend to misunderstand him. 'I must now resign myself to waiting for a reply.'

'If your father did write a new will, what would you expect it to contain?' he asked, following her into her office.

'Brackwood and its Home Farm are barely viable. The income is certainly not sufficient to pay for my brother's extravagant lifestyle without rents from the land and property that Papa purchased during his lifetime. My father never openly criticised Edgar, but he knew he was very wild and I think he may have put in place measures to stop my brother selling off the unentailed part of his inheritance, at least until Edgar is older and more settled.'

'As my godfather did with my inheritance.'

She sighed. 'Yes, but you were never profligate.'

'You think it will not answer?'

'One can only hope it does.'

'Brackwood means a lot to you, doesn't it?'

'Until a year ago, it was my whole life.'

'Rosina, I wish there was something I could say, or do—'

She put up a hand to cut him off. 'Thank you, but at present we do not know if my father *did* write another will.'

'But it seems very likely, given your brother's visit to the old valet.'

'Yes. Perhaps it is mere wishful thinking on my part. Mr Paxby may have misunderstood Papa.'

'Perhaps.'

Rosina was relieved he did not try to comfort her with platitudes. She fell silent, thinking wistfully of Brackwood and all she had lost.

'There is nothing to be done until I receive a reply,' she said at last. 'And that cannot be for some time, if ever. Thankfully, I have plenty here to occupy me.'

He did not respond to her attempt at a smile.

'I must leave for London at the end of the week,' he said. 'You will write to me, if you please. If—no, *when* you receive a reply.'

'As you wish, my lord.'

She saw him frown at the formality of her response but he made no comment, merely going out and leaving her to her thoughts.

Rosina did not have time to indulge long in idle speculation. There was plenty to be done at Morton Gifford and also at Bellemonte, where Matthew was continuing with improvements to the gardens. He had written to say he had secured more investors, which meant work could begin to turn the derelict house into an hotel.

She saw Conham only once more before his departure, when he returned the ledgers she had left with him for inspection.

'Your record-keeping is excellent, as always, and needs no clarification,' he told her, putting the books down on her desk. 'I leave tomorrow, at first light. You can write to me at the town house with any matters that require attention, I believe I shall be in residence for some time.' At the door he stopped. 'The countess expects me to remain in London for the rest of the season.'

Rosina knew he meant *The countess expects me to propose to Miss Skelton*, and could only reply with a little nod.

'Very well. I doubt we will meet again before I leave.
Do not forget to inform me when you receive a response
to your letter!'

And with that sharp reminder, he departed.

Davy was proving his worth at Morton Gifford, but Rosina remained as busy as ever. She was thankful for the occupation to pass each of the long days as June progressed.
Yet, no matter how full her days, she still found time to
scour the society pages of the London newspaper, looking
for a notice of the earl's betrothal.

It was on Midsummer's Day that she returned to her
office to find a letter from Edinburgh on her desk. She
quickly broke the seal and spread the pages, but she had to
sit down and read them twice more before the words actually sank in.

After expressing his condolences for her father's un-
timely death, Professor MacDowell confirmed that he and
his friend had called upon Sir Thomas:

> *We declined his invitation to remain the night, not
> wishing to put him to the inconvenience at such short
> notice. However, we did stay to dinner, and it was after
> we had dined that Sir Thomas asked us to witness his
> new will, although neither of us more than glanced
> at its contents. They did not concern us. After all, we
> were merely obliging and old friend.*
>
> *When it was done, I recall that Sir Thomas placed
> the document inside a packet that he had addressed
> to his attorney and he added it to the rest of his cor-*

respondence, ready for his servant to deliver or to post for him the following day.

I also remember that your dear father was quite insistent that we should sign a second copy that he had prepared and when we took our leave later that night, to return to our hotel, I distinctly recall that the copy was lying on the desk.

Rosina read that line twice, then sat back and closed her eyes. Her thudding heartbeat began to slow. She still had no idea what was in the new will, but it seemed clear to her that the will, and its copy, had disappeared during the night.

For a long time, she remained in her chair with only the quiet chiming of the clock in the hall breaking the silence in the study. She did not weep, there was no point in that. Instead, she tried to consider what must be done.

Professor MacDowell had informed her he had written to a Mr Palmer, the second witness, but he thought the man had gone abroad and he could not be sure his letter would reach him. Even if Professor MacDowell and his friend could be summoned and provide statements, if neither of them knew the contents of the will, what good would it do? No good at all, was her conclusion. There was no one to share her disappointment and only one person with any interest at all in knowing what she had learned.

Sitting up, she pulled a clean sheet of paper from the drawer and began a letter to Lord Dallamire.

Chapter Twenty

'I hope you have not forgotten it is Lady Skelton's soirée tonight, Dallamire. You are escorting me.'

'I have not forgotten, ma'am.' Conham did not look up, but he knew the countess would be fixing him with a gimlet stare across the breakfast table. 'I have business in the city today but I shall be back in time to dine with you beforehand.'

'Make sure you are,' she told him. 'Lady Skelton said most particularly that she expects to see you there tonight.'

'I shall not disappoint her.'

The countess let out an exasperated huff. 'Really, Dallamire, you might at least show a little more enthusiasm! How can you be so tiresome, when we are all going to such lengths for your benefit?'

He looked up then, his brows raised.

'When you are going to such lengths to sell me to the highest bidder. Do you expect me to be grateful for that?'

'Yes, I do,' she told him. 'It is your duty to marry well. And if you will not think of yourself, consider your half-sisters.'

'I would remind you, madam, that my father did not leave them penniless. They have at least another two years in the schoolroom, and there is money held in trust for them.'

She scoffed. 'Barely enough for their dowries! And who is to pay for their presentation, pray?'

'*You* might do so easily, with a little economy!'

His sharp retort had the countess sitting up in her chair, nostrils flaring and eyes darting fire.

'How can you say such a cruel thing, Dallamire, would you have me live as a pauper?' She began to hunt for her handkerchief. 'W-would you have me d-disgrace the sainted name of your dear father?'

Conham held on to his temper, knowing this little display of sensibility would turn into full-blown hysteria if he challenged her.

'Of course not. Be assured, I intend to do my duty.'

'But *when*, sir? You must marry, and soon. Heaven knows I have done my best since you came home. I have presented any number of young ladies to you. All of them pretty and amiable.'

'And boring!'

'Nonsense. They may be biddable, but at least they all have impeccable lineage. Unlike that female you were making up to in the West Country.'

Conham tensed.

'And what *female* might that be?' he asked with dangerous calm.

'The widow you followed to Bristol. Mrs Fawkes, or Fowles, or something...'

He relaxed. 'You mean Mrs Faulds.'

'Yes, that was it. Very flighty piece. My heart sank when I heard your name was being linked with hers. Your father would not rest in his grave if you had brought her home as your countess!'

'But she was rich enough to refill the Dallamire coffers.' Conham felt a slight lightening of his mood; he had not thought of Alicia for months now. 'Would you have objected if I had used Mrs Faulds's money to pay off the debts my father left?'

The countess eyed him resentfully, but after holding her gaze for a moment he laughed.

'You should thank your stars then, dear Stepmama. She would not have me!' He pushed back his chair. 'Now, if you will excuse me, I have papers to go through before I leave the house. But pray, rest easy, madam. When it is time for my half-sisters to be presented, I will make sure it is done properly.'

'And you will come with me to the soirée? I have your word?'

'You have my word, ma'am.'

Conham went out, resisting the urge to run a finger around his collar. It might as well be a noose that was tied about his neck, not the finest muslin.

He could not blame the countess for trying to find him a rich wife. She had lived in luxury her whole life and wanted nothing to change. She complained constantly about Dallamire Hall although she refused to leave it, declaring that she would not quit that stately pile until he brought home a wife. He felt a sudden sting of grim humour. The prospect of seeing his stepmother and half-sisters move into the smaller but infinitely more comfortable Dower House upon his marriage was by far the most pleasant thought that had come to him all morning!

Conham went into his study to find his secretary had left a neat pile of papers on his desk. He quickly flicked through them. Bills, letters from tenants and stewards at his various properties requesting help, polite notes from charitable groups seeking his patronage. So many calls upon his time and his purse.

His thoughts changed abruptly when he picked up the next letter and saw Rosina's neat writing. Walking around the desk, he sat down and broke the seal.

>...*in conclusion, my lord, with the second witness gone abroad indefinitely, my enquiries regarding a new will have met with no success. If neither the original document nor the copy exists, then to pursue the matter further would only cause distress to everyone involved and be of no material benefit to anyone save, perhaps, the lawyers.*

The letter continued with matters of business, a summary of the accounts for Quarter Day, questions about proposed new farming methods and a report on the efficacy of the new drains and ditches during the recent heavy rains.

He read to the end then lowered the paper and sat back in his chair. Poor Rosina, she had been hoping that somehow, her father might have found a way to protect Brackwood from the ravages of his irresponsible son. Conham could admit now that he had been hoping for something more. In some wild, fantastical and quite illogical way, he had hoped Sir Thomas might have done something to protect his daughter, too. Increased the amount he had settled upon her. Sufficient, perhaps, for her to marry an impoverished earl...

With an oath Conham threw the letter aside. How shameful, how *contemptible*, to think of himself in all this. Rosina loved Brackwood. Even if she had inherited everything, she would not want to sell her old home in order to restore his crumbling house.

For now, she had no option but to continue as land steward at Morton Gifford. It was possible that in a year or two

Bellemonte might be profitable enough to provide her with a comfortable income. Or it was not inconceivable that she might receive an offer of marriage. After all, she was highly respected in Morton Gifford.

That idea did not find favour with him but he could not deny it was a possibility, if she met someone she loved enough to give up her independence. He released a sigh, long and heartfelt.

'If only I was free! If only—'

Conham shook his head, determined not to think of what might have been. He picked up Rosina's letter again. There were estate matters here that needed a reply and he would dictate something to his secretary before going off to the city. Then he must put all thoughts of Rosina Brackwood from his mind and fulfil his destiny.

He must propose to Amelia Skelton.

Conham rubbed one hand across his eyes. The windows of Lady Skelton's drawing room had been thrown open but the night was sultry and with the candles adding to the heat, it was uncomfortably warm.

'It is gone eleven, Dallamire,' said the countess, coming up to him. 'Lady Skelton has sent Amelia off to the morning room. She will be quite alone there.' When he did not speak, her fingers tightened on his sleeve. 'She is expecting you, my lord.'

The message could not have been clearer. With a little nod he walked off and went down the stairs to the morning room. There was nothing else to be done. Amelia Skelton had indicated she was happy to receive an offer and both families approved the match. All he had to do was make that offer. Just a few simple words and everyone would be happy. Miss Skelton would be a countess and he would have the means to protect his family home and keep the countess and her daughters in the luxury to which they were accustomed.

And Rosina could remain at Morton Gifford.

'I can do that much for her,' he muttered as he walked the final few steps to the morning room. Even though it would be torture for him to see her there, so near and yet quite, quite unattainable.

His first thought on entering the room was thank goodness it was bright with candlelight and not a soft, romantic glow, but his relief was quickly replaced by the feeling that something was not quite right.

Miss Skelton was standing on the far side of the room. She had her back to him and he had the impression that her shoulders were shaking, although she turned to face him almost as soon as the door opened. He looked at her closely. She was a little pale, but her voice and her countenance were welcoming.

'Lord Dallamire.'

'Miss Skelton.' He closed the door and moved further into the room. 'I am pleased to have this opportunity to speak with you alone.'

'Yes.'

He smiled, hoping to put her at her ease. 'Forgive me, I have not had much practice at this sort of thing.'

She blushed. 'Do go on, my lord.'

Her tone was inviting, a faint smile curved her lips, but he noticed that the knuckles of her clasped fingers were white. It could be maidenly nerves, but something in her demeanour told him it was more than that.

He said quietly, 'Is anything wrong, Miss Skelton?'

Her eyes flew to his face. 'Wrong?' She gave a little laugh. 'Oh, no, no! It is merely…excitement, my lord.'

Conham looked at her then. Really looked. Her pretty face was wreathed in smiles, but it was what he saw in her eyes that gave him pause.

Pure terror.

He had seen it before in the eyes of his soldiers, men as well as boys, when they were facing a cavalry charge, or before going into battle. Then he had been able to do nothing about it. They were at war; his men had no choice but to fight and he had no choice but to lead them. It was his duty.

It is your duty now to go through with this!

The countess's voice rang in his head but he ignored it.

'Amelia, we don't have to do this, you know.'

'Oh, but we do! Mama has set her heart on it.'

'But what of *your* heart?'

Her face crumpled. Taking her hands, Conham led her over to a chair and she sank quickly onto it, as if her legs would no longer support her. He pulled up another chair, close enough to talk, but not to intimidate. He regarded her bowed head.

'Why is Lady Skelton so set on this marriage?' he asked her.

'Because you are an earl. She says it was always Papa's dearest wish that I should marry well. And there are no dukes or marquesses available this season.'

His mouth twisted in disdain at her final remark, and he could only be thankful that she was hunting for her handkerchief and did not see it.

'I beg your pardon,' she said. 'That must sound terribly unfeeling, when you are being so kind to me.'

'Let us be clear, your mother and my stepmother hatched a plot to marry us off.'

'Yes. Mama made me promise I would accept you. And…' She took a deep breath. 'And I thought I could. Only, this evening, when she told me to come down here and, and *wait*, I knew…' She blew her nose and gave a shuddering sigh. 'Oh, dear. There is going to be such a fuss when she discovers I have refused you. She will accuse me of breaking my word!'

'We shall not give her the opportunity to do that. You cannot accept my offer until I have made it, can you?' He pushed himself out of the chair. 'I think the best thing is for me to go away now.'

'But she will know we have been talking!'

'Not necessarily. Leave it to me.' For the first time that day he felt like grinning and he did so. 'I hope that when Lady Skelton comes in, she will have nothing but sympathy for you. All the opprobrium will be heaped upon my head, and you will be the hapless victim.'

She jumped up, relief lighting her countenance.

'Oh, thank you, my lord! That is… I hope I haven't offended you?'

'Offended, no,' he said with perfect truth. His next words, however, were not nearly as sincere. 'I am disappointed, naturally, but that will pass.'

She went with him to the door but before he opened it, he stopped.

'Tell me, is there anyone else?'

Another blush touched her cheek, but this time it was accompanied by a soft glow in her eyes.

'There *is* a young man. William. He is a neighbour of ours, and we have known each other forever! But he is only a baronet, and not nearly lofty enough for Mama.'

'But you and he would like to marry?'

She nodded. 'Very much, only, he understands that Mama has such plans for me.'

'How old are you now, Amelia?'

'I shall be one-and-twenty in October. Mama would have brought me to town last season, only we were still in mourning for Papa.'

'Then let me give you some advice,' he said. 'In a few months you will be able to marry whomsoever you choose. In the meantime, you must make it clear to your mama that you do not wish to receive any more offers of marriage. You only have to be firm; she cannot force you. Can you do that?'

She nodded. 'I think I can now, my lord. After all, there are only viscounts and barons left to choose from.'

A shy twinkle appeared in her eye, and Conham had a glimpse of the charming young lady Amelia could be, when she was not being browbeaten out of her wits.

'Indeed! I am sorry if things are a little uncomfortable for a few weeks. Lady Skelton might even think it expedient to take you home.'

'Oh, I should very much like that,' she exclaimed, clasping her hands together, but this time in happiness.

Conham smiled. 'Remember that none of this is your fault. I am the one who did not come up to scratch.'

With that, he slipped out of the morning room and across the hall, which was empty save for the footman dozing by the street door. Previous visits to the house had shown him there was a small library on the far side. It was in darkness, but taking a candlestick from the hall he soon remedied that.

He needed to marshal his thoughts. Relief was uppermost. He had not realised how repugnant the idea of a loveless marriage was to him until this evening, and if Amelia

Skelton had not shied at the last fence, they would even now be announcing their betrothal.

'Never again,' he muttered. 'There must be another way.'

Conham began to pace the room. He felt that he had been given another chance and he must take it. There must be some way to raise funds without selling himself to the highest bidder. He thought of Matt, throwing himself into restoring Bellemonte, and Rosina, who had already made a difference at Morton Gifford. The land was in much better heart and showing a return for all the changes she had made.

He stopped, saying aloud, 'If they can do it, why can't I?'

He set off again, a plan forming in his head. There were one or two properties he might sell. The town house, for example. It would fetch a handsome price and he could hire a residence if he wished to spend any time in London.

Conham heard the unmistakable sound of his stepmother's voice coming from the hall. No time to think any more about that now. He made his way towards the door, grabbing a book from one of the shelves as he passed and was in time to see the countess and Lady Skelton coming down the stairs, on their way to the morning room to congratulate the happy couple.

Opening the book, he strolled across the hall, pretending to be engrossed in the text. It took a moment for them to notice his presence.

'Dallamire! What on earth are you doing?'

The countess's voice floated down to him.

He looked up. 'Reading, ma'am. I have discovered the most fascinating book in the library. *The Principles of Morals and Legislation.*' Horror and confusion were writ large upon the ladies' faces and he smiled. 'I had not come across Jeremy Bentham's work before. Most enlightening.'

'But why are you not in the morning room?' demanded Lady Skelton, hurrying down the last few stairs.

'I was, er, distracted, ma'am.'

'Distracted, *by a book*?' She stared at him then looked at the countess. 'But it was all agreed, all arranged!'

His smile did not waver, but his voice contained an implacable note that he had seldom used since leaving the army.

'Yes, it was agreed between you and the countess, madam, *not* by me. In the end I thought better of it.'

'Conham!' Lady Dallamire shut her fan with a snap. 'You do not mean you have left that poor gel in there, waiting?'

'I fear I may have done so, ma'am.'

A frosty silence ensued. Lady Skelton flushed angrily, while the countess went by turns red and white as her emotions moved between anger and chagrin.

She drew herself up and declared in arctic accents, 'I think it is time we left, Dallamire.'

He bowed. 'I think so, too, ma'am.'

They took their leave of their hostess, who was clearly beyond anything other than a stiff nod of dismissal. Lady Dallamire waited in silence for her cloak to be fetched but once they had climbed into the carriage, she did not hold back.

She expressed herself fluently and at length, pouring scorn upon her stepson's ingratitude. Conham listened in silence while she talked herself almost to a stand, but when, after a few gusty sighs, she drew out her handkerchief and asked him in tearful accents just what he had been thinking of, he replied quite calmly.

'I discovered I did not like having my hand forced, ma'am.'

'But that poor girl. It was all decided!'

'Only between you and her mother. If Lady Skelton has been spreading it about, boasting of the impending match, then the best thing she can do is to take her daughter home until the matter is forgotten.'

'Yes, I have no doubt that is what she will do,' muttered the countess, dragging her handkerchief angrily between her fingers. 'And we must leave town, too. I will not remain here and have people laughing up their sleeves at me. And they will be, sir! Lady Skelton is not one to keep quiet about a thing like this. She will take great delight in telling all and sundry that you as good as jilted her poor daughter. And how, then, am I to arrange an advantageous match for you?'

'I do not want you to arrange any match for me.'

She sat up quickly. 'But you have to marry! How else are we to solve our predicament?'

'I do not believe our *predicament* as you call it, is as bad as all that. If we were to draw in the purse strings a little.'

'No, no, it is not to be borne!' The countess resorted to tears again. 'The shame of it, to be reduced to penury, at my age!'

'We are a long way from penury, madam!'

But she was beyond reason and continued to weep and bemoan the cruelty of Fate for the remainder of the journey. Only when they had reached their own entrance hall and Conham agreed to her pleas not to rush into any decisions did she manage to calm herself sufficiently to be delivered into the hands of her maid and helped up to her bedchamber.

Conham ordered brandy to be brought to him in the library and walked off. One problem had been resolved tonight, and although he disliked the thought of the talk and condemnation that would follow, in his eyes it was no worse

than the gossip and sly remarks that would have arisen if
he had married Amelia purely for her money.

He sat down and closed his eyes. He would far rather
face the French cavalry than the tears and tantrums of his
stepmother, or her constant reminders of how he had failed
his father, but tonight there had been no other way to deal
with a difficult situation.

Amelia Skelton was free to find happiness with her baronet and, although he dare not put too much store by it just
yet, if the ideas now whirling about in his head were practi-
cable, then he, too, might find a way to achieve his dreams.

As summer wore on, Rosina tried to occupy herself with
the estate. She looked eagerly through the post each day,
hoping for a reply from Conham. Her disappointment at the
disappearance of her father's new will went much deeper
than she had expected, and with no one but the earl to confide in, she was desperate to hear from him, to read a line
or two of sympathy.

When at last a letter did arrive from London, her hopes
were dashed the moment she saw that it was not the earl's
bold handwriting but that of his secretary, and dealt only
with matters pertaining to the estate.

For a while, she continued to hope that perhaps Conham
would write to her privately, but when after a week no letter arrived, she knew it was time to put aside her foolish
daydreams. The earl was too busy with his own affairs to
spare any more time on hers.

Thankfully, there was plenty to keep Rosina busy into
the autumn months. She decided to reinstate the harvest
supper that Hugo Conham had always held for his neighbours and tenants, which proved to be a great success. Everyone lamented the fact that Lord Dallamire could not be

present although Rosina had explained that the earl was exceedingly busy.

She had written to Conham, telling him of her plans, and was unsurprised to learn he would not be attending. However, he had written this letter himself; it was very brief but it ended with the words *warmest regards*, which gave her some comfort and she had folded it away for safekeeping.

A few weeks later, she added to it a letter that arrived from Mr Shipton, informing her that Lady Brackwood had given birth to a boy and that mother and baby were doing well.

Chapter Twenty-One

'Well, Conham, what do you think of Bellemonte now?' Matt Talacre handed his guest a glass of brandy. 'It must be, what, five months since you were last in Gloucester.'

'Yes.'

A full five months since Conham had seen Rosina, but she was never far from his thoughts. He had thrown himself into repairing his family fortunes, but even though it filled his days, Rosina was like a phantom, constantly at his shoulder. Sometimes he felt her presence so powerfully he thought if he turned his head she would be there, standing beside him.

He said, 'You are quite right, Matt. I haven't been here since May.'

Dinner was finished and they were sitting before the fire in Matt's rooms on the first floor of what had been the derelict house on Bellemonte Square.

'You have made great strides,' Conham remarked. 'Your plans for the hotel appear to be going very well.'

'Thank you. Only this wing is habitable at present, but I am glad to have my own apartment here now. I have good people working for me but I like to be on hand to look after the gardens and the baths. I like to help with the building work, too, where I can.'

Conham raised his glass in salute. 'Your efforts do you credit, my friend.'

They had spent the short November day touring Belle-monte and he was impressed by the improvement. Despite the wintry weather the pleasure baths were busier than ever under Matt's management. More walks had been opened through the gardens and there were new, rose-covered arbours designed for romantic trysts. The Pavilion was proving popular for its winter concerts and balls, as well as with patrons wanting to dine or sup there in the evenings.

'It is not only my efforts,' said Matt, pouring them both more brandy. 'Rosina has supported me throughout. She has an excellent grasp of business.'

'Has she now?' Conham interrupted him without thinking, then had to look away from his friend's knowing grin. 'I hope she has not been neglecting her own duties.'

'Of course she hasn't, you dolt,' retorted Matt with his customary lack of respect for his friend's rank. 'She has been far too busy looking after your interests at Morton Gifford to spare me more than a few hours, but her advice is always sound. She is a very intelligent lady.'

'I know it,' growled Conham.

Matthew laughed. 'You can take that frown from your face, Conham. Rest easy, I have no interest in Rosina, other than as a good friend.' He hesitated. 'Did she tell you her brother has had a son?'

'I had heard.' Conham was not going to admit, even to his best friend, that he scoured every letter from Rosina, reading it at least twice, even though he rarely penned a reply himself. He had resolved to keep their correspondence formal, businesslike, afraid that if he picked up the pen, he would not put it down until he had poured his heart out to her.

'Aye,' Matt went on. 'When Rosina and I last met she told me she hopes having an heir might be the making of Brackwood. Personally, I doubt it. From what she has told me, that brother of hers is bad, through and through. She is far better off making a life for herself, away from him.'

'My thoughts exactly.' Conham nodded, but he was not yet ready to explain himself. He said instead, 'But enough of that, we were talking about Bellemonte.'

As he suspected, Matt was only too pleased to expound upon his plans.

'Yes, I was saying, Rosina has been very helpful, as have you, Conham! The patronage of the Earl of Dallamire has worked like a charm with prospective investors! I have secured funding to continue with the improvements next year, too. As we thought, those living or visiting Clifton Village and Hotwells are hungry for more entertainment. And I mean to extend the stables. I will need more room when the hotel opens, for those using their own cattle.'

Conham smiled. 'You have it all planned out.'

'I have indeed, but everything is costed, I do not mean to outrun my funds. I have worked out all the figures and I am confident the gardens will be making a small profit by Lady Day. And if things continue to go well for the next twelve months,' he added, with a grin, 'you will be able to increase my rent.'

'Not many tenants would admit to that!'

'No, but I know retaining Bellemonte was not your original plan, and with Dallamire in dire straits...'

'Actually,' said Conham, staring down at the golden liquid in his glass, 'things are not so dire as I first thought. Selling the town house and two of the hunting lodges in the north has allowed me to clear the remainder of my father's debts, and I have spent the past few months going over all the accounts with my man of business and we have negotiated better terms on a new loan. Not a fortune, but it will help. I now have a full programme of repairs for Dallamire Hall. It will take some time to complete, of course, but that was always going to be the case.'

'And what does the countess say to it all?'

'The ongoing building work has…er…persuaded her to remove with my half-sisters to the Dower House. With the countess now running and paying for her own household, matters have improved a great deal. I have promised her I will fund the girls' come-out, and I am already making provision for that. I have assured her I shall be able to do my duty by my half-sisters.'

'So, you have no need to marry an heiress.'

'No.' Conham was unable to hide his smile any longer. 'An heiress is no longer necessary.'

Matthew laughed. 'I know a lady who will be delighted to hear you say that, my friend!'

Conham felt the heat rising in his cheeks. 'Oh, I hope so, Matthew. I do hope so.'

The short November day was coming to an end as Rosina made her way back to the Manor. An icy wind was buffeting her and she was glad she had her mannish greatcoat to wear over her riding habit. She had ordered it from the village tailor and it was far more practical than a cloak, although even with the collar turned up and her wide-brimmed hat pulled low, the icy wind still managed to sneak in and sting her cheeks.

A storm was brewing, the heavy clouds threatened rain, or even snow, and she wanted to get back to the Manor before the weather broke. Bramble needed little urging to keep up a good pace. She was eager to return to her warm stall, and Rosina was happy to let the mare pick her way over the ground while she turned her own thoughts to a problem that had been nagging her all day.

She had seen nothing of Conham since May, when he had come to Gloucester for the reopening of Bellemonte Gardens, and she had no news of him, except that he had quit London in the summer and returned to Dallamire. Whether or not he had proposed to Miss Skelton she had no idea. Matthew had not said anything about it, when she had seen him at Bellemonte.

Neither had she seen any announcements concerning the Earl of Dallamire in the newspaper, although that was not surprising. Throughout the summer the news had been all about the crowds flocking to see Lord Elgin's Parthenon marbles, the opening of Waterloo Bridge and the introduction of the Sovereign coin, as well as speculation over Princess Charlotte's forthcoming confinement, and if the child would be a boy or a girl.

Then, last week, Mrs Jameson had received a note saying that the earl would shortly be returning to Gifford Manor. Four days later he had still not arrived and Rosina could not decide if she was most relieved or disappointed. She feared that this would be exactly like his last visit, when he had arrived so suddenly with Lady Dallamire and the Skeltons.

For the past year Rosina had thrown herself into work, determined not to allow her growing affection for Conham Mortlake to ruin the life she was making for herself. And yet, her pleasure in living at Morton Gifford was diminished. She still valued her independence, enjoyed her work and the estate was thriving under her management, but she was haunted by Conham's presence. There were constant reminders of him everywhere. Memories of discussing estate matters with him in her office or riding out together to visit tenants, the hours flying by, even though she could not remember what they found to talk about.

And every time she walked back to the lodge, she remembered him accompanying her to the door, remembered him kissing her.

Nothing could come of it. Conham must marry well, and Rosina was prepared for that. She was committed to remaining at Morton Gifford until Lady Day, but then she would leave. She could not expect to find another position as a land agent, but by March she would have saved enough of her generous salary to augment her own meagre inheritance and keep her for a few months, until she could find somewhere to live and some sort of employment. Perhaps she might open a school, or take in girl boarders.

'Or my investment in Bellemonte will come good,' she said aloud, determined to be cheerful, 'Who knows? The profits might soar and overnight I shall become a woman of independent means!'

It was a nonsensical idea but it made her smile, despite the icy weather and the lowering thoughts that threatened to depress her.

When she reached the stable yard, Fred Skillet came hurrying over.

'Here, let me take 'er for you, Miss Brackwood!'

'Thank you, Fred.'

Rosina handed Bramble's reins to the elderly stable hand and jumped down.

'No sign of His Lordship yet,' he remarked.

It was an answer to the question uppermost in Rosina's mind, but one she had been determined not to ask. She nodded to the old man, murmured another word of thanks and set off towards the Manor.

It was of no consequence to her at all when His Lordship

should arrive, she told herself, not quite truthfully. Everything was in order. She was confident he would find nothing wanting in her accounting or the records she kept of estate business. She was his land steward and would meet him as such. His absence over the past months had made it quite clear that he required nothing more from her.

Sadly, her defiant thoughts could not dispel the gloom that descended over her spirits. A gloom that was never very far away these days. Martha Jones had become a regular correspondent, and while the news that Mr Paxby was recovered from his fall was cheering, everything else she wrote about Brackwood was not. Edgar was gambling heavily and had put much of the unentailed land up for sale. Much as Rosina told herself Brackwood was no longer her concern, she could not help feeling depressed at the thought of what was happening to her old home.

The butler was crossing the hall when Rosina entered, and he turned and came over to her.

'Miss Brackwood, you are back, and not a minute too soon, by the looks of it,' he said, taking her greatcoat from her.

'Thank you, Jameson. Yes, it is sleeting out there now and the wind is getting up. Is Mr Redmond still here?'

'No, ma'am, but he has only just left, so there is a good fire burning in your office and it won't take me a moment to relight the candles for you.'

'No need, thank you, I can do that.'

The old retainer wasn't fooled by her smile, which she had had to dig deep to find.

'Then perhaps you'd like Mrs Jameson to prepare some coffee for you, to warm you up?' he suggested.

His kindly look cheered her, and the smile became a little less forced.

She said, 'That would be very welcome, thank you.'

By the time the housekeeper arrived with the coffee, Rosina was putting the last of the ledgers away in the large bookcase.

'Thank you, Mrs Jameson, although I really should not have bothered you. Apart from a few letters that have arrived for me, Mr Redmond has left me with nothing to do today.'

The housekeeper chuckled as she put the tray down on the desk.

'Then you can sit by the fire and enjoy your coffee before you read your letters. You certainly don't want to be traipsing back to the lodge until this shower has passed. And the squire has sent over his London news sheet for you,' she said, taking the paper from under her arm and placing it next to the tray.

'How kind of Sir John. And it is kind of you, too, to bring me the coffee. I am very grateful.'

'Nonsense, it's the least we can do, when you are out and about in all weathers.'

When the housekeeper had left the room Rosina went over to the desk and picked up the newspaper. It was a little creased from having been through several hands, and she noticed that it was folded at one of the inner pages. The headline jumped out at her—*The Demise of Her Royal Highness, the Princess Charlotte.*

Forgetting her coffee and the wind howling around the house, Rosina turned towards the lighted candelabra and read the report of the princess's death, only days after giving birth to her stillborn son. The shock of this double tragedy brought on a wave of sadness that broke through the control Rosina had kept over her own feelings for so long. She put down the paper, leaned against the edge of the desk and let her tears fall unchecked.

Conham had hoped to reach Morton Gifford by early afternoon, but one of the glossy matched bays pulling his curricle cast a shoe and it was dark by the time he eventually reached the Manor. Gusts of wind were blowing sheets of sleety rain across the drive as he ran into the house. A footman was on hand to take his hat, gloves and greatcoat and he paused only to confirm that Miss Brackwood was in the house before hurrying to her office.

He opened the door, an apology for appearing in all his dirt already on his lips, but the sight of Rosina weeping unrestrainedly put to flight everything except the need to comfort her. He crossed the space between them in two strides.

'What is it? Rosina, what's wrong?'

With a sob she threw herself into his arms. He held her close, resting his cheek on her golden hair and murmuring soft words, but they were lost against the noise of the storm raging outside.

At last, her tears were spent and she muttered into his shoulder.

'I b-beg your pardon. I am not usually so lachrymose! You took me by surprise.'

'Thank goodness it was me, then, and not a stranger!' She gave a watery chuckle and he kissed her hair. 'Tell me who or what has upset you so?'

She pushed against him and he released her immediately.

'So silly of me,' she mumbled, searching for her handkerchief. 'It was the news, about P-Princess Charlotte. Heartbreaking, so soon after losing her baby.'

He frowned. 'I do not believe that is all, Rosina. You are not one to cry so easily. Tell me what has happened to upset you.'

'N-nothing!'

She jumped as the wind hurled rain against the window in a sharp tattoo and he reached out for her again, but she held him off.

'You can—you *should* go. Now. I am p-perfectly well.'

'Little liar.'

'Please, Conham, leave me.'

She ended on a sob, but her dainty hands were clutching at his coat and she did not resist when he put his arms around her.

'Look at me, Rosina.' He put his finger under her chin. 'Look up and tell me you want me to go.'

There was a momentary lull in the storm and his words fell into the sudden silence. The air in the room was stifling, charged with tension, and Conham's heart pounded like a hammer against his ribs. Slowly, she raised her head and looked at him. Her eyes were bright with tears, but in their blue depths he saw a hunger and such fierce desire, that it took his breath away. His arms tightened and he lowered his head, capturing her mouth for a kiss that expressed all the months of pent-up longing.

Rosina responded eagerly, slipping her arms around his neck, her lips moving instinctively against his, and she pressed her body against him with an eagerness that shocked her, as did the hunger that consumed her. Every nerve within her was crying out for more.

He sighed, murmuring her name over and over as he

planted butterfly kisses on her eyes, her jaw, and moved down to touch his lips to the erratic pulse in her neck.

'I have wanted this for so long,' she whispered, clinging to him. 'I have wanted *you*, Conham!'

His heart swelled at her soft words. He swept her up into his arms and when she laid her head against his shoulder and gazed up at him, smiling, a jolt of pure lust shot through his body.

'Oh, confound it, Rosina,' he muttered, his voice ragged, unsteady. 'I have never wanted anyone, anything, as much as I want you!'

'Then show me,' she whispered, her eyes glowing like sapphires. 'Take me to bed.'

Conham's heart soared. Holding his precious bundle he turned towards the door.

'Conham, the servants!' She clutched at his collar. 'We must be discreet.'

'Discretion be damned,' he said savagely, 'I am bedding my future wife and I don't care who knows of it!'

Rosina awoke slowly from a deep sleep. The storm had passed but it was still dark and very quiet. She took a moment to consider how she felt. Content. Happier than she had been for a very long time.

Everything came flooding back. Conham carrying her up to his room—quite fortuitously meeting no one on the way—the frantic kisses and caresses that accompanied their undressing and the delight of exploring each other's bodies.

Desire was pooling again, low inside her, as she remembered all they had done. The intimate caresses that sent her body out of control, the joyful ecstasy of their coupling, first on the woollen rug before the fire and later between the cool sheets of Conham's bed, where he had touched her as no one had ever done before, bringing her alive, awakening thoughts, feelings so new, so exciting, that she ached for more.

She dismissed his declared intention to marry her as the heat of the moment. Once he remembered his duty to his name, to his family, he would realise how impossible that was. Even if he did marry her, how long would it be before his conscience began to eat away at their happiness? She folded her arms across her breasts, as if trying to protect herself from the unpleasant truth. Everything was different, but nothing had changed between them. He still needed a fortune, which she could not give him. She knew him too well to believe he would be happy if he could not fulfil his duty to his family.

Conham was sleeping beside her and, seeking comfort, she turned towards him. She pressed herself against his naked body and closed her eyes. She was familiar with the hints of cedarwood and spicy cologne that clung to his linen, but now she breathed in the very male, musky scent of the man himself.

When he stirred and reached for her, she cupped his face in her hands and kissed him. As their kisses grew ever more urgent, she let her hands explore him, desire mounting as she smoothed her fingers over the muscled contours. Then she followed his lead, running her lips over his skin, exulting in her power to make him moan with pleasure at her touch even as he continued to caress her until they were both beyond thought and came together for a final joyous union.

Afterwards, Rosina lay in his arms, sated, replete, while silent tears spilled over her cheeks. The future could not be theirs, but she would carry the memories of this night with her forever.

* * *

As the first rosy fingers of dawn crept into the sky, Rosina slipped out of Conham's bed.

'Where are you going, my love?'

'Back to the lodge, before anyone sees me.'

'That no longer matters. We will soon be married.'

She pretended not to hear that and continued putting on her clothes. She walked over to the long glass and studied her reflection as she fastened her riding habit. Her clothes looked neat enough, but there was little she could do about her hair, save to use what few pins she could find to put it up in a knot.

'You are really going?'

Conham's deep voice came from the shadows of the bed and she went over to him.

'Yes, I am really going.' She kissed him briefly. 'Now, go back to sleep.'

He sat up and caught her hand. 'But you will marry me?'

'I must go back to the lodge and make myself respectable. Then I will come back to my office and we can talk.' She squeezed his fingers and slipped quietly out of the room.

Conham lay back against the pillows, his hands behind his head. Last night had not gone as he had expected. He had wanted to explain to Rosina about the changes he was making and his plans for the future. For *their* future. It would be slow work and hard, too, rebuilding Dallamire and reviving the estates from their previously dire position, but he did not think she would mind that. With Rosina at his side, working with him, he knew they would succeed.

Finding her in tears had thrown his thoughts into disarray. He had taken her in his arms, all his carefully worded speeches replaced by the overwhelming need to comfort her. A smile began to grow inside him. Comfort had soon given way to desire, for both of them. He had read it in her eyes, felt it in the way she had returned his kisses. Later, in the bedroom, she had shown a passion equal to his own. It had been a revelation; he had never felt this way about any woman before, the need to cherish her, to protect her and put her happiness before his, in all things.

Beyond the dressing room door he could hear Dawkins moving about. There had been no sign of his estimable valet when he had carried Rosina into the room last night. Did the man know what had happened here? It was likely that he would guess, from the pile of hastily discarded clothes, but it made no difference. The fellow had always been the soul of discretion and when Conham informed him he would be wearing his new coat of blue superfine today, Dawkins would know at once that something out of the ordinary was about to take place.

Conham curbed his impatience and forced himself not to rush through his morning routine before going down to breakfast at the usual hour. Rosina would need time to change and break her own fast before she returned to the Manor. He would go to her office and casually invite her to join him in the morning room. There they would talk, uninterrupted. With her excellent grasp of such matters, she would understand that he had little to offer her, apart from his heart and a great deal of hard work, at least for a few years. He only hoped she would think it was enough.

By ten o'clock Conham could wait no longer. He made his way to the land steward's office and was surprised to find Davy Redmond there alone. The young man jumped up as he came in and Conham waved him back to his seat.

'Is Miss Brackwood not arrived yet?'

'She has been and gone, my lord.'

'Gone?' Conham's brows snapped together.

'Yes, my lord. She left this for you.'

Conham almost snatched the papers Davy held out to him and walked across to the window. There were two sheets, pinned in one corner. The second was folded up beneath Rosina's message, which was brief and to the point.

My lord...

So formal!

I have gone to Brackwood to search for my father's will. The attached arrived yesterday from Mr Palmer, the second witness. He has only recently returned to England and learned of my enquiries from Professor MacDowell.

I should not be gone more than a few days and Davy knows what needs to be done while I am away.

I have taken your travelling chariot. Forgive me.
R

Stifling a curse, he read the letter she had pinned to her note. Then he turned to Davy.

'When did she leave?'

'I—I am not sure, my lord.' The young man stuttered, startled by Conham's abrupt tone. 'I arrived here soon after eight and she was already writing her note for you.'

Conham barely heard the last few words, he was already heading out the door.

* * *

The travelling chariot was comfortably sprung and the seats thickly padded, but Rosina was in no humour to appreciate its luxuries, or the passing landscape. She was going over and over Mr Palmer's letter in her head, and trying to reassure herself that she was doing the right thing. His reply suggested that Papa had hidden a copy of the will.

A very reasonable voice inside argued that Edgar would have searched for it thoroughly, but that did not mean he would have found it. Edgar had never done anything thoroughly in his life, except drink to excess. No. Rosina was convinced the will was still in the house, and she would not rest until she had visited Brackwood and made her own search.

Her attention was caught by a familiar landmark and she sat up. They were very close to the Crown, where she had ordered the driver to stop. She needed to eat something before arriving at Brackwood Court. Her reception there was unlikely to be cordial.

The chariot came to a halt before the entrance of the posting inn. Rosina collected her reticule from the seat beside her, but when she looked up there was no liveried footman waiting to help her out. Conham was holding open the door, and he looked furious.

Chapter Twenty-Two

'Lord Dallamire! What, what a surprise.'

After the slightest hesitation Rosina stepped down from the travelling chariot. Conham's riding dress and the two lathered horses being led away by his groom explained how he had caught up with her so quickly.

'It shouldn't be,' he said grimly.

He held out his arm and one look at his face told her not to ignore it. She placed her fingers on his sleeve and went with him into the inn, where a bowing landlord showed them immediately to a private parlour.

She preceded Conham into the room and spoke almost before the door had closed upon them.

'I am very sorry I took the travelling chariot without permission, my lord.'

'Damn the chariot!' he retorted, ripping off his gloves. 'What the devil do you mean by coming here without me?'

She made sure the large dining table was between them before she answered him.

'I did not wish to involve you in this.'

His eyes were the colour of granite this morning, and they glittered dangerously.

'By heaven, madam, I know you value your independence, but this is the outside of enough! Do you think your brother is going to allow you to search his house? The man has already tried to kill you once.'

Rosina shuddered at his words, but she overcame it.

'That is why I needed your carriage. Edgar is unlikely to harm me if I have your driver and footman in attendance.'

'I would not be so sure of that.'

They glared at each other for a long moment, then Rosina sighed.

'Let us not fight, sir. Mr Palmer's letter was on my desk when I went into the office this morning. It was in the pile of correspondence Davy left for me yesterday.' She blushed, remembering the reason she had not dealt with it last night. 'You had only just arrived at the Manor and I did not want to drag you away again so soon. For what might turn out to be a mare's nest.'

'And did you think I would be happy to learn you had come here alone?' he demanded.

'No, I knew you would not, which is why I set off early. I beg your pardon, I thought you might try to dissuade me.'

Rosina looked at him across the table and saw the genuine concern in his eyes. She walked around to him, putting out her hands.

'I must do this, Conham. I need to know what my father's last wishes were.'

'I can understand that.' He clasped her fingers and looked down at them, his thumbs rubbing gently across the backs of her hands. 'I know this is important to you, but you must allow me to help you.'

'Do I have any choice?'

He met her eyes, the hard look fading. 'No.'

A tiny thread of relief rippled through Rosina.

'I should be glad of your company,' she admitted.

'Good. I shall order refreshments and then we will discuss what you intend to do.'

Within a very short time they were sitting down with a pot of coffee and slices of cake on the table between them.

'You read Mr Palmer's letter?' she asked him.

'Yes.' He drew it from his pocket and looked at it again. 'Palmer quotes your father as saying he would not keep the will in his desk but that he would be *keeping it close*.'

'Yes. Mr Palmer remembered that particularly because it was such an odd thing for my father to say.'

'Do you not think that means he would be keeping it on his person? If so, it was sure to have been found when he died.'

'I did consider that,' replied Rosina. 'However, if that had been the case then Mr Paxby would have known of it. After all, he was with Papa when he was taken ill. He helped undress him and get him to bed for the very last time.' She frowned. 'No, I think Papa secreted it somewhere in the house.'

'But surely, if there was a will, it would have been found by now.'

She raised her chin. 'Not necessarily.'

Conham knew that determined look. It would be useless to argue.

'Do you have a plan?' he asked her.

She nodded. 'Today is market day. When Edgar moved back to Brackwood he formed the habit of drinking at one of the taverns in the afternoon, to throw dice and play cards with anyone who had the money to join him. I doubt if his marriage has changed that. It is in part the reason I was in such haste to come here. I thought I would go to Brackwood Court while Edgar is out and talk with Lady Brackwood. I hoped I might persuade her to let me look over the house.'

'And if your brother is at home?'

'I shall have to think of something else.'

He raised one eyebrow. 'Housebreaking, perhaps?'

A faint flush bloomed on her cheek.

'Perhaps.'

Conham sighed. It was madness, even to contemplate such a thing, but he knew how much this meant to her.

'Very well, let us hope it will not come to that.' He took out his watch. 'Once we have finished here we will make our way to the Court. The market should be over by then and the taverns will be filling up.'

The sun was dropping towards the horizon when they reached their destination but the sky was clear, and Conham judged that there was a good hour of daylight left. As he jumped down from the carriage he took his first look at Rosina's old home.

Brackwood Court was a large, rambling building, built of local stone. Much of it appeared to be old. Tudor, he thought, looking at the stone-mullioned windows and high chimneys, but some later modifications had been carried out, including a square porch over the entrance. It was a handsome house and he could understand why she loved it.

Conham handed Rosina out and went with her to the door, where he enquired if Sir Edgar was at home. Upon learning that he was not, Rosina asked to see Lady Brackwood, and they were left to kick their heels in the hall while a stately butler carried a message to Her Ladyship.

'I do not recognise any of these people,' she muttered. 'Edgar has dismissed all Papa's loyal retainers.'

He knew she required a clear head for what needed to be done next and kept his response deliberately cool.

'Did you think he would not, after what he did to you?'

His matter-of-fact tone worked. She squared her shoulders, hiding all signs of distress. Impulsively, he caught her hand and kissed it. 'Courage, Rosina.'

The gesture touched her heart. She was grateful for his support, but there was no time to tell him that. The butler returned and they were escorted up the ornately carved wooden staircase to the drawing room. It had changed little since Rosina had been here last. The furnishings looked more worn but the wood was highly polished and the flowers on the side table suggested that the house at least was well cared for.

The new Lady Brackwood was standing beside the fireplace, waiting to greet them.

'Sir Edgar is out,' she said quickly, twisting her hands together. 'I am not sure you should be here.'

'Thank you for agreeing to see me,' said Rosina, ignoring her remark. 'How is my little nephew?'

'He—he is doing very well,' replied their hostess, thrown off guard by this friendly enquiry.

'I am very pleased to hear that.' Rosina paused, then said, 'Lady Brackwood, how much do you know of my leaving this house?'

Harriet looked a little surprised. 'I know that you quarrelled with Edgar.'

'It was far worse than a quarrel, but never mind that now. When I left, I was unable to take all my personal belongings. Nothing valuable, but things that mean a great deal to me.'

'I am very sorry,' Lady Brackwood replied, looking genuinely dismayed. 'By the time I came here your room had been cleared. There can be nothing of yours left. Edgar said he wanted to remove every trace of you.'

Rosina shuddered. She felt Conham's hand on her back and was heartened by his presence. She tried again.

'Would you permit me to look in my father's study? He had some letters of mine, put away with the family papers.'

'No. That is not possible. The study is locked and Edgar keeps the key.'

'Ah, of course he does. But Lady Brackwood... Harriet. We are sisters, now. Surely you would not deny me one last look around the house, if I promise not to disturb anything?'

Rosina reached out to touch her arm and Harriet jumped away as if she had been burned.

'I c-cannot allow you to do that, Edgar would not like it.' She moved towards the bell pull. 'I am sorry. I think you should leave now.'

'Please, we wish you no harm,' said Rosina quickly. 'Surely you would not deny me the chance to say goodbye to my old home.' Harriet had stopped short of ringing the bell and Rosina added, 'I spent so many happy years here, you see. So many precious memories.'

She let the words hang, knowing she was playing on the other woman's sympathy.

Harriet stood, indecisive, wringing her hands. Then, just as she was about to speak, they heard the rumble of voices from the hall. Heavy footsteps sounded on the stairs and the door was thrown open so violently it crashed back against the side table.

'What the devil do you mean, letting that whore in here!'

Edgar came roaring into the room and Lady Brackwood fell back with a cry.

'Mind your manners, Brackwood!'

Conham stepped forward. Rosina knew his superior build and the sharp warning would be enough to make Edgar pause. From his flushed face and bloodshot eyes, it was clear that her brother was drunk. He glared at Conham then turned his head and addressed his wife.

'What are they doing here?' he demanded.

'Sh-she wanted to see her old rooms,' stammered Harriet, her face white. 'But I said no. Believe me, I was not going to let them. I was about to send them away.'

With a curse Edgar turned and glared at Rosina.

'You have no business here. Get out of my house.'

'Please, Edgar, I do not want to fight with you.'

'I said get out!'

'What have I done to deserve this?'

'You stole my birthright!'

Rosina stepped back as if he had slapped her.

'That's not true!'

'It is, damn you! Father made you mistress here, running the estate, organising everything. You turned him against me!'

'No, that's not true,' she cried. 'I helped Papa after Mama died, but that was only until you could come home and take over. I promise you, Edgar, he wanted to teach you, just as he had taught me.'

'Teach me? I never had a chance!' He raged at her, his lips flecked with spittle. 'You were always Father's favourite. So devilishly clever, so damned *c-capable*!'

Rosina stared, shocked at the malice in his voice.

'But you could have done as much, Edgar, if only you had applied yourself.'

'Why should I?' he threw at her. 'Why even bother when you do everything so much better?'

With a curse he swung away and began to pace the room.

'You were always in the way, criticising, meddling in the running of the estate,' he muttered, punching his fist into his palm. 'That was why you had to go. I couldn't let you stay here any longer. You were too good at everything.

Always interfering, overriding my orders. You put me to shame with the tenants, the neighbours!'

She was aware of Conham moving to her side as her brother came to a halt before her, menacingly close.

'Oh, Edgar,' she said softly, 'I am so sorry. That was never my intention.'

Her words made no impression. There was nothing but angry loathing in his face as he glared at her.

'Get out, madam. Get out and take your *lover* with you!'

Conham's fists came up but Rosina quickly clutched his arm.

'No! He is drunk, my lord. You must not fight him.'

'Aye, how would that look?' Edgar sneered. 'Attacking a man in his own house.'

Rosina felt the muscles tense, hard as steel beneath his sleeve, and hung on tighter.

'Conham, please.'

The red mist was clearing from Conham's mind. Brackwood was swaying unsteadily on his feet. The fellow was no longer a threat. It was beneath him to knock down such a pitiful wretch. He heard Rosina's voice at his side, soft, pleading.

'Come away, my lord. Let us leave this place.'

'Very well, we will go. For now.'

He glanced back. Lady Brackwood was hunched in a chair, weeping softly. Heaven help her, with such a husband!

'Aye, go and devil take you both,' Brackwood jeered. He turned to his wife, hauling her to her feet. 'Come along, my dear, where are your manners? We must see our guests safely out of the house.'

Lady Brackwood was shrinking away from Edgar and Conham hesitated, loath to leave any woman at the mercy of such a bully. He felt Rosina tug gently on his arm.

'He is doing this for our benefit,' she murmured. 'He *wants* you to strike him. We should leave, now.'

Conham nodded. He escorted Rosina from the room, conscious that Brackwood and his wife were behind them. He opened the door and paused, allowing Rosina to go before him, but as he followed her out onto the landing he heard Lady Brackwood whisper something to her husband. It was met with a snarling curse, then a slap and a scream.

Conham swung around. Harriet was reeling, on the edge of collapse. Instinctively he stepped back to catch her as she fell, and at that moment Edgar barrelled past him.

'Rosina, look out!'

She had almost reached the staircase but turned back at Conham's shout, to see her brother hurtling towards her.

By the time Conham laid Harriet gently on the floor, Edgar had caught up with Rosina. She was backed against the landing railing and threw out her hands to hold him off. Frantically, she pushed him away and he swayed, stepping back and missing the top stair. Conham ran forward but he was too late. Brackwood swayed, arms flailing like a windmill as he lost his balance and toppled headlong down the stairs.

Rosina slumped against the handrail. After the commotion there was now only a terrible stillness. The silence seemed to go on forever, but it could only have been moments before Conham was running down the stairs. She glanced across the landing as Harriet came unsteadily out of the parlour and stared down at her husband, lying at the bottom of the stairs.

Collecting herself, Rosina hurried down to join Conham, who was kneeling beside Edgar. She stared at her brother's lifeless form. There was a small cut on his head, but apart from that and his dreadful pallor, there was no outward sign of injury.

'Is—is he...?'

'No, he breathes.' Conham tried to sound reassuring.

He assured himself that she was not about to faint before addressing the two footmen who had come running over. He barked out his instructions and when he turned back, Rosina was kneeling beside her brother, her fingers on the pulse in his neck.

'Don't move him,' he warned, 'I have sent for a doctor.'

'Can we not put him to bed?'

'Not yet. I saw a lot of broken bones when I was in the army. The surgeons told me many injuries are made far worse by moving the patient.'

He heard footsteps on the stairs and glanced up. Harriet had descended to the lowest stair.

'He is safe enough here, my lady,' he told her. 'But we need to keep him warm.'

At first, he thought she had not heard; she was staring down at the broken body on the floor, her face ashen. Then she nodded. 'I will fetch blankets.'

'I shall go and help her,' said Rosina, rising. 'I can do nothing here.'

She was very calm, but there was such anguish in her eyes that it tore at his heart.

'Yes, yes. Go and help.'

He watched her hurry after Harriet, knowing they would be better for being busy. For himself, there was nothing to do now but wait.

It was some time before the surgeon arrived. The ladies brought blankets to cover Edgar and then joined Conham in the vigil at the foot of the stairs. The patient slipped in and out of consciousness several times, and they gave him sips of water, doing their best to keep him still.

Conham said nothing, but what worried him most was that although Edgar threw his head from side to side and thrashed his arms, his legs beneath the covering blankets did not move.

He said as much to the doctor, once he arrived and examined Edgar. The man shrugged.

'Only time will tell.' He knelt by the patient, shaking his head. 'Drunk when he fell, was he? No need to deny it, I can smell it on him. I was expecting something like this. Well, well, let us put him to bed and we will see how he goes on. He will need careful nursing, night and day.'

Rosina stepped forward. 'I would like to help with that.'

Conham wanted to object but was silenced by her look, pleading with him to understand.

He gave her a slight nod and she turned back to address the doctor.

'I will stay, if Lady Brackwood will allow me?'

Rosina glanced at Harriet. The two of them had worked together, fetching blankets and bandages, finding a board in readiness for carrying the injured man upstairs to his bed, and she was relieved when the other woman agreed.

An hour later Edgar had been put to bed and Rosina went down to the hall to see Conham, who was preparing to leave.

'I cannot stay long,' she told him. 'Lady Brackwood is with my brother now, but she wants to go to the nursery soon, to attend to her baby.'

'Yes, of course,' he said, pulling on his gloves. 'It is too dark to return to the Manor tonight so I shall put up at the Crown, but as soon as I get back to Morton Gifford, I shall arrange for your bags to be packed.' He patted his pocket.

'I have your instructions for Mrs Goddard, your luggage should be with you by tomorrow night.'

'Thank you.' She hesitated, then, 'I am sorry. I never meant... I never knew Edgar felt so, so *belittled* by me! I feel all this is my fault.'

'No, Rosina, you must not blame yourself. Your brother is eaten up with jealousy.'

'But if I had acted differently...if I had not undermined him—'

He caught her hands. 'You did what you thought was best for Brackwood, what you thought your father would have wanted. Nothing can excuse what your brother did to you!'

'I know that, but... Oh, Conham, I cannot leave him while he is like this!'

'Stay then, if you must.' He touched her cheek, smiling a little. 'Do not worry about Morton Gifford. I will look after matters there with Davy until you are free to return. You will want to concentrate on looking after Sir Edgar. He is still your brother, even after everything he has done.'

'Yes. And although Harriet is very capable, she has the baby to consider and will need someone to help her nurse Edgar. It seems she has no one else, her family cast her off soon after she was married. I must stay. I hope you understand.'

He caught her hands.

'I do understand,' he said lightly, lifting first one then the other to his lips. 'It is my misfortune that I fell in love with an angel.'

'Oh, pray, do not say that,' she cried, blinking away tears. 'You know we can never be together.'

'We can and we will,' he said, kissing her.

The wail of a baby floated down from the upper floors and Rosina reluctantly pushed Conham away.

'I must go. Harriet needs to look after her son.'

He nodded. 'There is no time to explain it all now, but when this is over, we shall be married, I promise you!'

His smile almost broke her heart, but she bravely hid her tears until he had ridden off into the darkness.

Chapter Twenty-Three

For a full week Rosina worked with Harriet to nurse Edgar. At first he was too ill to know who was tending him, but as his mind recovered, he became increasingly angry to find her there, and she suggested they bring in one of the women from the village to help.

Rather than cause him distress, she took over the night watch, sitting with him while he slept during the long, dark hours between midnight and dawn. During the day, when she was not sleeping, she resumed the management of the estate. She dare not interfere too far, but her knowledge of Brackwood allowed her to fend off any immediate problems.

She also found herself growing closer to her sister-in-law. Harriet began asking her questions about Brackwood, and Rosina was only too pleased to talk about her old home and the village. She even drove Harriet around the land, something that Edgar had failed to do.

By the end of the third week, the doctor declared that Edgar was out of immediate danger and Rosina wrote to Davy, asking him to send the carriage. Despite the worry over her brother, she had taken some pleasure in seeing Brackwood again, but she knew she would be very glad to get back to Morton Gifford after one final night watch.

The doctor had said it was not strictly necessary now but Rosina wanted to do it. She felt she owed her brother that much. It was not too onerous a task, as long as Edgar was sleeping. A coal fire kept the room warm throughout the night and a lamp beside her chair gave sufficient light for her to occupy her time sewing or reading. She had been pleased to see that most of Papa's books remained in the small library, and she found one he had been particularly fond of, during his later years. She had read it before, several times, but still enjoyed it for its witty and sometimes cutting depiction of country society. She trimmed the lamp and settled down with her novel.

She had not read very far when one line jumped out at her:

> *If I could love a man who would love me enough to take me for a mere fifty pounds a year, I should be very well pleased.*

Rosina lowered the book, suddenly feeling slightly sick. Conham was such a man, she knew that, but there could be no happy ending to their story. Since taking her to his bed he was determined to marry her and count the world well lost. But that was impossible. A rich bride was not just desirable for Conham, it was a necessity. His mother had said as much. He had been born into a different world; he would be derided and despised by society if he neglected his duty. His friends would turn their backs on him.

Rosina might try to dismiss it as mere arrogance, but she knew Conham could not shrug off his obligations so easily. He might love her now, but it would not last. Not if it meant behaving in such a dishonourable way to his family, people that he loved.

Edgar stirred and Rosina went across to the bed. He murmured something, but did not wake. After straightening the bedcovers, she went back to her chair but she did not pick up the book again. There was not time to read the whole, so it was best to put it aside now, although she had no idea how else she would fill the remaining hours, save with her own thoughts.

They were not happy. Nursing Edgar had not taken all her time these past three weeks and she had visited Mr Paxby and his sister. There she learned even more about the discontent in the village and on the farms. It confirmed her own impression that matters at Brackwood were going from bad to worse.

Rosina leaned back in the chair and closed her eyes, remembering her original reason for coming here, to search for a new will. Since her brother's accident she had made no attempt to look for it, thinking it would be wrong, somehow, with Edgar being so ill. But now she began to think of the matter again. After all, it was not only Edgar who was suffering from Brackwood's ailing fortunes, there was his wife and son to consider.

She turned her mind to her father's last days. He had collapsed in this very room the night after he had dined with his friends. What if he had managed to hide the will somewhere in here?

She got up and wandered around the room, noting that the heavy dark wood furniture had been replaced by newer pieces with brass inlay and lions-claw feet. She saw Papa's mahogany dressing case sitting on Edgar's new dressing table and felt a sudden constriction in her throat. It brought back a host of memories, of happier times when Papa had been alive.

She gave herself a little shake. This was doing nothing

to help her find the will and she forced herself to consider where it might be. If Papa had hidden it in any of the drawers or cupboards, or even between the mattress and the bed frame, it must have been found by Edgar or one of the servants when they turned out the room.

That only left the floorboards or the wainscot. She picked up the lamp and began to inspect the panelling. Beginning on one side of the door she made her way slowly around three of the walls, running her hands over the wood. It was worn smooth with age and polishing, but she could discern no gaps or loose panels. Edgar's bed was pushed against the last wall and she went back to it carefully, wary of allowing the light to disturb him. Nothing. Rosina moved around the bed. Hope was fading, but she thought that she might as well finish what she had started.

She had reached the final section of wainscot when her fingers felt a distinct ridge. The edge of one of the panels was definitely standing proud, but she had to move into the corner, where the wall adjoined the door frame, to see beneath it. She crouched down, holding the lamp towards the slight gap and her heart almost stopped.

Was that really something under the panelling or was she merely imagining it, because she wanted it so badly? She took a moment to steady herself and looked again. It was not easy to hold the lamp still, but yes, she was sure there was something in there.

Quickly, she went back to the dressing table and opened the dressing case. Inside were the usual silver-topped jars for holding powders or lotions and a selection of combs and brushes with ivory handles. She pulled out the small drawer beneath to reveal a row of smaller instruments, all necessary to a gentleman's toilet and each piece in its place on the green baize. She lifted out a pair of tweezers.

Her heart was pounding with anxiety that Edgar might wake as she went back to the gap in the panelling. Cautiously, she tried to extract the paper lodged beneath the wood. It was slow work, the folded sheet was tightly wedged into the narrow space, but finally she pulled out enough for her to be able to grip the document and ease it free from its hiding place.

Carefully she unfolded the paper.

I, Thomas George Brackwood of Brackwood Court in the County of Somersetshire, being of sound and disposing mind and memory...

Rosina was already in the hall when the Dallamire travelling chariot came to a halt on the drive of Brackwood Court. Taking her leave of Harriet, she stepped outside, only to stop in surprise when Conham jumped out of the carriage.

'I have come to take you home.'

His smile and the simple words set her heart soaring. It would be useless to deny her pleasure in seeing him, her countenance gave it away, but Rosina tried to contain her happiness. Despite everything she had to tell him, nothing had changed between them, except that her feelings for Conham had grown even stronger in the past three weeks. She knew it would be quite unbearable to remain at Morton Gifford knowing they could never marry.

He helped her into the carriage, gave orders to the driver and jumped in, sitting down beside her as the chariot moved off.

'Have you missed me?' he asked.

As if I had lost part of myself!

She could not say that of course. She held him off as he reached for her.

'Oh, Conham, I have so much to tell you. I have found the will.'

'The devil you have!'

Conham sat back and listened as she explained everything and showed him the paper she had extracted from behind the panelling.

'We should take this to Mr Shipton immediately,' he said, when he had read it. 'As executor and your father's attorney, he is by far the best person to deal with the matter. With your permission, we will go there now.'

Rosina nodded and he let down the window to give fresh instructions to the driver.

'There, it is done,' he said, resuming his seat. 'It is not so far out of our way.'

'Thank you. There will be enquiries to be made, and we do not know yet if the will is legally binding.'

'Have you told anyone else about it?' he asked her.

'No. Edgar is not well enough. He cannot leave his bed and it is not yet certain he will ever walk again.' She paused, saddened by the thought. 'I confess it did trouble me not to tell Harriet. We have become friends, you see. She did not confide in me, but I believe Edgar has been bullying her dreadfully. She has become a different person since the accident, far more assured.'

'I am very glad to hear that. But you know what this means?' He nodded towards the paper that she was still clutching in her hands. 'Your father has left all the unentailed land to you, for your lifetime.'

'Yes. If the will is proven then I shall have control of everything save Brackwood Court and the Home Farm. Having helped Harriet with the accounts for the past three weeks, I know my brother has already spent most of the dowry she brought with her, and without the rents and income from the farms and villages, he will not be able to pay his way.

'Edgar would have to listen to me, then. I am sure he must want Brackwood to thrive, if not for his own sake then for his son. Do you not think so?'

'No, I don't,' said Conham, bluntly. 'Are you not concerned he might make another attempt to harm you?'

'I thought of that.' She folded her hands in her lap. 'I am going to make a sworn statement, with all the facts of his previous attempt, and our other encounters since. I shall have it signed and sealed and give it to Mr Shipton for safekeeping, in case anything should happen to me. I think it will be as well to be prepared,' she told him. 'I should have done it before, rather than rely solely upon your protection.'

'But I *want* to protect you, Rosina. More than that I want to make you my wife!'

'Please, say no more!' Her anguished cry silenced him. 'I have too much to think of at present. Edgar may not even survive! If that is the case then his son will inherit, and Harriet will need my help whether the will is proven or not.' She gently pulled her hands free. 'I have a duty to my family, my lord, as you have to yours.'

'Duty!' He uttered the word like a curse. 'That damned word has always haunted me. But if we are to talk of duty, what of my obligation to you, now? I took you to my bed, madam. I *seduced* you!'

'I went willingly,' she replied. 'You owe me nothing because of what we did that night.'

'If you are with child—'

'I am not.' She was sitting very straight and still, only her hands, clasping and unclasping, betraying her agitation.

'My body has shown me,' she said, her cheeks flushed. 'You have no duty towards me, sir. I am not carrying your child.'

Conham shut his eyes. He had really thought she loved him, but it was not the case. She did not want to marry him, she would not even let him propose to her.

'By God, what a coil!'

She shrugged. 'Not at all. It is quite clear what we have to do.'

He said, after a moment, 'It is likely, then, that you will go back to Brackwood.'

'Yes, but not to the Court. Even if Edgar was not married, I would not live under his roof again. As it is, Harriet is mistress there now and she has the baby, too. She would not want me under her feet.' Rosina turned and looked out the window. 'But I could take a house close by. That would be essential if I am to run the estate. In either event I should have the one thing I have always wanted more than anything. To be independent.'

Conham listened to her cheerful voice and felt the leaden weight of her words on his spirits. She had always maintained she preferred her independence to marriage. He had thought he might change that, conceited fool that he was. She could have a comfortable life in Somerset, looking after the people and the land she loved. Had she not said more than once that Brackwood was her life?

When she looked back at him he dredged up a smile from somewhere deep inside.

'You would have your dream, then.'

'Yes.'

Rosina turned away again, pretending to study the familiar landscape. Now it was within reach, she realised that particular dream had been replaced months ago with another one. Something far more unattainable.

* * *

It was late by the time they reached Morton Gifford and Conham ordered the chariot to drive on to the lodge where, despite Rosina's protest, he insisted on walking with her to the door.

'Thank you for coming to fetch me, Conham.'

'Think nothing of it.'

She waited, wondering if he would kiss her, but he merely squeezed her hand before jumping back into the carriage.

'It is for the best,' she muttered to herself as she let herself into the lodge. 'If the new will is proven, Brackwood will need the income from the surrounding land. It has been neglected for the past year but I can change that. I must make it profitable, if not for Edgar's sake, then for Harriet and the child.'

And for herself, too, because independence was all she had left now. Even if her conscience would allow her to ignore the plight of her family and divert the funds to her own use, it would never make her the wealthy bride Conham needed.

With Rosina back at Morton Gifford, Conham knew there was no real need for him to remain, but he could not bring himself to leave. She would be heartbroken if the will should prove to be invalid, and he wanted to be there to support her.

He did his best to avoid Rosina, afraid she would see the hunger in his eyes. When it was necessary for them to meet and discuss estate matters Davy was usually present, and their encounters were always businesslike. On inclement days he found himself prowling the house like a prisoner, but when the weather was fine he was out of doors, visiting neighbours or spending the daylight hours riding through the Gloucester countryside.

However, he knew he could not stay forever. His man of business was urging him to come to London to deal with pressing financial matters. Also, his stepmother might have removed to the Dower House, but she was still writing to him, complaining of the slow progress in restoring Dallamire, and begging him to reconsider his decision not to marry an heiress.

After two weeks he decided it was time to leave the Manor. The latest correspondence from Berkshire concerned the next phase of improvements at Dallamire and he needed to decide how best to spend the limited funds at his disposal. Besides, Rosina was growing ever paler and more gaunt as she waited to hear news from Somerset: keeping his distance, not being able to comfort her, sliced like a knife into his soul.

Having made up his mind, Conham waited until Davy had left the Manor one morning before seeking out Rosina in her office. He knocked on the door and entered to find her sitting at her desk, staring at a letter in her hand.

'I beg your pardon, am I interrupting you?' She looked up and one glance at her face chased all other thoughts from his head. He said sharply, 'What is it?'

She said, in a colourless voice, 'Mr Shipton has written to me.'

'What does he say? Is the will invalid?'

Conham could not prevent a very selfish and ignoble burst of hope.

'Quite the opposite. Edgar has declared he will not contest the new will.'

'Oh.' He firmly squashed his disappointment. 'Is your brother fully recovered, then?'

'No. Harriet wrote to tell me that the doctors despair of his ever walking again, but he is sitting out of bed now and she says he is far more docile than before his accident.' She glanced down at the letter. 'I think this must be due to her influence. Mr Shipton says it will take time for everything to be finally settled, but my brother has agreed to my taking charge again and Harriet wants me to do so as soon as I can.'

'Well.' Conham strolled over to the window. 'That is good news for you.' He stared out at the winter landscape. It looked as dark and bleak as his mood, but he forced himself to say cheerfully, 'I am glad. You must be very pleased.'

Rosina had never felt more like weeping, but she said, in her brightest voice, 'Oh, good heavens, I am!'

He turned to face her. 'Well then. I will not stand in your way.'

'I beg your pardon?' She heard his words, but Conham was standing with his back to the wintry light coming in from the window and she could not see his face.

'Brackwood needs you. You should set to work, immediately.'

'But I am contracted as land steward here until Lady Day.'

'That can be changed. I worked with young Redmond while you were away and he proved himself very capable. I am sure he will make an excellent land steward.'

Rosina was well aware that Davy could easily take over as her successor at Morton Gifford, but hearing Conham express the idea did not please her at all.

'You want to be rid of me!'

'There seems little point in you staying longer.'

He had stepped closer and she could see now that his face was inscrutable.

No, she thought, after a second look. He was *indifferent*.

Since her return from Brackwood he had been avoiding her. She knew it was partly her fault, she had given him to understand that she did not wish to marry him, but now it was clear why he had so readily accepted that. What she had thought was a grand passion, thwarted by his sense of duty, had been nothing more than infatuation. Now it was over and he wanted her gone with all speed. Odious, odious creature!

She was angry that he could think so little of her but there was something else, deep down. Panic. She was not ready to leave Morton Gifford. She did not really want to go.

It took every ounce of her control to maintain a businesslike demeanour.

'I think not, my lord. My contract runs until the twenty-fifth of March and I shall honour that. There are matters to be dealt with here that I should like to see through to completion.' She gave him a cool, enquiring look. 'Unless you are dissatisfied with my work here?'

Rosina noted his scowl with satisfaction; her challenge had surprised him.

'Your work here has been exemplary, as well you know.'

'Thank you. Then Davy shall take over from me on Lady Day and not before. As you say, he is perfectly capable now and, should it be necessary for me to travel to Brackwood in the coming months, you will be able to rest easy, knowing that he will look after your interests here.'

'If that is what you wish, madam.'

'I do.' Having won that point, Rosina felt her resolution faltering. If he remained here much longer, she feared she would burst into tears. 'If that is all, my lord…'

'What? No. I came to tell you that I am leaving for Dallamire tomorrow. I intend to stop at Bellemonte on my way, to speak with Matt Talacre. Would you object if I told him now that you have heard from the attorney?'

She hesitated, but only for a moment. With Conham in Berkshire it would be useful to have someone nearby whom she trusted. Not that she could ever tell Matthew everything, of course.

'Yes, thank you, Matthew has proved himself a good friend to me. I have told him nothing of my visit to Brackwood and it would save me trying to put it all down in writing.'

'Very well. Goodbye, Rosina.'

'Goodbye, my lord.'

He held her gaze for a moment, as if waiting for her to say something more.

Go, Conham. Please go.

If he did not walk out soon she knew she would be lost. All pretence would be gone and she would throw herself at him, and beg him not to leave her at all.

Finally, just when she felt she could stand no more, he turned on his heel and strode out of the room.

Conham left Morton Gifford the following morning. He made no effort to see Rosina, merely leaving word with Davy that he could be reached at Dallamire, if she wished to contact him. He drove his curricle out through the gates and along the lanes at a smart pace, glad to concentrate upon keeping the spirited bays under control rather than allowing his thoughts to dwell on what he was leaving behind him.

There were no mishaps on the journey and he reached Bellemonte at midday. Leaving the curricle with his groom he set off in search of Matt, finally tracking him down to the little office he had set up for himself in the Pavilion.

'Conham, damme, this is a surprise! Come in, man, sit down and take a drink with me.'

'Thank you, no.' He threw his hat and gloves down on a chair. 'I cannot stop, I am on my way to Dallamire.'

Matt grinned. 'Off to tell your stepmama the good news, are you?'

'There is no good news.'

'Never tell me Rosina has refused you!'

'Yes—no. I did not ask her. That is why I have called, to stop you saying anything to her about the matter. It would only cause her distress.'

Conham swiftly told him about the new will.

'So, you see, Rosina will be leaving Morton Gifford in a few months.'

'I am astounded!' exclaimed Matt, when he had finished. 'The two of you have only had eyes for each other since we came into Gloucestershire. Rosina loves you, my friend, I would stake my life on it.'

'Then you would lose. Rosina's heart has always been at Brackwood. That is where she wants to be.'

But Matthew would not believe it.

'Have you told her that things have changed?' he demanded of Conham. 'That you are no longer in need of a rich wife?'

'What good would it do? Her brother is not contesting the will, which is almost an admission that it is valid. Rosina wants to return to Brackwood and continue with her father's plans to make the place profitable. It is what she has always wanted.'

'And if Sir Edgar dies?'

Conham felt his mouth twist into a bitter smile. 'Then she will devote herself to helping his widow, and providing a secure future for Edgar's son and heir.'

'The devil she will. Have you not told her how you *feel*? Surely you will not let her go without a fight!' Conham put up his hand, as if to ward off a blow, and Matt exploded. 'By God, man, don't be a fool. Go back now and talk to Rosina. Tell her you love her!'

'Confound it, how can I?' Conham raked a hand through his hair. 'Yes, I believe I can restore Dallamire without marrying a fortune, but it will take years. Possibly a lifetime of hard work and toil.'

'Much she'd care about that!'

'But *I* would care! And that is not the point. Rosina does not love me. Oh, she cares for me, a little. It would pain her to refuse me, and I do not want that. *If* she cannot go back to Brackwood, if it becomes a choice between working for someone else or marrying me, then perhaps, *perhaps* she might say yes. Until I know how things stand in the matter I will hold my peace. And so will you,' he finished, picking up his hat. 'You will say nothing about any of this to her. Promise me, Matthew, on your honour as an officer!'

Chapter Twenty-Four

It was Rosina's second spring at Morton Gifford, and bitter March winds were scouring the countryside. However, the days were growing longer, spring flowers dotted the hedgerows and Rosina clung to the hope that the weather would soon improve. That might lift her spirits, which had been uncharacteristically low throughout the winter. Her plans were all in place to quit Morton Gifford at the end of the month and move to Somerset. After that, all her ties to the Earl of Dallamire would be cut, with the exception of their mutual interest in Bellemonte.

She had heard nothing from Conham himself since his departure last winter. News of the earl was scarce, too. She scoured the London newspapers but there was no mention of him. The only news of any interest was that Miss Skelton had married Sir William Cherston. A baronet, not quite the noble rank Lady Skelton had wanted for her daughter, but Rosina hoped Amelia was happy with her choice.

From her office in the Manor, Rosina looked out at the leaden skies. Matthew was supposed to be calling today, to discuss his new plans for Bellemonte, but when she had walked across from the lodge this morning, a flurry of snow had caused her to think he might postpone his visit.

An hour later it was snowing heavily, and Rosina was

just lighting the candles in her office when her visitor arrived.

'Matthew!' She went over to him, hands held out. 'I had quite given up on you.'

'It takes more than a little snow to stop me,' he said, kissing her cheek. 'To be truthful, I was more than halfway here when the snow began, and I decided it was easier to carry on than turn back. Although I may have to beg you to put me up tonight.'

'You know that will be no problem, Mrs Jameson is always pleased to see you here. She thinks almost as much of you as her master!'

Matt chuckled and put his case of papers on the desk. 'Talking of Conham, have you heard from him recently?'

'Why, of course.' Rosina went back to the fireplace. 'I correspond regularly with his secretary at Dallamire.'

'I am not talking of business letters, Rosina!'

'But what else should we discuss?'

She picked up the poker and stirred the coals. Matthew was a very good friend, but she could not bear to expose her wounded heart to him or anyone. When she looked up she saw that he was frowning at her and she fought hard to find a convincing smile.

'Pray sit down, Matthew. I will ring for some coffee and we can get to work!'

'So you see, Rosina,' said Matthew, smiling at her across the desk, 'Bellemonte is already showing a profit in its first full year under my control.'

'Oh, Matthew, I am so pleased for you.'

'And that's not all,' he went on. 'Your investment will return you a full fifty pounds this year. Almost as much as if you had invested it in government bonds.'

'Truly?' She pressed her hands to her cheeks. 'That is wonderful news!'

'Aye. Not a fortune, of course, but I expect the returns to improve next year, if you can afford to leave the money with me.'

'That is my intention.'

'You are sure you do not need it?' he asked her. 'For your new life in Somerset?'

'Ah, you have heard.'

'Yes. But I am grieved that you did not think fit to tell me of it yourself.'

'I beg your pardon. There never seemed to be the right time...'

He waved away her excuse.

'Too late for that now. Tell me instead what your plans are.'

'I move to Brackwood on the twenty-fifth, when my contract here ends. There is a small house in the village, which I shall make my home. I plan to allow myself a small salary from the estate funds and the rest will go back to Edgar. Or, more truthfully, to Harriet, who is slowly taking over the running of Brackwood Court. She is proving herself an excellent manager.'

'And Conham?'

'What about him?' She began to gather up the papers on her desk. 'This has nothing to do with the earl. We are agreed that Davy Redmond will take over here as manager. Now, I believe that is all our business concluded, Matthew, is it not?'

She smiled at him, holding his gaze and her breath, praying he would not say anything more about Conham. Finally, he nodded.

'Yes, that is all I need to discuss with you.' He glanced towards the window. 'However, since it has not stopped snowing all day, I shall not even attempt to drive to Belle-monte tonight.'

'I should think not,' she told him, relaxing a little. 'If I know Mrs Jameson, she will already have instructed Cook to prepare dinner for us.'

'Very well. I shall go and see if I can charm her into sending up some hot water for me, but I am afraid I shall have to dine with you in these clothes.'

Rosina chuckled. 'I am very glad. It means I shall not feel obliged to make my way back to the lodge and change!'

Matthew went off and Rosina set about putting away her ledgers. The news about Bellemonte was encouraging. The gardens had performed well, even through the winter, the Pleasure Baths were also showing a profit and Matt hoped to open the hotel in the coming months. She was pleased for him; he had worked so hard to make Bellemonte a suc-cess. And she was glad to see, when he had walked in ear-lier, that the ugly limp that had troubled him so much had disappeared. He looked like a man content with his lot.

'And so should you be content, Rosina Brackwood,' she told herself as she went around the office, snuffing the candles. 'Your future is more than secure now. You have sufficient income to live comfortably, should you need it.'

She extinguished the final light to leave only the glow from the fire.

'And you are returning to Somerset, your old home,' she went on. 'That should be enough for anyone.'

But the words had a hollow ring to them and they did not lift the leaden weight from her heart.

Dinner with Matt Talacre proved a welcome distraction for Rosina. They talked about Bellemonte and the weather, politics and art. She was genuinely glad to have Matt's company and when the covers were removed, she happily agreed to have a final glass of wine with him. Anything to delay returning to her lonely bed, where her thoughts would fly, as they always did, to Conham.

'I am very pleased you could come, Matthew,' she said, when he had refilled her glass from a fresh bottle. 'I have enjoyed talking with you this evening.'

'So, too, have I, although there is one subject we have not touched upon,' said Matt, his dark eyes suddenly serious. 'What the devil happened between you and Conham?'

'N-nothing,' she replied, startled.

'Did you know he wanted to marry you?'

She hesitated, staring down into her glass for a long moment.

'Yes. But he was just trying to be kind.'

'Kind be damned! He loves you, Rosina.'

'That's not true.' She shook her head. 'He likes me. Perhaps for a while he thought it was something more...but not now. And it could never have come to anything. He needs to marry a rich woman.'

'Not any more.' Matthew leaned forward. 'Do you know what he has been doing these past months, Rosina? The steps he has been taking to improve his fortunes?'

'Of course I do. I know he has sold several properties, for example.'

'Did you also know he has persuaded the countess to decamp to the Dower House with the children? Or that he has sold timber from his estate to fund the latest repairs to Dallamire Hall?'

She raised her head. 'I do not need to know what is going on at Dallamire. My concern is Morton Gifford. Or it was,' she amended. 'From next month Davy Redmond will be land steward here and I shall be in Somerset.'

'And that is what you want?'

She pinned on her brightest smile. 'Of course it is. I shall be independent, which has always been my ambition.'

'But at what price, Rosina?'

She raised her hand. 'Stop this now, Matthew. This is none of your business.'

'But it is, when I see the two people I care about most in this world tearing themselves apart.'

'No, you are wrong. Conham cannot even bestir himself to see me before I leave Morton Gifford.'

'What?'

She bit her lip. 'I received a letter from his secretary. The earl is too busy to leave Dallamire. He is content for me to arrange matters as I wish in handing over to Davy Redmond.'

'I cannot believe he does not care. Rosina, I—'

'No more!' She pushed herself to her feet. 'I have had enough of this. Good night, M—'

'Believe me, madam, Conham is breaking his heart over you!'

She froze. Matthew went on.

'I have known Conham for ten years. We fought together, buried comrades together… Confound it, we are as close as family. Closer, in fact. He is not a man to wear his heart on his sleeve, but I *know* he loves you.'

Rosina sank back onto her chair. 'He has never said so.'

'Not at first, because he had nothing to offer you. Less than nothing.'

'How foolishly noble of him!'

'Aye, it was. But then he set about changing all that.'

'But why did he not write to me? Why did he not tell me about his plans?'

Matt laughed. 'Have you seen his letters? Conham is a man of action, Rosina. He does not express himself well with pen and ink. And besides, he was not sure he could do it and did not want to raise false hopes. Then in November, when he *did* think that he might be able to make it all work, he came back to propose to you.'

'But he didn't.'

'No, because you dashed off to Brackwood in search of that damned will.'

He refilled his glass and took a long drink. 'He has now convinced himself that you do not love *him*.'

Rosina crossed her arms, hugging herself. Conham had announced he was going to marry her, he had taken her to bed, but he had never said he loved her.

'He should have proposed, told me everything.'

Matt huffed. 'Did you really expect him to do so, when you were so intent on saving your old home?'

'I was trying to save *him*!'

She remembered how he had tried to kiss her, when he collected her from Brackwood. She had held him off. And she had refused to listen when he said he wanted to marry her, refused to let him explain.

I played my part too well. I pretended that Brackwood was all I really wanted, when really...

She looked up. 'Why have you not said anything of this to me before?'

'Conham swore me to silence. He believes that you want to return to Brackwood. That you do not love him.'

Tears started to her eyes. 'But I do. I do love him. Far too much to stop him from taking a rich wife. Someone with a large fortune.'

'And I am telling you he does not *need* to marry a fortune.' He pushed her wineglass towards her. 'If anyone should understand what is required to restore his neglected property, it should be you, Rosina! Thanks to your improvements, Morton Gifford is making more than enough to sustain itself and Conham is using some of the income to repair Dallamire Hall. Bellemonte, too, is showing a return. Not a great deal, to be sure, but enough to convince him there is a way forward that doesn't involve him marrying an heiress.

'He thought you could help him, Rosina. He thought you could work together to bring Dallamire back from the brink of ruin. But you have convinced him that you would prefer to live at Brackwood.'

'Yes, so he is free to find a more fitting wife.'

Matt threw out his hands and looked up at the ceiling.

'Damnation, woman, can't you see? He loves you, and if he can't have you, he won't marry anyone! He would rather tackle the restoration of Dallamire on his own than marry when his heart is elsewhere. Trust me, I know him better than I know myself.'

She shook her head, trying to make sense of everything she was hearing. Could it be possible? Could he truly love her? He had never said as much.

But he has shown you...time and again he has shown you how much he cares.

She frowned. 'But... Matthew, if you are such great friends, if Conham swore you to secrecy, why are you telling me this now?'

He grinned and held up his glass. 'Because I am drunk, madam, and not even a gentleman can be expected to keep his word when he is drunk!'

The snow was already melting when Rosina walked back to the Manor the next day. She was pleased to see it had not flattened the clusters of daffodils that glowed butter yellow in the early-morning sunshine. She always thought daffodils a very cheerful flower, a sign of hope for better things ahead, and today they exactly matched her mood.

She entered to find the butler in the hall and greeted him with a smile. A far more genuine smile than she had managed for some time.

'Good morning, Jameson, has Mr Talacre broken his fast yet?'

'No, Miss Brackwood, he is still in his room. Breakfast is set for ten o'clock.' His eyes twinkled. 'Mrs Jameson insisted he should eat a good meal before setting out for Bellemonte.'

She nodded. 'An excellent idea. I shall take breakfast with him, if you will have another place set.'

'It shall be done. And Mr Redmond is already in the office, ma'am.'

'Thank you. Perhaps you could have coffee sent in for us. We have much to discuss!'

'I am sorry if I have delayed your departure, Matthew,' said Rosina, walking with him to the door of the Manor.

'Think nothing of it. The sun is shining, you see. There should be no difficulty in getting back to Bellemonte before dark.'

'Then I wish you a safe journey, my friend.'

She held out her hand and he kissed it.

'Thank you, Rosina. You will be quitting Morton Gifford yourself, soon. Is there anything I can do to help?'

'Nothing, thank you, it is all in hand. There is a great deal to be done here before Lady Day, but I shall manage, with Davy's help.'

'And when you leave? Perhaps you would like me to accompany you to—'

'That is very kind of you, Matthew, but no, I do not want you to come with me.'

He grinned. 'Because you wish to be independent?'

'Oh, no,' she said, twinkling up at him. 'Because I am going to find the earl, and I think you would be very much in the way!'

Chapter Twenty-Five

'There's some water here, sir, if Your Lordship is thirsty.'

Conham accepted the proffered flask with a word of thanks and drank deep. He was indeed thirsty. Hungry, too, having been on the roof of Dallamire Hall since daybreak. He had started by inspecting the gutters and the new lead flashing, and for the past half hour had been helping to haul up replacement coping for the stonemasons to repair the low parapet that ran around the edge of the roof. It was hot work, but he was discovering that he enjoyed hard, physical labour.

He had spent the past few months helping on the farms, laying hedges, mending fences and rebuilding barns. There had been no time for gentlemanly sports and pastimes but he found the work rewarding, even in the bad weather. It was honest toil and he was not ashamed of it, nor of helping the builders at work on the Hall. It gave him valuable experience and knowledge of how things were done and what was needed to keep Dallamire working. The exercise also tired him out and allowed him to sleep soundly.

Most nights, at least.

Conham wiped the sweat from his brow and glanced up at the sun. It was gone noon. He would go down soon and partake of his solitary nuncheon in the dining room while those working on the roof enjoyed the basket of cheese and bread and pickles that he had ordered to be sent up.

He gazed out over the countryside. There was undoubtedly a wonderful view from up here. The ornamental lake gleamed like a mirror, and he could see over the woods to the lush green hills beyond. How long was it since he had ridden out over his land, just for the sheer pleasure of it? In truth, he could not recall ever having done so since he became earl. As soon as he returned from France he had been beset by the obligations of running Dallamire.

He was about to turn away when a movement in the distance caught his eye. A carriage had emerged from the trees and was bowling along the drive towards the house.

'Oh, Lord, who is this now?' he muttered. His lawyer, perhaps, with more urgent papers to sign. Or another creditor, come to remind him of an overdue bill. 'I suppose I must go down and meet them.' He made his way across the roof to where a series of ladders was lashed to the scaffolding. 'Hell and damnation, 'tis All Fools' Day and I am clambering around on my own roof. Well, let them see me in all my dirt, perhaps that will convince them that I am not shirking my responsibilities!'

Rosina gazed eagerly out the window at the park that stretched to the horizon in every direction. They had left the main road some time ago and now, as the carriage emerged from the leafy shade of the woods and into the bright sunshine, she caught her first glimpse of Dallamire Hall.

The meandering drive was designed to give visitors an excellent view of the magnificent West Front. The main body of the Palladian mansion rose up, square and imposing, flanked by two low wings that stretched out like arms on either side. She felt a slight tremor of nerves. The house was even larger and more impressive than she had imagined. As the drive curled about again, she could see a lattice of scaffolding covering the south front, behind the Pavilion, and a number of figures moving about on the roof.

Rosina began to have doubts about the wisdom of her plan. What was she doing, arriving unannounced? With the amount of work being done on the house, it was unlikely that the earl would even be here. She clasped her hands together, prayer-like, and pressed them against her mouth as the carriage rattled around in a final sweeping curve and came to a halt in front of the house.

The coach rocked as one of the servants climbed down to open the door. Rosina took a deep breath and stepped out onto the drive. The magnificent central portico towered above her, while on either side, curling stone steps led up to the covered entrance.

No one appeared from the house to greet her, which heightened her apprehension that the earl might not be at home. Then she heard footsteps on the gravel and turned to see Conham striding quickly towards her.

Her heart missed a beat at the sight of him. He was dressed in serviceable boots and buckskins, but he wore neither coat nor waistcoat over the billowing white shirt that made his broad shoulders look impossibly wide. His auburn hair glinted in the sun, one unruly lock falling forward over his brow, and as he drew closer she could see his face was set and unsmiling.

'Miss Brackwood.'

His formality was not encouraging. All the rehearsed greetings she had prepared withered away as he crossed the final few yards and stopped before her.

Rosina's mouth dried. The top buttons of his shirt were undone and she could not keep her eyes from the smattering of dark hair exposed there. Heat surged through her body as she remembered the feel of it beneath her fingers when they were lying together in his bed, their naked bodies touching…

Oh, heavens, she was lost!

'Why are you here? Is something wrong?'

'N-no,' she stammered, dragging her gaze away from his chest but unable to look him in the eye. 'Nothing is wrong, exactly.'

Conham saw the rosy flush blooming on her cheek and cursed. He should have put on his coat before coming out. Rosina was the last person he had expected to see, and she was clearly upset to find him half-dressed. They were not lovers, after all.

Much to his regret.

A servant ran up, interrupting his thoughts. 'I beg your pardon, my lord, we was clearing the hall, and no one heard the carriage!'

'Thank you, Robert.' Conham forced his befuddled brain to think. 'Escort Miss Brackwood to the drawing room, if you please. And order refreshments to be taken in. Excuse me, ma'am. I will join you momentarily, once I am more…dressed.'

With that, he turned on his heel and strode off.

Rosina followed Robert up the steps, trying not to feel disheartened. She had gambled everything upon Conham being in love with her, but was he, really? He had not looked happy to see her. In fact, he had been distinctly ill at ease. Perhaps he had decided that his noble plans were unworkable. That he would prefer a rich bride after all.

Her heart sank. She thought he had never looked better, his skin tanned by the sun, those powerful long legs encased in buckskin and the white shirt rippling over his muscled shoulders. She felt quite weak with longing. He would have no difficulty finding a wife. How could any woman reject such a man? Perhaps he had already proposed to some beautiful heiress.

The drawing room was shady to the point of gloom. Opaque muslin sub-curtains covered the windows to prevent the light from fading the expensive furniture, and no fire burned in the hearth. Rosina took off her bonnet and gloves but she was not tempted to remove her pelisse. She did not feel at all welcome here.

When the refreshments eventually arrived, she ignored the cake but took a glass of wine. With nothing better to do, she carried it over to one of the windows, where she held aside one of the muslin curtains. The drawing room looked out over the gardens and lawn to a shimmering lake. It was a pretty view, but she thought the grounds sadly neglected. Not that it would take a great deal of work to restore the gardens, if someone was interested.

Since she did not expect to see Conham again for some time, she amused herself by planning the best way to set about it. She was busy mentally cutting back the shrubbery and restocking the flower beds when she heard the door open. She let the curtain fall and turned as Conham came in.

He was dressed now in a blue coat, grey satin waistcoat and a snowy white shirt and neckcloth. He had changed his buckskins and boots for tight-fitting pantaloons in dove grey and glossy black Hessians that would not look amiss in Piccadilly. It was a far more formal appearance, but it did not prevent her heart from skidding erratically at the sight of him. She said the first thing that came into her mind.

'Well, that is certainly a little more appropriate.'

His smile was perfunctory, a faint crease in his brows as his gaze swept over her. Then he looked towards the hearth.

'Ah. I beg your pardon, I quite forgot there is no fire. This room has not been used since the countess moved out. Also, we cannot light one because the men are repairing the chimney. I wondered why you were still wearing your pelisse. We could go to the morning room, if you would prefer?'

So polite, so formal!

'No, thank you, this is perfectly satisfactory.' Rosina felt her courage ebbing away. 'You are busy. I will not take up too much of your time.'

'Where is your maid?'

'I left her in Pangbourne. At the posting inn where we put up last night.'

His frown deepened. 'You should not be here alone, Rosina. You are no longer my employee.'

'No, but I thought I was your friend.'

He ignored that. 'You have come from Brackwood?'

'Yes.'

'And have you settled upon a house?'

'I am not going to rent a property there.'

'Oh? You have decided to live at Brackwood after all.'

'No, I would be very much in the way there.'

'I see. How is your brother?'

'The doctors do not think he will walk again.'

'I see. I am very sorry.'

Her hand fluttered. 'He is much altered, and Harriet is very firmly in charge. She is truly fond of Edgar and determined to keep to her marriage vows. She is also proving to be a very good housekeeper.' Rosina finished her wine and carefully placed the glass down on a table. 'We have advertised for a land steward.'

'May I ask why, when you are perfectly capable of doing the job?'

'Edgar would not welcome my…interference. Harriet and I have decided the best thing is to employ a capable steward to manage both Brackwood and the land Papa left to my care. Since most of the income I receive from it will go back to Brackwood, it is the most sensible solution.'

Conham frowned. She always put others before herself.

Except where you are concerned.

He thrust that thought aside.

'That need not prevent you from returning to the area, to be near your old home, your friends. You have sufficient money to live in comfort and independence. Why should you give up your dreams for your brother, after all he did to you?'

'Edgar will be far happier if I am not there.'

Her smile slipped a little and he exclaimed, 'Confound it, Rosina. Brackwood is all you have ever wanted!'

'It was, but I find now that it is not what I want at all.' She came a step closer. 'I wondered…that is, I came here to ask if, perhaps, you would like to marry me after all.'

Conham stared at her.

'Is this some sort of joke?' he demanded. 'Some fantastical jape for All Fools' Day?'

'No, no!'

Rosina had envisaged several answers to her question, but never that! She gave a ragged laugh.

'Oh, dear, I am making a mull of this. I am not quite a pauper and I thought, if you have not set your heart on a rich bride, that is…'

'No, Rosina, do not go on. It is too late for that!' She raised her brows at him and he said impatiently, 'Oh, Dallamire is safe, but it will take years to return the house and

land to profit. There is little money for finery. I have reduced my staff, sold most of my horses and quite given up
on visits of pleasure to the capital.'

'Do you think I care for that?'

'No, but I would care. You would be giving up your hard-
won independence for…what? A life of damned hard work,
full of debt and responsibilities.' He glanced down at his
hands, rough and calloused from hard labour. No longer
the hands of a gentleman. '*I* can bear the deprivation, but
I will not inflict such hardship upon *you*.'

Her nerves already on edge, Rosina's temper snapped.

'Damn you, Conham, allow me to make my own decisions on that!'

Her unladylike language had shocked him. It had
shocked her, too, but she could not stop now.

'How can you be so, so pompous, so nobly self-sacrificing?'

'Because I do not want you to suffer.'

'But I am already suffering!'

The words were out before she could stop them. He
turned away, putting up a hand as if to silence her, but
she had come this far and would say what she must. She
thought bitterly that Edgar would approve. One last throw
of the dice.

'I love you, Conham.'

She saw the slight shake of his head, sensed she was
losing him and suddenly everything spilled out in a raging torrent.

'What would you have me do to prove it? Shall I…shall
I build a willow cabin at your gate? Or, as I drove in, I noticed a pretty little gatehouse standing empty. You could
rent that to me…'

'For God's sake, stop, Rosina!' he exclaimed. 'Do you
think I haven't considered this, that you aren't constantly

on my mind? I am not the husband you deserve. *I have nothing to offer you!*'

'Except love.'

The words fell into the abyss that yawned between them. She fixed her eyes on his broad back and went on quietly.

'If you can offer me that I would be satisfied.'

Rosina waited. She thought she heard a faint exhalation and saw the slightest lessening of tension in his figure. She stepped closer and put one hand gently on his shoulder.

'You see, I love *you*, Conham. Not your title. Not your wealth, or lack of it. I want to *be* with you. To live with you, work with you. If you will have me.'

Silence. Conham did not move. Her hand dropped. Matthew was wrong, he did not love her.

'I beg your pardon. My coming here has embarrassed you. I had best leave.'

'No, don't go.'

He turned, fixing her with a look from his grey, stormy eyes. She held her breath and waited for him to continue. Instead, he silently reached out and cupped the back of her head, pulling her close.

He kissed her, long, hard and very thoroughly, and the whole world exploded. He teased her lips apart and their tongues danced together. Rosina responded, feeling the heat of desire rushing through her body. She was almost swooning with it as he swept her up into his arms. He carried her over to the sofa, where he sat down with her on his lap and continued to plunder her mouth. Rosina sighed against his lips; every nerve end was on fire, she was trembling beneath his hands. When at last he broke off, she buried her face in his shoulder and clung to him.

'Oh, I thought you didn't want me,' she whispered.

'Want you! I have wanted you from the moment you cannoned into me in Queen Square.' She could feel his words, a rumble deep in his chest. 'I love you, Rosina, never doubt that, but I thought you wanted Brackwood and your independence more than you wanted me.'

She sighed. 'I thought so, too, at first. And then I had to persuade myself it was true. Because I knew I couldn't have you.'

'Even after I had taken you to bed? After I had said I would marry you?'

'I thought you were merely being noble.'

'There was nothing noble about it.' He settled her more securely on his lap and rested his cheek on her hair. 'I had come to Morton Gifford that day with the sole intention of throwing myself on your mercy and begging you to accept the hand of an impecunious earl. When I found you crying, I could not help myself. I wanted only to comfort you.' He sighed. 'I should have explained first!'

A chuckle escaped her. 'How could you? We were too busy kissing.'

She looked up then, but that was a mistake, because he immediately captured her mouth and for a long while she forgot everything, save the pure pleasure of his kiss. He unbuttoned her pelisse and she gave a little mewl of pleasure as he trailed a line of light butterfly kisses down her throat, gasping when his hand slid inside her bodice and cupped one breast.

He stopped. 'I beg your pardon, my hands are roughened with work.'

'Don't apologise,' she muttered, her voice ragged. 'And please, don't stop now!'

Conham lowered his head and kissed her again. Her body on fire, Rosina's fingers set to work on the buttons of his waistcoat. Clothes were abandoned amid a frenzy of passionate kisses, until they were lying naked together, oblivious of the cool air or the distant thud of hammers from the workmen on the roof.

When at last they were dressed again and Rosina was seated once more on the sofa with Conham's arm around her, she gave a long sigh.

'What a great deal of time we have wasted. If only I hadn't dashed off to Brackwood to search for that will!'

His arm tightened. 'When I read your note, I was afraid for you. I cursed your damned independence in going off alone.'

'My independence has caused a great deal of trouble,' she said in a small voice.

'But it also brought us together,' he reminded her.

'It did, but if I had not gone to Brackwood, Edgar would not have been injured.'

'And your father's estates would be in a fair way to being ruined,' he told her. 'We cannot live our lives on what might have been, my love. I regret, most deeply, that I didn't explain sooner that I had found a way out of our problems. That I could marry you and still fulfil my obligations. But it was never the right time, and after you found the will, I did not think there was any point in making you an offer. I thought I knew what your answer would be.'

'You see, I was right.' She raised her head and smiled up at him lovingly. 'You are nobly self-sacrificing.'

'But no more,' he declared. 'In future, I am going to take advantage of you, shamefully! I shall start by accepting your offer of marriage. You will keep your own income, of course. That must be included in the marriage settlement. But I warn you, there will be very little extra money to spare for fripperies or furbelows. No new carriages or grand tours of the Continent.'

'Unless my investment in Bellemonte comes good,' she murmured.

'Yes, but that will take years. I do not want to mislead you about our future, Rosina.'

'I know, and I am perfectly content,' she told him. 'All I want is to be allowed to help, to work with you to restore Dallamire. To be by your side day and night.'

'Especially at night!'

Rosina shivered deliciously at the wicked glint in his eyes.

'Well, madam,' he continued, 'will that do for you?'

'Oh, yes, Conham,' she said, melting back into his arms. 'That will do very well!'

* * * * *

If you loved this story, be sure to pick up one of Sarah Mallory's other charming Harlequin Historical reads

The Laird's Runaway Wife
The Duke's Family for Christmas
The Night She Met the Duke
Snowbound with the Brooding Lord
Wed in Haste to the Duke